CW01624627

LOST SECRETS *of the* ITALIAN POST OFFICE

Amanda Weinberg
& Silvia Mazzola

embla books

First published in the UK in 2025 by

embla books

An imprint of Bonnier Books UK
5th Floor, HYLO, 105 Bunhill Row,
London, EC1Y 8LZ

Copyright © Amanda Weinberg & Silvia Mazzola, 2025

All rights reserved.
No part of this publication may be reproduced, stored or transmitted in any form or by any means, electronic, mechanical, photocopying or otherwise, without the prior written permission of the publisher.

The right of Amanda Weinberg & Silvia Mazzola to be identified as Author of this work has been asserted by them in accordance with the Copyright, Designs and Patents Act, 1988.

This is a work of fiction. Names, places, events and incidents are either the products of the author's imagination or used fictitiously. Any resemblance to actual persons, living or dead, or actual events is purely coincidental.

A CIP catalogue record for this book is available from the British Library.

ISBN: 9781471419751

Also available as an ebook and an audiobook

1

Typeset by IDSUK (Data Connection) Ltd
Printed and bound in Great Britain by Clays Ltd, Elcograf S.p.A.

MIX
Paper | Supporting responsible forestry
FSC www.fsc.org FSC® C018072

The authorised representative in the EEA is Bonnier Books UK (Ireland) Limited.
Registered office address: Floor 3, Block 3, Miesian Plaza, Dublin 2, D02 Y754, Ireland
compliance@bonnierbooks.ie
www.bonnierbooks.co.uk

The LOST SECRETS *of the* ITALIAN POST OFFICE

To the late Julia Casterton, our inspirational mentor.
To Julian and Stefano.

Prologue

Bastiani 1937

The only girls in a sea of young boys, Nina Caruso and Ambra Tizzani had sat side by side in class since the very first day of school, *compagne di banco*, deskmates since the age of six. They met every morning at the *lavatoio*, the laundry house, walking to school together, skipping along the alleyways. In summer, they would stop to gather blackberries and hazelnuts, dipping their feet in the fresh waters of the River Fastino; in autumn, they collected red and yellow leaves to fashion into skirts. Their afternoons were spent sitting on the bench outside Bar Renzo in Bastiani's main square, sucking almonds and dreaming about life beyond the black silhouettes of the Mainarde mountains.

Today, Nina, eyes fixed on the page in front of her, prodded her friend sitting on her right. 'Ambra, help me. What's the subjunctive of the verb "to do"?' she whispered. The air in the classroom was heavy despite a breeze coming from the open windows. Ambra's lips curled in an expression of contempt. 'Leave it out! It's only a stupid grammar test. No one uses the subjunctive in this hole of a village.' She tossed back strands of light brown hair, mouth half-covered by fingers with bitten nails.

There was a knock on the classroom door. The headmaster, *Preside* Bartelli, stepped inside with a long stride.

His features were sterner than usual, his mouth stretched in a hard line across his jaw. The class rose like a wave, their arms darting forward in the Roman salute, their feet stamping the floor as their bodies stood to attention. He motioned to the teacher, *maestra* Anna Martinucci. They stood together in front of the desk mouthing words too soft for the class to hear.

Maestra Martinucci turned her face towards the class, her eyes wide, her rosy cheeks pale. She motioned to the rest of the class to sit down. 'Will the class please continue with the assignment? Caruso, Tizzani, go with *Preside* Bartelli.'

Ambra strolled to the front of the class, hands deep in her pockets, unfazed by her classmates' eyes glued to her. Nina, head bent and socks rolled down to her ankles, anxiously twirled the blue ribbon of her school apron. She trudged behind Ambra.

The girls followed the headmaster, past the framed photograph of *il Duce* hanging on the wall above the blackboard, next to the wooden crucifix. They passed the poster issued by the *MINISTERO EDUCAZIONE NATURALE*, displaying the image of a boy with a rifle slung across his shoulder.

Preside Bartelli ushered Ambra and Nina from the empty silence of the corridor into his office. As he related the news, Nina dug her nails into the palm of her hand. Her father, tall, hook-shouldered Gaetano Caruso, was no more. 'Dead in Action' in the Spanish Civil War, fighting for freedom. Her father was the one who had protected her before he left the fields and the family to volunteer in a country that wasn't theirs. Fighting for the Socialists and the peasants in a faraway war to uphold his principles and beliefs. Were they more important than her? She glanced at Ambra standing tall, statue-like, as if she in turn had not been robbed of her mother, Agostina, by cancer. As if her world, both their worlds, had not shattered into a million pieces.

Ambra walked through the glass doors into the warmth of the early October afternoon. She marched ahead, the hem of her skirt rising and falling against her calves, her shoulders hunched and tight. Nina staggered forwards, trying to catch up with her friend. The shared destiny of the half-orphan added yet another layer to their friendship. They were both alone, both burdened by unexpected sadness and loss.

'We are the same, both half an orphan!' Nina said, catching up with her friend. 'And both only twelve years old.'

Ambra reached out and wound her fingers through Nina's. With a voice of stone, she said, 'Let's walk for a while together. I can't go home yet. I can't face the smell of my mother's medicines and know they haven't cured her.'

Nina understood why Ambra couldn't go home to the Post Office and encounter the silence. She had watched Ivo, Ambra's father, move the sick bed into the storeroom, bringing with it the odour of medicines and body sweat. The door was always ajar, and the rattling of Agostina's sickly breathing had oozed through the gap into the main Post Office—uneven, rasping, unsettling.

Fingers laced, they followed the bend in the road, past the Sansone villa, where Nina's mother Marta was employed as housekeeper and where Nina had spent every summer for as long as she could remember, playing with Nicolò, the Sansones' son; past the Post Office, where Ambra's father worked and the Tizzani family lived. Ambra was holding Nina's hand, squeezing it tight. Nina listened to the crunch of their combined footsteps on the gravelled road, her body following the sway of Ambra's motion.

They approached the old *lavatoio* at the edge of Bastiani, the stone slabs smooth and shiny, where for centuries local women had scrubbed and beaten garments in scorching heat and wintry cold. Below, the Fastino rippled like a smooth, turquoise jewel. Ambra stopped and placed her satchel on the ground. She rummaged through it and extracted a pair of scissors from her box of pencils. Then she whipped out a handkerchief patterned with green and white flowers. She sank to the ground, fine grains of earth coating her shins, and began to cut her handkerchief into thin strips.

'What are you doing, Ambra?' Nina whispered, voice tight.

'Get your handkerchief out. And you'll see.'

Nina dug her hand into the pocket of her skirt and slowly pulled out a small square handkerchief dotted with pink baby rabbits.

'Are we making something?' she asked, watching Ambra's steady hands.

'Yes, take this.' Ambra passed the scissors to Nina. 'Cut it up and we'll braid the strips together.'

'Why are we doing this?'

Ambra exhaled slowly and brushed the earth from her legs. 'Because I lost my mother today.' Her voice wavered. 'You've lost your father. A disease and that stupid war have robbed us. But we have each other. This will be our pact, our *fazzoletto*, our friendship handkerchief. We must remember to always be there for one another. Best friends, forever.'

The idea of a pact kindled in Nina such a sense of excitement she almost felt ashamed. Hadn't she just lost her beloved father? She had never had a friendship pact before. In truth, in Ambra, she'd only had a *compagna di banco* and now here was Ambra inviting her to be her best friend. She could hardly breathe.

'Then let's make two handkerchiefs,' Nina suggested. 'So we both always remember our promise.'

Fingers touching, they plaited the strips one by one into two small knots. They placed their hands on the two tight braids they had formed.

'Best friends?' Ambra said.

'Best friends,' Nina replied.

'Always?'

'Always.' Nina nodded.

'I'll hide my friendship handkerchief in my chest of drawers at home, underneath my underwear. My father will never know it's there. It will be our secret.'

'And I'll hide mine under my mattress. No one will find it, and whenever I feel sad or lonely, I can hold it close to my heart and know I'm not alone.'

'Because I'll be there.'

'Because you'll be there.'

'No matter what?'

'No matter what.'

'Shall we scream?' Ambra asked.

Nina blinked. 'What do you mean, Ambra?'

'Scream out the pain, the loss of my mother and your father. We're alone. No one can hear us.'

The autumn sun beat down on Ambra's head, streaking her hair with flecks of red. Her eyes were wide, almost vacant. Was it fear, anticipation or loss? Nina wasn't sure. Her eyes darted around the *lavatoio* and beyond to the empty alleyways of Bastiani. The air was still, the cobbled streets silent and empty.

'I have no mother; you have no father. We can face this together. Our scream will cement our friendship pact.'

Ambra raised her eyes to the sky above. 'They will hear it up there.' She held out the friendship handkerchiefs. 'Hold them with me.'

Nina did as Ambra asked.

Ambra made two plump fists around Nina's hands. Her eyes softened. She tightened her grasp around Nina's fingers.

'Friends forever.'

'Friends forever.'

The sound of their voices hovered above Bastiani's Santa Croce church, over the Sansone villa, the stone walls of the Post Office, the olive groves surrounding the farm where Nina lived; soft at first, then gaining momentum as it rose above the River Fastino, the hay fields, the peaks of the Apennines, in a long explosive cry of friendship.

Nina and Ambra raised their gaze as the echoes of their pact lifted up to the deep blue of the sky, their bond sealed by the symbolic knotting together of two handkerchiefs. At that moment, their connection deepened, and they believed it would be unbreakable.

*

Two coffins left the central nave of the Santa Croce church, side by side on a single carriage pulled by two dark horses and governed by Nina's brother Gino and Renzo, the owner of Bastiani's Bar Renzo.

Nina and Ambra walked together, eyes cast down. Black cotton veils the women of the village had crocheted for the funerals covered their heads. They weren't holding hands. Instead, they were united by the tips of their friendship handkerchiefs, clenching them in their fists as they walked outside the walls of Bastiani up to the cemetery. The villagers thought it was to dab their tears. Only they knew it was their rope of strength gifted by mutual loss.

At the graveside Ambra pulled it. Nina responded with a tug. She stared at her father's coffin, an empty wooden box carrying his boots and his work overalls. Her mother had been right to insist on a formal funeral after all. Yet Nina had never expected to mourn a pair of boots.

At Bar Renzo, on the terrace overlooking the River Fastino, the mourners refreshed themselves with glasses of ruby Tintilia wine. Nina and Ambra sat together on a weathered bench, each sucking on a sweet Renzo had offered them, their faces solemn, friendship handkerchiefs dangling between their fingers.

A shadow fell in front of them; a hand, light but firm, touched Nina's shoulder. Nicolò Sansone stood before her, his deep blue eyes creased with concern. He had always been there, for as long as she could remember. The Sansones arrived in Bastiani from Campobasso every summer and Nina's mother Marta worked at the villa preparing dishes, pressing linen and polishing silver.

'Nina, I'm so sorry about your father.' His voice was low, almost intimate. He leaned in, his thick curls tickling her cheek. Placing his lips close to her ears, he whispered, 'I heard from Gino . . . Your father died fighting in Spain.'

Nina stiffened. The Sansones were a renowned Fascist family. Her father and Gino had always warned her—never speak about politics in front of them. Bow your head, smile sweetly, say nothing. Tears pricked her eyelashes at the thought of her father dead in a foreign land. She hoped she could stop the tears from flowing. She didn't want fifteen-year-old Nicolò to see her cry. 'I wish my father were still here with me,' she said finally, her voice steady despite the tightness in her throat.

Nicolò's gaze flickered, as if searching Nina's face for something unspoken. Then he turned towards Ambra. 'I'm sorry for your loss too,' he said softly.

For a moment, they remained silent, surrounded by the distant hum of conversation, the clinking of glasses. Nicolò's lips curled into a smile, boyish and familiar. 'Why don't you come with me to the river? Remember how we used to dive into the water and race each other to the other side? I bet I could beat you both.'

'Let's go.' Ambra tugged Nina's hand.

They glanced down at their formal funeral clothes, the stiff black skirts hanging below their knees. Smiling at each other, they rolled up the pleated material and knotted it at the back.

'Our veils?' Nina pointed to the black fan-shaped head covers draped over the back of the bench.

'Leave them. Someone will pick them up.'

Ambra and Nina followed Nicolò Sansone down the slope to the river, the tips of their knotted handkerchiefs sticking out of their pockets like wings of flying birds. They held hands, oblivious to the distant rumbles of the war that was shaking Abyssinia and parts of Europe, a war still far away from Bastiani and the bucolic landscape of the Molise region.

Friends and Enemies

Bastiani 1943

Post Office

Day by day, month by month, year by year, the torn pages of the calendar drift to the floor like dead leaves. I am a rural Post Office, at the heart of Bastiani, where a smattering of stone cottages cling to the hillside, their terracotta roofs bleeding into the ochre of the earth; a village nestled in the foothills of the rugged mountains of Molise, where the wind whispers secrets through olive groves and time ambles. Our region contains the highest peaks and most rugged terrain of the Apennines. Squashed between the Adriatic and the Tyrrhenian seas, we are often forgotten, overlooked by bigger cities and more prosperous lands. We are a '*terra di contadini*,' a land of sharecroppers, between the Matese and Mainarde mountain ranges.

My postmaster, Ivo Tizzani, drops a sack full of mail on my counter each day. The letters I cradle are more than words on paper—they are lifelines. Some are wrapped in foreign stamps, their envelopes worn soft from travel, telling tales of opportunity in other cities, other lands. Others are government decrees, stamped with the eagle of Mussolini's regime, cold and unbending in their authority. The villagers read them with the same wary eyes they cast toward the weather—uncertain of what might come.

I keep the secrets of my villagers; the letters they entrust to me carry the weight of their lives—confessions of love, whispers of rebellion, pleas for salvation. Renzo, the owner of the Bastiani bar, traces each line of his brother's letter from America, memorising its promises of a better life. Don Simone, the priest, sends reports to the bishop, balancing faith with the growing demands of the state, and snippets of news to his sister Teresa in the nearby village of Castelnuovo al Volturno.

I dream of the journeys my letters take, slipping beyond the confines of this rural village, sometimes crossing seas and borders and always carried by the hands of strangers. I am rooted here, as immovable as the mountains, as enduring as the sky. I am more than a building. I am a lifeline, a confidant, a bridge between the known and the unknown. And though the Fascist banners flutter in the breeze and the world beyond threatens to seep in, I remain steadfast, a beacon of continuity and hope in a village where change comes slowly.

My wooden door opens onto the main piazza I share with my neighbours: the baker Pietruzzo Marra, moustache always sprinkled with specks of white flour; red-cheeked Don Simone, the bald-headed parish priest of our Santa Croce church with its octagonal steeple; old Santino, the cobbler hammering torn soles onto worn-out shoes; Renzo, small-eyed but with an inviting smile; Tommaso and Rita, our cheesemakers, who lead their mule to the piazza, wicker panniers of ricotta and *caciocavallo* astride its mottled-grey back; Antonio, the carpenter, sawdust flecking his eyebrows.

From the window overlooking the square, I observe the clear waters of the River Fastino. Its crooked stone bridge shines like gold in the summer sunshine and in winter rests under layers of powdery snow. Surrounded by a perfumed garden, Villa Sansone, the summer residence of *Avvocato* Sansone's family, is Bastiani's largest and most imposing home. With its square and solid ochre walls and forest-green shutters, the villa sits on one side like a sentinel to the activity of the piazza. At the far end, a tall arch made of bricks and stone leads to the olive groves and potato fields of the Caruso farm where Nina lives with Gino and her widowed mother.

The villagers congregate in the Post Office to exchange snippets of information about the war, gossip, news of their loved ones fighting in far-flung corners of the world. Names of countries flutter through my walls: Abyssinia, Albania, Greece. Words drift in the air: hunger, wounds and the dream of an Italian empire. The *Foglio D'Ordine*, the order sheet of the Fascist Party that Ivo had hammered to my outside walls in 1938, is now torn and yellowed. The printed words are still visible—so harsh are they, that even the passing of time and the inclement weather can't erase them. Words unfurl, stark and unyielding—*Il Gran Consiglio del Fascismo orders: Jews dismissed from government and schools. Jews banned from marrying Italians. Jews cast out of the military. Foreign Jews imprisoned. Jews erased from media and public life.*

Then in 1940 news of the war trembled through my walls. The Pact of Steel between Hitler and our *Duce* is bearing its fruit. 'The Italian people will have their empire again. *Viva il Duce*.' Voices murmured. The notes of the Fascist hymn '*Giovinezza*' vibrated through my walls. In the piazza, *Carabiniere* Giorgio Palotta, arm outstretched in the Roman salute, shouted, 'This is good for our country. A quick war, over by autumn. Our *Duce* assures us victory.'

That's what they'd thought. They confiscated our factories and private residences to imprison anyone they considered an enemy to the regime in internment camps in Molise. The Italian Fascists took the little we had and stained our villages, our fields and olive groves with their brutality and greed.

Three years have passed, and war is still raging and my people have no choice but to obey *il Duce*'s commands, despite the poverty and famine that runs through the villages and towns of Molise. Celestina and Pietruzzo, Bastiani's bakers, are still forced to give up their grain to the regime with tight lips and furrowed brows.

The radio is hidden in the Post Office storeroom, emitting bursts of static, crackling sounds at a low volume. Esther, the Polish Jew with curly black hair, translates the latest announcements from the BBC into Italian for Ivo, Gino and Mariolina, her sister-in-law, hair sprinkled with grey and soft flesh padding her jowls and neck. The radio is transferred into the safe when not in use.

News of the war seeps under the storeroom door, spreading an eerie mood like winter fog. Blackshirts, their polished boots striking sharp notes against my floor, bring orders and propaganda posters of *il Duce* with his jaw set and his hand raised, demanding loyalty even from these forgotten hills. But I know the truth of this place. The people here are tethered not to politics but to the land, to the church bells that call them to mass, to the cycles of sowing and reaping. I watch their faces, weathered as the mountains themselves, and see that their fealty to Mussolini is a mask worn out of necessity.

Today, the brass bell chimes. The sunlight wavers, casting golden streaks on the cobblestones, but the air feels heavy. Gino strides in, chestnut hair in messy tufts, nails blunt and scoured with earth. Sweat drips from his forehead. He is chewing filaments of hay. The scent of dry earth and crushed leaves mingle in the still afternoon air. He clenches his fists and digs them into his trouser pockets with such fury it seems he intends to hit someone. When he opens his mouth he roars like a caged animal, his wide forehead scrunched, cheeks crimson, lips puckered.

'There is a rumour that *Avvocato* Sansone has been appointed the new supervisor of the five internment camps set up in our region.' The words are hissed with fury, spittle flying into the air. 'We must be more cautious with our anti-Fascist propaganda, now that an official of the regime is here permanently in our village,' Gino says and punches the counter with his fist.

Ambra and Nina, changed from girls to young women, are slouched over my granite counter, leafing through the pages of a fashion magazine and dreaming of summer dresses. They look up in alarm at Gino's outburst, their faces red with heat, lips smudged with crushed berries to imitate the lipstick they can't afford.

Ivo places a hand on Gino's shoulder and squeezes it. 'But we can't stop. We need to keep an eye on Esther. Not only is she an anti-Fascist like us, she's a Jew. *Avvocato* Sansone might send her to one of these internment camps. Or worse. Remember, she had to give up her job as a teacher in Castelnuovo because of the *Leggi Razziali*, the Racial Laws.'

I know what they mean. When darkness descends the storeroom transforms. The wireless is carried from the safe to the table. Leaflets with inflammatory words against the regime like '*Via i Tedeschi. Contadini*, Unite Your Forces!' are stored in piles to be delivered clandestinely around the villages of Molise. Sometimes Don Simone pops his head around the door, twiddling the fringes of his sash.

In daylight things change. The storeroom is cleared of compromising material, the radio is packed away. The brass bell over the main door clangs as my usual customers walk in.

The shadow of war stretches over Bastiani, over Castelnuovo, over my villagers. The weight of an unknown future feels unbearable. In the distance, a wolf howls, its mournful cry echoing across the mountains.

The leaf of the paper calendar hanging on the back wall crumples in the heat.

It is the 3rd June, 1943, Saint Clotilde Regina's feast day.

Today is another summer month under Mussolini's Fascist rule.

Chapter One

The sunflowers, withered and dry, turned their charcoal faces towards the scorched earth. Nina found comfort in their reassuring presence, with so many Bastiani men having left to fight in places she didn't even know where to find on the map: Abyssinia, Eritrea, Rhodes, Libya, Albania.

Standing in front of Villa Sansone, Nina watched the black Fiat 1100 of the Sansone family pass through the wrought-iron gates and slide along the gravel drive, its sleek bonnet reminding her of the elongated snouts of the dogs roaming Bastiani.

The car stopped in front of the villa. *Avvocato* Sansone opened the door and helped his wife out of the passenger seat. Carmela Sansone, her hair coiffured in perfect blonde waves reaching her neckline, stepped out with the elegance and confidence of the film stars in the magazines Nina read with Ambra bent over the counter in the Post Office. The signora was wearing a navy frock with pale yellow polka dots, with a crisp neckline.

A young man stepped out of the back seat and stretched his legs. He was wearing chocolate brown slacks and a white cotton shirt. His chest was square, his legs long; the hands that he passed through his dark hair were large.

Nina remained still, shielded by the old oak tree by the gate; the smell of car exhaust mingled with the sweet scent of jasmine from the nearby bushes. Memories of past summers spent together with Nicolò and Ambra flooded back, tripping over each other in their hurry to be recalled. Nina thought of those summers, their arms and legs ripened by the sun, their noses brown and freckled, deep layers of reddish gold in their hair. He was the one who had taught her how to ride a two-wheeled bicycle when she was only five and he a boy of eight. She had been the first to offer him a bunch of dock leaves to soothe his stinging legs after he'd fallen into a patch of nettles when they played hide-and-seek with Ambra and the other children of the village. Nina recalled how one year Signora Carmela handed her mother trousers and shirts Nicolò had grown out of. Nina had cried all the way to the villa, dressed in a white shirt and patched-up flannel trousers in the height of summer. But when Nicolò had said, 'They're mine, now we match,' the tears had stopped flowing and they'd run together down to the River Fastino to swim in the swirling waters. It was the shape summer made when the Sansones left their residence in Campobasso and came to Bastiani.

Since his family had left Bastiani the previous summer, he had faded from her mind like the lines of a beloved poem learnt by heart in elementary school. The years they had spent together had been eclipsed by the unfurling of wartime events in Italy and her special friendship with Ambra.

She stared at Nicolò. His long skinny legs looked thicker, more muscly, his shoulders stronger, his face more chiselled, his jaw studded with a soft stubble. She was surprised how loudly her heart was clanging in her chest.

Nina waited until the Sansones had climbed the wide sweeping steps of the front entrance. She didn't want Nicolò Sansone to see her at eighteen, with hair still fashioned in two hanging plaits, socks rolled down to her ankles, her plain grey smock hanging loosely on her slim body. She should have listened to Ambra and worn her raven hair loose down her back.

She slipped out from behind the trunk of the big oak tree and its protective branches and headed towards the back door of the villa, which led to the kitchen. She passed the ornate flower beds full of deep-red roses, bunches of lavender, pink and white geraniums. The lawns were clipped and the smell of lemon trees hung in the air. It was the scent of summer.

In the kitchen, her mother Marta was standing by the stove, hands immersed in a bowl of flour. Her face was lined and stretched tightly over prominent cheekbones. Purple shadows circled her eyes. Nina couldn't remember seeing her mother any other way—permanently worried, with a pinched and tight mouth, fingers knotted with arthritis. How could Nina blame her? She'd spent her entire life in Bastiani, a widow with a farm to cultivate, helping Gino in the fields and olive groves, organising the Sansone household, worrying about bringing up a family during wartime. A widow, alone day after day.

'What do you think you're doing, dilly-dallying in the garden? There's so much to do. Put the water on for the pasta and slice the potatoes,' her mother commanded.

'Did you know Nicolò was joining his parents this early in the summer?'

'Nicolò? Signora Carmela never mentioned it. Quickly, take the bed sheets up and prepare his room.'

'I thought you wanted me to cut up the potatoes!'

A sweet smell of perfume drifted through the air. Signora Sansone popped her head around the door.

'We're earlier than expected. And Nicolò is with us. Apologies, Marta, I forgot to tell you.'

'Don't worry, Signora. Nina is just going up to prepare his room.' Marta flicked her head towards Nina. Tufts of grey hair escaped from the tightly knotted bun at the back of her head.

Only then did Signora Sansone turn towards Nina and greet her with a cold tilt of her chin, the blue of her eyes shining with confidence and presence.

'It's a different summer this year; war changes things, often for the best. The regime has appointed my husband head supervisor of the internment camps of the region. He has an important role to fulfil for the war effort.'

'Maybe for the best for you, Signora, but not for us. Since my husband died in that foreign war, life has been wretched. And very lonely.' Marta hissed the words from between clenched teeth, deepening the grooves of pain and worry permanently etched into her skin.

'We don't speak of the Spanish Civil War in this household, Marta. Remember which side we are all on.' She swivelled her head towards Nina. 'And you should know that too, Nina. You are the new Italy, part of the Fascist youth. *Credere, obbedire, combattere* – our *Duce*'s slogan is your slogan. Believe, obey and fight.'

Arms clasped around the sheets, Nina shrugged and hid her face away. She was glad it was her mother who had to deal with Carmela and not her. She climbed the back staircase that led from the kitchen up to the main hall. Signora Sansone's words and her perfumed scent hovered like a cloud above Nina's head, intermingling with Gino's warnings of Mussolini's Fascist youth, the arrogant, bullying Blackshirts who roamed the cobbled alleys of Bastiani from time to time, scaring chickens, goats and people alike.

Chapter Two

Ever since the death of her mother, Ambra had been known in Bastiani as the Post Office girl, a name she detested. Sorting mail, sticking stamps on envelopes, weighing packages and sometimes delivering mail to the villagers of Bastiani and Castelnuovo al Volturno had previously been chores undertaken by her mother Agostina, but they now fell on her shoulders like leaden pebbles.

She had bigger dreams. Ambra could hear her mother's words as she lay dying on the sick bed in the storeroom: 'Don't let Bastiani suffocate your dreams, Ambra. Live well. Love well.'

Then the war came and held those dreams in its claws.

Until today.

Her father was expecting a delivery for the Post Office; for her a promise of an abundant future within the bleak landscape of Molise. She swiftly made her bed, tidied her clothes and straightened the photograph of her mother in a wooden frame, her eyes smiling at Ambra before the cancer had fogged them with pain. She lifted the frame and planted a kiss on the glass. 'Don't worry, *mamma*, this war won't stop me. I'll move from this godforsaken village to a city where life pulsates, I promise. I'll have a wardrobe full of the latest fashions and makeup galore.'

She checked her appearance in the mirror, smoothed her white cotton skirt, applied a dab of compact powder to her cheeks to cover the two spots that had sprouted overnight. She covered her mouth with the stub of red lipstick that had belonged to her mother. Ready for the day ahead, she felt a pang of excitement as she closed her bedroom door and skipped down the stairs to the kitchen. She poured a cup from the pot of chicory her father had prepared and kicked open the door leading into the main Post Office. The musty heat overwhelmed her. She leapt over to the window, opened it wide and took a gulp of summer air, inhaling the smell of chestnut bread from Pietruzzo's bakery on the opposite side of the piazza. The scarcity of grain meant the villagers had to be more resourceful with the food they ate. Bread made from the skins of broad beans or chestnuts, hay for tobacco, chicory and barley to replace coffee—these had become the staples of the Molise diet.

Ambra unbolted the main door leading onto the street. She had a clear view of the square. At one end, the closed iron gates of Villa Sansone appeared forbidding in the soft rays of the early morning sun. On the opposite side, Renzo was arranging tables and chairs on the terrace overlooking the river. The octagonal bell tower of the Santa Croce church cast a long shadow on the cobblestoned square.

Ambra returned to the granite counter that stretched the width of the room and began to refill the pads of the rubber stamps with ink. When she was younger, she loved to play with them and enjoyed licking the stamps on envelopes as she sat on her mother's lap. Then the Post Office was her own magical playground where she was free to rummage through boxes of papers, rearrange ink bottles and sort the nibs into neat piles. After her mother died, the walls began to peel; the wooden floors remained dusty and unvarnished.

The honk of a horn startled her. Her father had arrived. She watched him with trepidation as he dragged the sacks of parcels out of the van, muscled arms tensed, his square face contorted with the effort. Ambra saw her father, his hands as large as vine leaves, heave a brown box sealed with yellow tape and labelled in capital letters: TIZZANI IVO, *POSTE E TELEGRAFI*, BASTIANI.

'I'll take the big package, Ambra, it's heavy. You carry the small parcels.' He arched his peppery eyebrows as he beckoned her to join him.

Ambra ran out to help him, hoping it was what she'd been waiting for, for weeks.

'It's arrived.' Ivo winked at his daughter and placed the box on the counter.

'A new beginning,' Ambra whispered to herself, grateful her father had decided to supplement the Post Office with a brand-new portable Olivetti ICO typewriter.

'I'll move it to the storeroom.'

'The storeroom?' Ambra stamped her foot on the wooden floor. 'But I want to use it too. The storeroom is often locked. You always hide the key.'

'The typewriter is portable; that's the beauty of it. I can move it from the storeroom to the Post Office easily and you can use it then.'

'It's my surprise for Nina. We're going to learn to type and get out of this hole of a village as soon as the world calms down.'

'Oh Ambra, if only the world would calm down and our poor village could return to how it once was, free of Blackshirts, German soldiers and Mussolini's commands!'

A metallic taste arose on Ambra's tongue. Why was her father always so pessimistic? She wished her mother were alive, sitting there at the counter; her mother had always had faith in Ambra and in the future. Her father's voice faded into the silence of the Post Office as he slowly began to unpack the typewriter.

Carabiniere Palotta walked past the open window, whistling the Fascist song '*Giovinezza*'.

'I wish he wouldn't whistle that tune near me,' her father cursed. 'I'm sure he does it to annoy me.'

'I think it's a jolly tune.' The words '*Giovinezza, giovinezza, primavera di bellezza*!' rolled off Ambra's tongue.

'Are you trying to annoy me too?' He glared at her.

'Not if you let me use the typewriter wherever I want.' She smiled sweetly and kissed him on the tip of his nose.

Chapter Three

The Sansones had owned the villa for several generations. Nina remembered Nicolò telling her that his great-great-grandfather had bought it and insisted it was never sold, but passed down through the family. Nina loved the long glass windows that stretched from floor to ceiling opening onto the garden, the beautifully decorated rooms with velvet curtains and swinging chandeliers. As a child she had held Nicolò's hand and pretended she lived there with him, roaming the corridors, swinging from the bannisters or sharing *caramelle* together on the wide stone steps that fanned the entrance of the house. Sometimes she had to share him with Ambra. Ambra was her best friend; they had their handkerchiefs hidden away to prove their pact. Yet when Nina was alone with Nicolò she felt a lightness she couldn't explain even to herself.

The Sansone villa exuded a sense of opulence and abundance, unseen anywhere else in Bastiani, where food was sparse and so were men, metamorphosed from *contadini* to soldiers. Here with the hall chandelier swaying above her and the oak staircase inviting her to dream, she was part of this other life, Nicolò's life. Her shoulders relaxed despite the weight of the fresh sheets and towels she was carrying to Nicolò's room.

Nina climbed the stairs, her eyes skimming over the Fascist flag hanging in the entrance hall and resting instead on the paintings flanking the wall. There were many depictions of Bastiani surrounded by rolling hills, the glittering River Fastino in the background, houses perched together like the dominoes she had played with as a child with Nicolò. Idyllic settings, suffused in the yellow blush of the rising sun, splashes of red and purple flowers dotting the fields. These were the inventions of artists, not the Bastiani Nina lived in, a Bastiani with rows of stone houses, surrounded by bland potato fields, aged olive groves, drooping sunflowers and withered basil pots. Yet it was her village.

Nina sighed, shifted the pile of laundered sheets in her arms and walked down the corridor. Nicolò's room was the first door on the left. It hadn't changed much since she had last seen it. His toy soldiers were still arranged in rows on the shelves lining the room. The wall displayed a poster of his favourite football team, Lazio. She wondered if he supported them now or had changed his support to the Campobasso squad. She was relieved there were no propaganda posters or images of Mussolini adorning the walls.

The bed was pushed into a corner of the room. She remembered last seeing it in the centre. With Nicolò she had jumped on that bed, giggling till her mother called them for their afternoon snack of bread and butter dusted with sugar, a treat she was not used to in her own home.

She turned her gaze to the wide window. The view of the lawn and lemon trees laden with fruit were as she remembered. She inhaled the garden's heady fragrance of jasmine and roses and left the wooden shutters ajar. Fragments of harsh light stretched across the wooden floorboards and flickered like flies on the white sheets. Nina made the bed, fluffed up the pillows and pulled the light cotton bedcover tightly over the mattress. In the penumbra, she folded the towels neatly and placed them on the chair by Nicolò's writing desk. A footstep creaked on the floorboards and made her turn.

'It's you!' His lips curved into a half-smile, his eyes wondering, almost startled.

'So you're here!' She pulled at the hem of her skirt.

'Yes, and I will be for a while.' His voice was laced with a rasp that reminded her of the rustling of autumn leaves; his cheeks shaded with fine golden stubbles of beard. He lowered his eyes and swung his suitcase onto the freshly made bed making ripples on the sheets.

'Oh Nicolò, I've just made your bed. You're ruining it.'

He laughed and caught her arm playfully, the corners of his lips creasing as he smiled. He pulled her towards the window and pushed the shutters wide open. Again the citrus smell of fruit mixed with the sweetness of the flowers enveloped Nina. Beyond the walls of the villa, she had a glimpse of the expanse of the River Fastino, its waters glittering in the steaming heat of the day.

'Nina, do you remember the fun we used to have, diving from up there?' he said, his eyes fixed on the stone bridge linking the village to the countryside beyond.

'And I was always the best swimmer,' Nina teased, her mouth an upward arch.

'You were, but only because you are smaller and lighter.' He looked straight at her, a smile dimpling his cheeks.

A rush of heat rose to Nina's throat. Nicolò turned back towards the view, his hands perched on the windowsill, head stretched as if he were about to leap forward.

'It's lovely here, the river with its clear waters, flanked by hazelnut trees.' He let out a long sigh. 'I breathe freedom in Bastiani.'

'I barely breathe when I see German soldiers drinking at Bar Renzo, sprawled over the chairs as if they owned the place.' Nina hesitated and tilted her head, wondering whether she had spoken out of turn. But she was relieved that Nicolò was in Bastiani and not at the front fighting for their country.

As if reading her thoughts, he said, 'I'm not going to fight in the war now. My father has seen to that.'

'Is that why you're here? We weren't expecting you.'

'For all his beliefs in *his Duce* and *his* promises, my father, the great *Avvocato* Sansone, didn't want to risk *his* only son and heir being shot on the battlefield.' A look of contempt muddied Nicolò's face before his features softened into a smile. 'Don't misunderstand me, I'm relieved. I don't have to fight in this blasted war. It's his hypocrisy I can't stand. The good news is, I'll be here with you all summer. Maybe longer.'

With a swift movement, Nicolò walked to the bed. He clicked open his suitcase, rummaged inside and took out a pair of woollen swimming trunks.

'Come on, Nina. Come with me to the river. We've always felt free there. We can collect Ambra on the way if you like?'

The mention of Ambra's name caused a slight clenching of Nina's belly, a rippling up to her chest. 'I can't, Nicolò. I've got to help my mother. And Ambra will be working with her father at the Post Office.' She hated the stiffness in her voice.

'Let's go and ask Marta to spare you, just for an hour,' he pleaded.

He led her by the elbow and ushered her along the corridor and down the stairs. She could hear the echo of her feet, his feet, tripping down the stone steps, breaking the silence of the house with their rhythmic thumps. Nina wished she could control the beating of her heart.

She noticed Signora Sansone before Nicolò did and tugged at his hand.

'Nicolò, where are you going?' The sourness in the signora's voice hit Nina like a bullet. Her pristine look and polished manners had intimidated Nina since childhood, making her feel uncouth and out of place.

'*Mamma*, we're letting Marta know we're going for a quick dip in the river.'

'Don't be absurd. Your father has invited the director of the Agnone internment camp for lunch. Neither of you is going to the river. Nina, you should be in the kitchen with your mother. And you, Nicolò, go and change. Make sure you look presentable.'

Nina blushed a deep crimson and fled, wondering why she felt like a thief, caught in the act of stealing a precious possession.

Chapter Four

The sky was tinged with orange. Ambra tapped her fingers impatiently on the sill and leaned her head through the open window frame. Nina should have arrived half an hour ago. Where was she? The smell of sunbaked earth, a hint of twilight birdsong drifted through the window. Earlier that day, Ambra had noticed the black Fiat enter the main gates of Villa Sansone and understood the signori had arrived. Usually, Ambra couldn't wait to hear the latest details of Signora Sansone's wardrobe from Nina, but today she had something to show Nina that was even more important.

She scanned the square: it was bustling. Men in black shirts loitered in clusters and sipped from stemmed glasses. German soldiers stretched out their limbs, the tip of their boots gleaming under the rays of the sun. Cigarette smoke swirled above their heads, their lips curled around the rims of wine glasses.

The large iron gates of the Sansone villa opened and Nina emerged.

'At last,' Ambra sighed.

She watched Nina cross the square and nod at Don Simone, who was sweeping the dust outside the church. Her lips parted into a '*buona sera*'. The eyes of the German soldiers followed Nina as she walked. Her socks were bunched down at her ankles, her hair in two long braids swung untidily around her shoulders, but even Ambra recognised there was something alluring about the natural sway of her hips, the perfect heart-shaped face with a small button nose and eyebrows that curved effortlessly over her eyes like velvet half-moons. Nina made little effort with her appearance, yet the eyes of the Bastiani men and the foreigners in their midst were always glued to her shapely calves, her delicate features. Young and old could not take their eyes off her. Ambra often heard villagers whispering of Nina's aura of beauty combined with vulnerability.

Well, if Nina had beauty and vulnerability, Ambra had style and class. And the knowledge to use what she had to get where she wanted to be. That was the difference between them. But they were friends; differences didn't matter.

Ambra greeted Nina and pulled her through the Post Office door. 'Nina, I have something to show you.'

'And I have something to tell you.' Nina's cheeks were flushed, her deep brown eyes flecked with gold seemed vibrant, excited.

'Is it the Sansones? Tell me later.' She took Nina by the hand and led her past packages and envelopes piled on the countertop, past the large brass till that towered over the scales used to weigh parcels. 'I have something that is going to change our lives.'

At the red wooden door leading to the storeroom, Ambra stopped and ran her fingers across the lintel above the door frame.

'I watched my father this morning, hiding the key here. Let's be quick, so I can show you what is waiting for us in the storeroom.'

'I have never been in the storeroom,' Nina said as Ambra unlocked the door.

'Come with me, it's in here.'

'It's very dark.'

Ambra switched on the light and Nina lifted her gaze to the walls lined with shelves and filing cabinets. A sepia-coloured photograph of a young Ambra with her parents stood on top of a large metal safe screwed into the wall. It was where Ambra's father kept valuable documents and money from the till at the end of the working day, Ambra told Nina.

'The documents must be very important.' Nina had never seen a safe before; a shiver mixed with excitement ran down her spine.

'That's my father's domain. He doesn't even reveal the code to me—his daughter, the Post Office girl, as everyone keeps saying.' Ambra scoffed. 'But look what we've got here.' Ambra pointed to the shiny typewriter that gleamed on an old kitchen table functioning as a desk, in the middle of the room. 'A portable Olivetti. They are all the rage at the moment.'

With the tips of her fingers, Ambra caressed the rows of round black keys rimmed with silver. She took a white sheet, slid it behind the roll and turned the knob. The paper moved along and came up at the front, as if it had a life of its own.

Then she pressed down the letter 'a'. The key tilted backwards before hitting the roll with a clunking noise. It reminded Nina of the long, green stick insects that clung to the hazelnut bushes down at the riverbank.

'You strike briskly and firmly like so.' Ambra let go of the lever and looked up at Nina.

'Now you try, Nina. It's easy.'

Nina lowered a finger towards the key of the letter 'n'; she missed it, and her finger landed in between the gaps of two keys, which sprang up, and became entangled. Ambra laughed and Nina couldn't help but giggle along with her.

'Imagine when we learn to type with both hands.' Ambra hovered her hands above the keyboard as if she were about to play a piano concerto.

'What a beautiful dream.' Nina sighed. 'But I don't have a typewriter.'

Ambra grabbed her by the shoulders and looked straight into Nina's eyes. 'You don't need one. You have this. Nina, look at me. Remember, we're in it together.' Ambra turned and walked through the door, down the narrow corridor, up the rickety staircase to her bedroom at the front of the building. She returned waving their knotted handkerchief. 'It's our pact. We made it at the *lavatoio* when we were twelve. Me with no mother, you with no father. Remember?'

'How can I forget? That piece of cloth is still under my mattress. Even now, I touch it before I go to sleep to feel less alone.' Nina grabbed the other end of the handkerchief, and they twirled around and around the barely lit storeroom, heads thrown backwards as their speed increased.

'The power of objects,' Nina laughed. Then Ambra stopped abruptly, making Nina stumble.

'Yes, the power of objects.' Ambra patted the typewriter. 'Our future is here. If we learn to type, we can find a job and get away from Bastiani. This war won't stop us dreaming, despite Mussolini's doctrine to keep women suppressed.' Then she remembered. 'What did you want to tell me, Nina?'

'He's here.'

'Who?'

'You know, the Sansones' son, Nicolò.'

Ambra rolled her eyes. 'You mean the *signorino* is gracious enough to pay a visit to our sleepy village. Shouldn't he be fighting for our country, supporting our *Duce* in the war effort?'

'He told me he is not joining the war.'

'Only the privileged ones!' Ambra snorted.

'But Ambra. He's handsome; wait until you see him.'

'Handsome or not . . . we've got our typing to do.' She stopped and smiled, eyes half-closed. 'Nina, let's make this summer our summer. One of us could be the next Signora Sansone if we play our cards right.'

'I hope not. She wears the right clothes and jewellery, but she's as cold as the river in winter and less inviting. Can you imagine she didn't even say hello to me?'

'But tell me. What was she wearing?'

Nina's words reached Ambra's ears like the refrain of the love songs she heard on the wireless at Bar Renzo: fashionable neckline . . . polka dots . . . the latest, latest, latest.

Ambra closed her eyes. The drab and lacklustre Post Office with its dawn-grey walls, chipped counter and unvarnished wooden floors had turned into an elegant drawing room with velvet curtains. On a plush silk sofa lay Ambra, dressed like Signora Sansone along with pearls and a gold-plated brooch.

Chapter Five

The mellow heat of the morning turned into a sultry July afternoon. The air in Campobasso, the capital of Molise, lay thick and cloying, pressing down on the city like an invisible hand. The sun blazed above the tiled rooftops, kindling them burnt orange. It deepened the scent of dust and hot stone. Waiting for her father outside the Post Office, Ambra sought refuge beneath the broad shade of a fig tree, its branches swollen with unripe figs. She shifted from foot to foot as the leaves above her stirred with a teasing whisper of breeze, too fleeting to bring relief. She lifted a hand to fan her face. The effort was futile.

A rustle of movement. Footsteps on sunbaked cobblestones. Before she even glanced up, she noticed the slate-grey trousers and black boots of the German army. She raised her eyes.

'*Fräulein,*' he said smoothly. 'I saw you standing here in this heat. I wondered if you might appreciate this—it will cool you down.' He clicked open a black and gold cloth fan, the silk rippling like the wings of a butterfly. With a slight bow, he extended it towards her. 'Please do me the honour of accepting it.'

His voice carried the ease and familiarity of practised Italian and Ambra could tell by the coloured stripes on the olive jacket that this man had an important role. His Italian was lilting, melodic, more refined than the clipped words of the soldiers who stumbled through Bastiani and slurred their elementary Italian—*ciao, buongiorno, bella signorina*—over glasses of grappa at Bar Renzo. Nor the brutish Blackshirts who kicked at stray cats and hens as if the village belonged to them and them alone. No, this one was different.

Ambra hesitated. The voice, the manner, the curious glint in his eyes—something about him unsettled her. Despite herself, a strange pleasure uncurled in her limbs, feather-light and dangerous.

His lips curved into a small smile. 'Are you new to Campobasso? I don't believe I've had the pleasure of meeting you before.'

She swallowed, shifting her weight. 'I come from Bastiani, a village in the hills near Castelnuovo.' A pause. Then she asked, 'Do you know it?'

A flicker of something, a watchful, amused quality to the slant of his eyes. 'I know all the villages around Campobasso. Bastiani, Castelnuovo, Fornelli, Vinchiaturo and many more.' He tilted his head. 'It is my job to know them, discreetly and deeply, if you see what I mean.'

She didn't. But she nodded anyway.

Up close, she took in the sharpness of his jaw, the fine bones of his face. Not brutish, almost delicate. The coloured stripes on his uniform set him apart from the common soldier. He was a man of rank. A corporal, perhaps? He noticed her gaze.

'My name is Werner,' he said, 'Werner Schuster, a serving officer in the German army, stationed here in Campobasso.'

'My name is Ambra. Ambra Tizzani.'

'A beautiful name. And what brings you here, Signorina Tizzani, to the cafés and streets of Campobasso?'

She hesitated. Then, as if testing the shape of the words, she answered, 'I'm waiting for my father. He is the postmaster in

Bastiani. He's collecting letters from the *prefettura*, the censorship office.'

Werner's eyes traced the shape of her lips as she spoke. There was a glint in his gaze—watchful, curious, almost amused. 'An important duty,' he murmured. 'Delivering censored letters, bringing news to those waiting for a word from their loved ones. I understand. It takes several weeks for me to receive news from my family in Koblenz.'

Ambra shrugged, lifting her chin. 'It's actually very dull. I want to leave Bastiani. Find work here in Campobasso.'

He studied her, as if turning her words over in his mind. Then, with a sudden warmth, he said, 'If there is anything you need, my *bella signorina*, I would be happy to oblige.' A pause, then he added, 'I love this country. And the women. Your language—it is like poetry, like music. I studied Italian literature at the university in my hometown. Giovanni Verga, Gabriele D'Annunzio and the sensuous elegies of Giacomo Leopardi, such a philosophical and sensitive poet.'

The names of Italian writers and poets drifted into the summer air and floated past Ambra's ears like wisps of clouds. Only one phrase rang in her head: if there is anything you need, *bella signorina*.

A reckless heat stirred in her chest. Without thinking, she blurted, 'Stockings. I need stockings. Preferably silk.'

The moment the words left her lips, Ambra blushed, embarrassed by her audacity. But Werner only laughed, his face creasing into dimples. 'You Italian girls are very direct,' he mused. 'I'll see what I can do. As long as you promise to see me again.'

A shadow flickered at the edge of her vision. Ambra turned her head. Her father was staggering down the steps of the *prefettura*, arms laden with parcels. His eyes scanned the street, searching for her.

Panic rose in her throat. Without thinking, she snapped the fan shut and thrust it back into Werner's hand.

'I must go,' she said quickly, stepping away.

'Wait. Please wait. I want to see you again.' His voice followed her like an anguished thread in the breeze.

But she didn't stop. Her skirt flapped behind her as she ran towards her father, leaving Werner standing alone beneath the relentless July sun, the embroidered German imperial eagle above a swastika adorning his chest.

Chapter Six

That Sunday afternoon, the streets and square of Bastiani were filled with a heaviness that made people more languid and melancholy than usual. In the stifling warmth of the Post Office, the window was wide open to allow wisps of fresh air to cool the room.

Ambra and Nina sat side by side in front of the Olivetti, their moist fingers tripping over the keys like partners in a dance. It reminded Nina of couples waltzing in the square during the olive harvest festival at the end of October. Their friendship handkerchiefs lay on each side of the typewriter, small, shrivelled knots of cloth—their reminder of the pact they had made years before.

'Now type without looking at the keyboard,' Ambra said and began to dictate the exercise: '*Pranzo d'acqua fa volti sghembi*.'

Tongue pushed between her teeth, hands cold and clammy, Nina managed to touch-type the sentence.

'Well done, Nina. At this pace, we'll soon be ready to apply for a job. I would love to work at the *Posta Centrale* in Campobasso.' Ambra smacked her lips as if she were already tasting a sweeter life.

'Gino says the city is swarming with German officers; surely that's not what you want.'

'There is a world outside the Bastiani hills, you know. It's waiting for us. And that's exactly what I want.' Ambra lowered her voice and leaned toward Nina. 'I'll tell you a secret. I met a German officer in Campobasso last week. He might even be a corporal. He began to talk to me when I was waiting for my father outside the censorship office. His Italian is fluent. He told me he studied Italian poets at university. His name is Werner Schuster. I think he holds an important role in the German army.' Ambra sighed and half-closed her eyes. 'Maybe he'll buy me some silk stockings and, you never know, he might find us a job.'

Nina's fingers caressed the keyboard with her fingertips. 'Ambra, I could never accept anything from a German officer, not even silk stockings. Gino would never forgive me. And remember, my father died fighting against the Fascists in Spain. And at the moment I'm enjoying working with my mother at the villa.'

Nina silently recalled how that morning, Nicolò had swirled her around the kitchen until they were breathless, his hair dappled by the reflection of the morning sun through the glass window.

'I don't want to work for the Sansones. I want to be Signora Sansone. I want to be on the right side of power.'

'How could you, Ambra? She's stern and remote. And she is a Fascist.'

'They are all Fascists.' Ambra swivelled around and stared at Nina. 'Nicolò included.'

'Nicolò is different.'

Ambra shrugged. 'Don't be so sure. He's from a well-known Fascist family.' She unfurled the paper from the typewriter. 'My wrists are stiff.' She twirled her wrists around to release the tension.

'Mine too,' Nina snapped. She tugged the sheets of paper and with a thump, placed them on the counter next to the typewriter. A strange sensation settled in her chest. Could Ambra, her friend, really think so differently, be willing to befriend a German officer for her own benefit? What would her father, Signor Ivo, think? And now here was Ambra, putting doubts in Nina's mind about Nicolò. He had always seemed different from his family, distant from their views. But was that what she desperately wanted to believe? Maybe Ambra was right. After all, Nicolò's father was the new supervisor of the internment camps dotted around the region.

'We've been typing for long enough. Let's go down to the river. A team of young boys from Molise are playing a game of football against some German soldiers.' Ambra smiled. 'And Nicolò Sansone is one of the players.'

Nina nodded, relieved at the opportunity to see Nicolò again. Nina leaned against the Post Office counter, the granite top cool against her back, and waited whilst Ambra placed the lid over it, ready for her father to transfer it into the storeroom. Hand in hand they left the Post Office and sauntered across the square towards the River Fastino.

Under a blazing blue sky lined with thin strands of white clouds a football match was taking place in the dry and dusty fields by the riverside. Improvised posts made of heavy rocks served as a goal.

Nina jumped when Ambra elbowed her in the ribs. Ambra's voice rose in excitement. 'Here he is, Nicolò Sansone with the ball. Look how fast he is running.' Nina's eyes followed Nicolò as he dribbled the ball, his movements fast and furious like a leaping tiger. He had always been a fast runner, Nina remembered. How many times had she lost when they had raced against each other? To console her he would give her a daisy picked from the lawn and when it was hot, he would cup his hands under running water to help her drink from the stone fountain at the *lavatoio*.

Ambra woke Nina from her reverie. 'You're right, he is a dashing young man. Convince him to come out with us this evening. Come on, you can ask him when you're at the villa.'

Nina's hands felt clammy despite the heat. The last thing she wanted was to share Nicolò with her friend. Over the past week at the villa an unexpected tenderness towards him had unfurled within her. Only that afternoon, he had brushed his hand against her shoulder. It had stirred within her a longing that had not left her since.

She pretended not to hear Ambra's suggestion and kept her gaze fixed on Nicolò. Suddenly, as he flipped backwards, he kicked the ball up into the air, his shoulder hitting the ground as his legs curled. The ball flew between the posts. The Bastiani boys cheered. The German soldiers, shirts rolled up to their elbows, heels of their boots stamping into the dried earth, cursed loudly in German.

Nina narrowed her gaze. Something flickered next to Nicolò's knee. It looked like a piece of wire. It slithered closer.

Nina screamed, '*Nicolò, attento*! There's a viper.'

Nicolò held his leg close to his chest, panting. 'It bit me.'

Within seconds she was by Nicolò's side. She grabbed his leg, lowered her mouth and sealed the wound with her lips. She began to suck the blood from the two tiny crimson dots just below his knee. She spat into the air. Nobody dared move her.

Her lips were still shielding the wound when a tall German soldier with an angular face bent down and pulled her away.

'What are you doing. *Fräulein*?' he chuckled in broken Italian. 'It's a simple grass snake . . . not poisonous.' His index finger pointed towards a green reptile slithering through the dried tufts of grass.

'No need to suck out the venom,' somebody said.

Shame flooded through Nina, cheeks flaming with embarrassment. She shook herself free from the soldier and broke into a run.

'Nina, wait!' Ambra called out.

Nina ignored her. She cut across the wheat fields, burnished gold in the afternoon sunlight, towards the winding streets of Bastiani. She turned into the steep, cobbled path leading to the old *lavatoio*, hoping none of the Bastiani women were there, washing their sheets in the stone troughs. But the troughs were empty; there was nobody to be seen. Nina sat on the cold stone steps.

'What on earth made you do that to Nicolò Sansone?' Ambra arrived panting, hands on hips.

'You followed me?'

'Isn't that what friends do?'

'Friends also understand when you need to be left alone.'

'What's the matter with you? You never want to be alone, without me.'

Ambra's voice was pinched, her skin crinkled with worry or annoyance, Nina couldn't tell. Ambra reached out and touched Nina's arm, moving closer to comfort her, but Nina shrugged her away with a flick of her wrist.

Ambra's coal-black eyes narrowed; two tiny red spots appeared on her cheeks. 'You're acting strange.' She turned and walked away, her footsteps receding into the distance, mingling with the words, 'See you later this evening, if you feel like it.'

Nina was glad her friend had gone. All she wanted was to be alone, to recall the sweet roughness of Nicolò's skin against her mouth; the salty taste of him on her lips; and to cleanse the naked shame invading her. She scooped some water out of the trough with cupped hands and let it trickle through her fingers. She didn't want to lose the taste of his blood, bittersweet in her mouth.

Chapter Seven

Nina only managed to swallow a few spoonfuls of bean soup. The emotions of the afternoon swirled inside her, creating a storm of thoughts that left her restless and agitated. The attraction she'd felt for Nicolò when her lips had brushed against his skin still excited her. When their eyes locked, the world around her seemed to fade away, leaving only the intensity of their connection. Was this what falling in love felt like? Nina wondered as she cleared away the remains of the meal she had shared with her brother Gino.

After washing up the terracotta bowls, she sprinted up to her bedroom, her footsteps echoing through the house. She brushed her hair in front of the mirror. With a comb, she made her parting straight down the middle. Her hair settled naturally across her forehead, draping over her left eye. Gino, head folded over the daily newspaper, *Il Giornale d'Italia*, didn't look up when she returned downstairs. Only when she walked towards the door did he mumble, 'Where are you going?'

'To meet Ambra in the piazza.'

'Nina, be careful; sometimes Bondi, the *questore* of the Agnone internment camp, comes to Bar Renzo to meet *Avvocato* Sansone. Keep away from them. And don't let the German soldiers flirt with you.'

'I know, I know. You tell me all the time.'

'You have to be vigilant. Trust me, Nina. I'll come by soon to keep an eye on you and make sure you get home safely.'

Out in the courtyard Nina breathed freely, unshackled by Gino's warnings. The musky scent of dusk mingled with the anticipated pleasure of seeing Nicolò again. But would he be happy to see her or would he ignore her, embarrassed that she had run up to him, pressed her lips to his knee? As children, hand in hand, they used to dive into the river. Linking arms they would run through the wheatfields around the villa. But they were no longer children. She was an eighteen-year-old girl and he was a young man of twenty-one. That afternoon at the football match she had crossed a line. And so had her heart.

Nina passed through the arch and arrived at the Post Office as the sun dipped behind the roof, flashing the terracotta tiles a blazing ochre. She knocked on the door. No reply. Ambra must have left for Bar Renzo. Perhaps, she was offended by Nina's reaction at the *lavatoio*. But Nina had needed time without Ambra; alone, to keep alive the intimacy she had felt with Nicolò. Sharing it with Ambra would have made the magic feel less real.

She knocked again, louder this time. The door opened and Ambra pulled her inside. The Post Office was ablaze in golden light; it felt alive to Nina despite the absence of customers. There was a vibrancy to it that she hadn't noticed during the day. She wondered if it was only the effect of the twilight. The storeroom door was half-open. She heard the tapping of keys and the murmur of soft voices. The door shut abruptly.

'Is your father still working?'

'Working? Something secretive no doubt. He's in there with Esther and her sister-in-law Mariolina. They are always here with him in the storeroom.'

'Do you think he's trying to protect Esther?' Nina leaned closer and whispered, 'She's a Polish Jew, you know.'

Ambra shrugged. 'Who knows what they're doing there? Anyway, what happened to you this afternoon? Why did you run off?'

Heat rushed to Nina's cheeks and neck. Should she confide in Ambra? Or should she keep it to herself, guarding the secret within her heart? Fears of being ridiculed battled with the hope of being understood by her friend.

She decided to keep her feelings to herself. The silence thickened and Ambra's eyes flashed with a momentary look of irritation, before it swiftly disappeared. 'Never mind,' she said, her tone lightening. Her eyes softened. 'Let's go out. It's such a beautiful evening.'

Nina took Ambra's arm, relieved the tension between them had dissolved. They strolled across the piazza, unspoken words of friendship flowing silently between their linked arms. Swallows crisscrossed the sky and dark bats flapped the warm air. The river far below had turned the colour of sunset, a shimmering red gold. The mountains above were bruised with the onset of night.

Outside Bar Renzo, the priest Don Simone Torti and the cobbler Santino Meriggi were drinking and playing cards. Cigarette smoke drifted above the priest's cap and Santino's pointed nose. Nina scanned the piazza, hoping to find Nicolò amongst the villagers, wishing she hadn't changed her hairstyle, afraid it didn't suit her. Ambra walked towards the bench, wiggling her hips from side to side seductively, flirtatiously, her shoulders swaying in a circular motion to emphasise her breasts. Who was she trying to copy? Greta Garbo?

A German soldier with long legs and a sallow complexion lifted his cap to Ambra as she sidled past. She smiled and waved her fingers at him as he nodded with approval.

Then Nina spotted Nicolò striding out of the wrought-iron gates of the villa, his large, strong hands pushed deep into his pockets. He was observing Ambra flirting with the tall soldier. Then he turned his gaze towards Nina. Their eyes met. It was as if silence had dropped in the piazza. His blue eyes sucked her in. They seemed lighter than usual. With long steady strides, Nicolò walked over to greet Nina and Ambra.

He grasped Nina's hand. 'I have to thank you for looking out for me before. It could have been a viper, you know. Luckily the bite was only from one of the common grass snakes you get around here.'

'I was silly. Sorry.' Nina hoped her voice sounded calm and clear, despite the turmoil she felt within as he cradled her hand in his.

'Nina, you cared. Look.' Like a child Nicolò rolled up the leg of his trouser and showed her the tiny red marks on his knee. He rolled it down. 'Can I offer you something from Bar Renzo, to say thank you?' He beamed at her.

'That would be lovely, Nicolò.' Ambra wedged herself between Nicolò and Nina. She leaned forward, and with curled fingers, gripped Nicolò's arm as if he were her prey. 'A *chinotto* for both of us, please.'

Nicolò returned from the bar, two glasses of the caramel-coloured soft drink balancing on a metal tray. 'I've just heard the news on the wireless. The Allies have landed in Sicily.' His hands shook as he handed over the drinks.

The voices in the square dulled to a hushed silence. Don Simone dropped the cards he was holding.

'I can't stay. I have to go home.' Nicolò turned his back and hurried across the piazza, a purple shadow following his long strides.

Gino marched out of Bar Renzo, cheeks red. He placed a hand on Nina's shoulder and whispered, 'Best you leave now. I'll walk you home.' Then he lifted his cap to Ambra in a display of gallantry and smiled. 'Good night, Ambra. You should go home too.'

Outside the villa, Nicolò was engrossed in a conversation with a German soldier and two local Blackshirts and didn't turn his head to look at Nina. Why did he not look at her? Why didn't he say goodbye?

Gino took her by the arm and quickened his step. 'Nina, if this is true it could be the dawn of the end of Fascism.' There was a twinge of hope in his voice. 'But be careful what you say at the villa. Not everyone will feel the same way as we do about an Allied invasion of Sicily.' Nina followed her brother home past the Post Office and through the grey stone arch to their farm.

'Does this mean the war will soon be over?' she asked.

'It's too early to be hopeful. Things could get worse, not better. I'll leave you here at the entrance. I need to speak to Ivo now.'

Nina watched Gino turn back along the path towards the piazza, his footsteps crunching on the gravel path. The moon cast a silvery shadow on his broad shoulders. For a moment she wondered how safe he was. An owl hooted from the nearby forest. A sensation of something much bigger than herself was taking shape within her. And she wasn't sure if it was her feelings for Nicolò or the news of the sudden invasion of Sicily.

Post Office

The night air thickens and the earth around the olive trees in the fields outside holds ridges as deep as knife wounds. Not even the coolness of night can quench thirst. Gino appears by the main door. He stubs out his cigarette with deliberate slowness, the muscles in his jaw tightening. He knocks three times on my locked door, then disappears around the side of my building through the secret passage that leads to the storeroom.

He coughs twice and shouts out a code name, '*Oggi piove*.'

'The Allies have landed,' he says. 'I have just heard on the radio in Bar Renzo.' He settles himself on a chair in between Esther and Mariolina. The air is suffused with the scent of sweat and dust, the low hum of voices rising and falling.

'Yes, we know. Esther is about to translate from the BBC.' Ivo hushes Gino with his hand and, with swift movements, he adjusts the long metallic aerial. The radio crackles and Ivo's fingers fly over the dials, fine-tuning the frequency. For a moment static noises reverberate in the air.

Esther's heavily accented voice layers Italian words on top of the foreign announcements spilling from the radio. She looks up, her black curls limp, beads of sweat on her upper lip. 'General George Patton's Seventh US Army landed before sunrise between Licata and Gela; General Montgomery's Eighth Army, between Pachino and Syracuse, encountering little resistance.' She breathes out and continues. 'It was a massive amphibious assault on the southern shores of the island. Only two German divisions were waiting in Sicily.' She stops and removes the thick-rimmed glasses balancing on her nose. 'The Allies were clever to trick them. The Nazi leadership believed the main attack would be in Sardinia and Corsica. The Canadians had to cope with fairly choppy seas in the area of their operation, but the British were protected by the bay at Passero and were able to land their equipment ashore fairly easily.'

Her voice fades as she listens once more to the broadcast, her head bent low over the radio. Mariolina, Ivo and Gino stretch their necks in anticipation. When Esther raises her head, her deep brown eyes sparkle with hope. 'Hundreds of ships are sailing across from North Africa carrying thousands of troops, weapons, armoured vehicles and heavy artillery.'

'Soon the Allies will reach Palermo, and liberate the whole of Italy.' Gino rises from his chair and whispers a song I have often heard seep through my walls during their secret meetings. The muffled lyrics of four voices, deep refrains of Ivo and Gino and the softer sounds of the sisters-in-law resonate through my wooden floorboards.

Fischia il vento, urla la bufera,
scarpe rotte eppur bisogna andar
a conquistare la rossa primavera
dove sorge il sol dell'avvenir,
a conquistare la rossa primavera
dove sorge il sol dell'avvenir.

The wind whistles, the storm rages,
our shoes are broken but we must march on,

to conquer the red spring,
where the sun of the future rises,
to conquer the red spring,
where the sun of the future rises.

The leaf of my paper calendar lies limp.

It is the 10th July, 1943, Saint Amalia's feast day.

Today is the day of Operation Husky and brings hope for my people.

Chapter Eight

The following morning, Nina passed the yellow wheat fields and took the road through the arch that led to the piazza, swerving round the goats and sheep littering the path. The braying of donkeys pricked her ears. Nina waved to Ambra's father as he loaded his old, battered delivery van with mail and parcels for the morning rounds. The warm air was sweet and fragrant at this time of day. Nina inhaled deeply.

It was as if the news from the night before had dissolved in the darkness, giving way to a fresh sense of hope and possibility.

Nina opened the wrought-iron gates of the villa and glanced up at the window of Nicolò's room, wondering if he was still sleeping. She kicked the pebble stones on the gravel path and entered the kitchen. The copper pans lit by the clear morning light gleamed like small suns on the hanging rack. Her mother was pouring egg and oil into the dough, ready to shape it into *cavatelli*, the Sansone family's favourite pasta dish. For a moment, Nina lost herself in the sight of the flour's pure whiteness, so different from the darker bran flour her mother used at the farm.

'Here you are at last,' her mother exclaimed, brushing away white flecks of flour from her chin. 'There is a pile of ironing on that chair. But first get the tablecloth and press it as smooth as a sheet of paper, the way Signora Carmela likes it. I'm going upstairs to clean the rooms.'

Marta downed forks and wooden spoons, covered the egg bowl with an upturned plate and wiped her hands on her thick black apron.

Nina set the kitchen table with a heavy undercloth and spread the tablecloth over it. It was large and she had to stand on tiptoes to fold it in two. She ironed one side and began to lift the tablecloth to turn it over. It was too long, and its ends brushed against the green and red hexagonal-tiled floor. With a dash of nostalgia, she thought of summer days when she and Nicolò used to skip barefoot on those tiles as children.

The door squeaked open, and Nina glanced up, her heart stirring. 'Here, let me help you,' Nicolò said, stretching out his arms to grab a corner of the cloth, his eyes twinkling. He behaved so normally that Nina could feel herself relax. She put the embarrassment of the football match behind her, as well as the deep and unfamiliar emotions it had stirred within her.

'Good morning, Nicolò,' she greeted him, happy to see him well disposed towards her. 'I was just thinking of the game we used to play on these tiles. Do you remember?'

'Of course,' Nicolò said, placing his foot right in the centre of a green tile and observing the intricate geometrical patterns at his feet. 'We were only allowed to step on the green tiles.' Then, gingerly, he hovered one foot over the red tile. 'And if, by mistake, we stepped on the red one . . .' he chuckled.

'Our wishes wouldn't come true.' Nina giggled as she placed the neatly folded tablecloth on the chair.

'My first wish of the day is coffee,' Nicolò said and reached for the Napoletana stored next to the sink.

'Chicory is all we can afford at home. It's like drinking dried soil,' Nina sighed.

'That's the beauty of living in a Fascist household. With my father's contacts in high places, he has access to the black market. But let me be your *barista*,' he added, with a playful smack of his lips. 'You can't say "barman". Mussolini controls our Italian language: no infiltration of foreign words.' Nicolò frowned, his wide forehead creased with light lines. 'Call me unpatriotic, but I prefer the word barman. I learnt English at school, and I like the sound of the word.'

Nina smiled. She thought of Gino and how incensed he would become at the mention of Mussolini's rules and laws. It was called autocracy, he'd told her. She was about to share this with Nicolò when she remembered Gino's warnings: 'Be careful what you say at the villa.' She bit her lip and passed Nicolò the bag of ground coffee.

Nicolò unscrewed the coffee pot and filled it with water. He spooned in two tablespoons of ground beans. Soon, the rich aroma of coffee brewing on the stove wafted around the kitchen. Nina inhaled the scent as if it were the mountain air of the Matese peaks. Was she really about to savour real coffee? She wished her mother and Gino could taste it too.

Nicolò poured the brown liquid into two small ceramic cups and handed one to Nina. Perched on a stool at the kitchen worktop, drinking coffee in the same room as Nicolò, him so close to her, stirred a sense of intimacy and excitement in Nina. War news could wait; here she was now, with Nicolò next to her, sipping real coffee. She swilled the liquid in her mouth to savour the intense toasted aroma of the brew on her tongue. She felt so privileged.

'Nina, quickly. Come to the dining room and bring me the freshly ironed tablecloth.' Her mother's voice boomed from upstairs, shattering the precious moment, bringing Nina back to reality.

The bittersweet aroma of coffee still lingered in the air when Nina returned to the kitchen. Their two empty cups stood on the kitchen counter. Nicolò was no longer there. She cursed her mother under her breath for taking her away from the kitchen, from him. A sinking feeling took hold of Nina. She tried to recapture the vibrations she had sensed when by accident her fingers had brushed against his, the linen of the tablecloth warm under his palms. She smiled to herself and began to rinse the cups.

A rustling noise startled her. It seemed to come from the kitchen pantry. A mouse, probably. 'They are desperate for food just like us,' she muttered as she turned off the tap. She dried her hands, took hold of the straw-bristled broom with the long wooden handle and tiptoed towards the pantry. She was about to wield the broom when she saw the whiteness of a shirt standing out in the semi-darkness of the pantry. Her heart pounded. It was Nicolò, crouching in the corner, back rounded over a small wicker basket. With swift movements he reached for the upper shelves, clasping items of food in his large hands and placing them in the basket.

Nina stepped back and retreated into the kitchen. A gasp caught in her throat. What was Nicolò doing? He didn't need to steal food; he had all the food he could wish for. Was he preparing a gift for someone? A thought rushed into Nina's mind. What if he was hoarding food to sell on the black market for profit? Perhaps Ambra was right, and he was more like *Avvocato* Sansone than Nina had realised. The idea saddened and appalled her at the same time. A bitter aftertaste of coffee rose to her throat and filled her mouth.

'Nina, come and help me set the table.' Her mother's plea came as a relief. Nina hurried out of the kitchen, doubts about Nicolò roiling within her.

That afternoon, when she stepped out of the villa onto the piazza, a wearied sensation took hold of Nina. Beads of sweat clung to her cheeks. She wasn't sure if it was from the oppressive heat of the day or the storm within her troubled mind. The pots of basil perched on the windowsill of the Post Office stood, withered and frail, under the relentless afternoon sunlight. She pushed open the Post Office door, hoping that typing with Ambra would bring her solace.

Chapter Nine

Inside the Post Office, Celestina handed Ambra a small package wrapped in rust-coloured paper and tied with string. Her usual mop of grey hair was hidden under a knotted scarf, her cheeks glazed with a patina of sweat from the stifling heat in the room.

'It's for my Giovannino. I've knitted him a pair of woollen socks. I hope they reach him in Albania in time for the colder months. I hear it freezes there in the mountains, much colder than here.'

Ambra placed the parcel on the brass scales. 'Of course I'll send this for you, Signora Celestina, but you haven't heard from Giovannino in months. Forgive me for being blunt but the battalion may have moved and he might never receive your woolly socks.'

Celestina's lips tightened, then her features softened. 'I will not stop sending packages to him. Each stitch I knit, each parcel I send, brings me closer to him and gives me hope.'

A film of sadness clouded Ambra's eyes. Hope? She had put so much hope in the medicines to cure her mother, but to no avail. Hope had failed Ambra, and Celestina's optimism seemed pointless. She should be practical, rational and think clearly instead.

'Have you contacted the Red Cross? They might be able to locate him,' Ambra asked, trying to be helpful.

Celestina shrugged, head cocked to one side. 'What can the Red Cross do for me?' she huffed. 'I go to mass every day. The Madonna of Loreto is my Red Cross. She is my true helper.'

Rita the cheesemaker's wife entered the Post Office, leaving her husband lingering outside in the piazza with their sleepy mule. Hearing the mention of the Madonna, she added her voice to the conversation. 'Every morning, at dawn, before I churn the cheese in the barrels, I murmur my prayers to our Madonna. She has never failed me.' Her short black curls bobbed around her smooth forehead. The scent of salted curd followed her, filling the room. Ambra sneezed. She passed some stamps to Rita and bid farewell to both women, relieved to see Nina step across the threshold.

'Thank goodness you're here,' Ambra said as soon as Nina closed the door behind her. 'These Bastiani women believe the Madonna is the answer to everything.' Ambra rolled her eyes. 'I only go to church for one reason—to get a glimpse of the few boys still left in the village.' She giggled and added, 'But most of them are too young. Apart from Gino, all the others are fighting for our country.'

The typewriter stood on the counter positioned in between the till and the brass scales. Ambra dragged two chairs towards it and gestured to Nina to sit down. She slid several blank sheets of papers into the typewriter carriage.

'Let's begin. I'll dictate, and you type first, Nina,' Ambra instructed.

She cleared her throat and began to read the sentences of the exercise aloud. '*Pranzo d'acqua fa volti sghembi*.'

The rhythmic clatter of the keys mingled with Ambra's voice. Nina's fingers hesitated over the keys, then she tapped and tapped. Her brow furrowed, her lips twisted in frustration. Over and over again, she failed to press the correct keys. She rubbed her hands on her smock. Ambra swallowed several times, forcing herself to stay calm despite Nina's clumsiness.

At Nina's umpteenth error Ambra's patience faltered. She slammed the book on the counter.

'Nina, what's wrong with you today? You seem distracted.'

'It's the heat,' Nina admitted, her voice low. 'I just need water. Then I'll be fine. I promise, Ambra.'

Ambra returned from the kitchen with a glass, watching as Nina drained it in one gulp. Ambra cleared her throat to begin, again. She hated wasting time when it came to typing. She was determined to master the skill swiftly if she intended to ask Werner to find her work in Campobasso. Nina poised her hands above the keys ready for the exercise, then dropped them to her lap.

'What's wrong now?'

'I can't, Ambra.' She blinked. 'I need to tell you something,' Nina said, her pointed chin raised towards Ambra, eyes pooling with tears.

'It's Nicolò, isn't it?' Ambra asked her with a sly grin. 'You've become strange since he arrived here this summer. It's like he's bewitched you. At the *lavatoio* you acted so peculiarly.'

'I fear you might be right.'

'Right about what? That he bewitched you?'

'No, no.' Nina's laugh was tinged with disquiet. 'That Nicolò Sansone is a true Fascist like his father and mother.'

In the stifled room of the Post Office, Nina shifted her body on the chair, pinned her elbows to the counter and recounted to Ambra what she had seen Nicolò doing. 'Imagine, selling food on the black market!' Nina concluded, lips puckered, a scowl crossing her face.

Ambra stretched and yawned. 'So, what if he is? What's wrong if he supports *il Duce*?' Ambra flicked a hand, waving Nina's worries away like smoke. 'Nicolò is lucky he can make money out of it. I would probably do the same thing in his shoes. Besides, *il Duce* is leading Italy to greatness.'

'Ambra, how can you say such things? Have you forgotten the Allies are approaching? And don't you understand Fascism represents everything my father and my family oppose and still fight against?'

Ambra looked at her friend, surprised and amused at her fiery speech.

'Politics mean nothing.' Ambra fanned herself with a sheet of paper. Couldn't Nina see the Sansones were leading a more prosperous life than anyone else in the village? How could she fail to see the allure of being them, regardless of politics?

'Perhaps to you, but not to me,' Nina replied.

'Besides, you don't know for certain where he truly stands, and I repeat, what's wrong with being on the side of the Fascists? Why not use it to your advantage? Tell him you'll guard his secret in exchange for food. Picture us, typing away, with sugar crystals on our tongues.' Ambra's eyes sparkled with a glint of mischief.

'I'll never do that.' Nina shook her head. She shot to her feet in protest, knocking over her chair.

'You are too moral, Nina,' Ambra retorted, pulling the chair upright. 'Look at me. I've got my German admirer. He calls me *bella signorina*; he promised me treats—"anything you need," he said in his beautiful, refined Italian. I suggested silk stockings and I am already thinking of asking for lipstick, a bottle of French perfume, perhaps, and even some real silk to sew myself a pretty blouse with flattering darts at the waist.' She twirled around the room. 'A rich woman's wardrobe during wartime? You see? It's easy, Nina. You should learn to play the game.'

'You astonish me, Ambra.' Nina's voice quivered. 'But I can't play the game. It's just not who I am.' She rested her chin in her cupped palms, closed her eyes, a pensive quiet look smoothing her features. 'Maybe I am disappointed in myself; I thought I knew him.' Her voice was wistful.

Ambra's throat tightened. Nicolò. Nicolò. Nicolò. It was always Nicolò. A sharp pang of jealousy tinged with irritation surged through her chest.

'Look, I can help you.' Ambra's tone was brisk yet measured. 'From the window here I have a clear view of the piazza and Villa Sansone. I'll keep an eye on him, but for now let's concentrate on the typing. War or not, we still need to secure our future, and I'm hoping my German friend will help me,' she added with a grin as she slid a fresh sheet of paper into the typewriter.

'If he wins the war,' Nina teased, a cheeky smile playing on her lips.

Ambra's wink was her only reply. The air between them fizzed with unspoken differences.

Chapter Ten

The fields around Bastiani turned from gold to dusty brown; the olive groves and vineyards sketched hazy silhouettes in the sultry mid-morning air.

'Another day of heat,' Nina exhaled, making her way through the stone archway into the piazza, toward Villa Sansone. Ever since the morning she had stumbled upon Nicolò in the pantry, she had kept a deliberate distance from the kitchen, fighting against the desire to spy on him in the villa, dreading what she might unveil.

But today her mother had been insistent: Nina was to sit at the kitchen table and shell the broad beans gathered from the villa's vegetable garden. Protests were futile; even Nina's offer to polish the marble floor in the drawing room was met with dismissal. 'Nina, waxing the marble floor is not a task for you. Do the broad beans. Off you go,' her mother commanded.

Trepidation fluttered in Nina's chest as she opened the kitchen door. Her hands trembled, her stomach flipped. The room, spacious and awash with light, was thick with the warm, inviting aroma of tomato sauce bubbling on the stove. Pangs of hunger stirred in her belly. She took a white serving bowl and seated herself at the long wooden table, beans on her lap, bowl before her, back turned away from the pantry. She began tearing the pods, deftly peeling away their outer skins, allowing the tender, vibrant-green beans to tumble into the bowl like beads slipping off a rosary. The rhythm of her hands, paired with the earthy fragrance of the beans, carried her away into a memory with her father. She was brought back to the time when as a child she accompanied him to the potato fields. She could still see his strong arms wielding the shovel, breaking the soil around the potatoes, while her tiny hands eagerly unearthed the spuds like hidden treasures in a game of pirates. Then under the shade of an oak tree, they had shared lunches of Pecorino cheese and beans. She struggled to recall the coarse texture of her father's fingertips brushing against her cheek as he passed her the plumper beans, his hands shaped by labour and love.

A sudden thud broke her reverie. She flinched. The sound had come from the pantry. Her chest tightened. Nicolò?

She hesitated, the impulse to flee gripped her. But no, she could no longer bear the weight of uncertainty. If it was Nicolò, she had to confront him, face the truth, no matter how unsettling. She set the beans and the bowl back on the table, rose to her feet and crept towards the pantry entrance. She nudged the door, already ajar, a little wider.

In the dim light of the pantry, she glimpsed the stark white of Nicolò's shirt, a fleeting flash against the shadows.

'Nicolò? What are you doing?' her voice, hoarse and quivering, barely escaped her lips.

He spun around, startled, cheeks pink with embarrassment or shame, she wasn't sure. His piercing blue eyes locked onto hers. He twisted his body as if attempting to hide the basket brimming with wedges of cheese, a loaf of bread, apples and a packet of coffee.

'What are you doing with all this food, Nicolò?' she repeated, her voice scratchy, fearful of what his answer might be.

Nicolò placed the basket on the floor, a finger on his lips to intimate silence. He reached for her and pulled her close.

'Can I trust you?' he whispered.

He squeezed her hand with urgency, fingers digging deeply into her palm. The warmth of his breath brushed her cheek. Nina faltered. She didn't want to surrender to her feelings, not until she knew where his loyalties lay. She had to steel her heart against the pull of her emotions. Resolute, she withdrew her hand from his grasp.

'I need to trust you, Nina.' His tone was soft now. The intimacy in his voice stirred her. She longed to reach out and stroke his lips with her fingertips, tell him he could trust her, that she would guard his secret as her own. That she cared for him. But she held back.

'It depends,' she replied simply.

'We've always been friends, you and I,' he said, his words carrying the memories of their shared history.

'Of course. But I need to know why you are doing it.' Nina kept her tone measured; her expression guarded.

A sudden clenching of his jaw. Nicolò blinked several times. Nina braced herself, her heart hammering in her chest, as she prepared to hear the words she had been dreading.

'Only last week, I accompanied my father to Isernia. He was visiting the internment camp set in the former Benedictine convent. We used to cycle there, the two of us and Ambra. Remember?'

Nina nodded; her heart quickened. 'And?' She stiffened, still unsure of where Nicolò's words were leading.

'I was waiting for my father in the piazza.' Nicolò exhaled sharply, wringing his hands. 'There, sitting on a bench staring at the water spurting out of the jets surrounding the Fraterna fountain, was a man, one of the internees on his daily outing within the established perimeter of the village. I sat next to him. He inched away afraid he might be caught talking, which is strictly forbidden on pain of imprisonment. I told him who I was, and he need not be afraid. Only then he seemed reassured and told me his name. Tonino.' Nicolò paused, his gaze dropped to the floor. 'I felt sad for him. I offered him a cigarette. He took it. His fingers were thin and long; nails chipped.' Nicolò's voice faltered.

'Is this basket of food for him, Nicolò?'

'Yes, Nina. I want to smuggle food into the camp.' His deep blue eyes burnt with an intensity and clarity Nina had not seen before. The grey-black rings around the irises gave him a wild quality. Nina sensed how strongly he believed in what he was saying. Relief washed over her, her shoulders relaxed, a warm feeling spread in her belly. She had been wrong to doubt him. Ambra had been wrong too. Nicolò didn't share his parents' political views.

Then a torrent of sentences gushed out of him, like a river breaking its banks.

'The internees there survive on small rations. Morra, the director of Isernia, is irascible and bad-tempered and allows the internees to eat only milk and rice. He even refused a request for light bulbs to illuminate the cramped room where seventy internees sleep on the floor. They really are in prison. I know, I have been inside with my father.' Nicolò exhaled as though the weight of his words were too heavy to bear.

'The camp is swarming with different types of people from different countries: Roma, Sinti, Jews and Italian anti-Fascists like Tonino.' He continued, his tone a mixture of anger and despair, 'So many different people huddled together in dormitories. Think, Nina. I am here playing football with German soldiers, drinking black market coffee as if I were oblivious to their injustice.' He stopped and drew a long breath. 'I must help these people. And now the time's right. The Allies are on their way. You heard the other night at Bar Renzo?'

Nina knew she was free to talk now she knew she and Nicolò were on the same side. 'Gino has always talked about the camps ever since they were installed here in Molise when war was declared, three years ago. I hear him discussing them with Don Simone and Ivo as they play cards at Bar Renzo. But when he mentions them at home, our mother tries to silence him, afraid even the walls can hear his criticisms, afraid he might disclose his views against the regime, afraid she might lose the only strong arms left in the family. I don't blame her; we lost our father fighting for his political beliefs, you remember?'

'And you must be proud of him for that! Would your father have turned a blind eye to innocent people interned for being against the regime or for having a different religion or ethnicity? I can't.'

Nina was touched when Nicolò remembered her father and felt flattered he spoke to her as an equal, as if she understood everything he was saying.

'It sounds risky, Nicolò . . .' Nina whispered.

'It is risky, you're right. But being *Avvocato* Sansone's son is useful; it gives me access to the internees and I'm protected at the same time.'

'But still, what if your father or the *questore*, or the *podestà*, or even the *carabinieri* find out? You could be in real trouble and end up in the anti-Fascist section of the camp yourself.'

'That's why I need you to trust me, and I am asking you not to tell anyone, not even Ambra. Keep it a secret, you understand? Our secret.'

Our secret. The words tolled in Nina's ears, giving her the confidence to reach out for Nicolò's hand. His skin was rougher to her touch than she'd expected yet still sent a quiver of tenderness down her spine. *Our secret.*

'Say, you'll help me,' he urged, 'and you'll keep this between us.'

Nina thought of the handkerchief under her mattress, its knots old and soiled by the passing of time. Was it wrong to keep this pact with Nicolò from Ambra? After all, wasn't it for a cause greater than their friendship pact? Perhaps.

'Of course I will, Nicolò,' Nina declared then added, 'I have access to the pantry. It will be easy for me to get the food you need for the internees. You go now. Leave the basket hidden behind that sack of onions and I'll pack it for you.'

'It has to be this afternoon. I've got my *motorino* ready. At four, Tonino will be sitting on the same bench. Bring me the basket. I'll meet you at our usual place with my scooter.'

Nina's heart skipped, her lips stretched into a smile. He had remembered. As children they used to meet at the stony riverbank where they would fish and swim till dusk, the row of hazelnut trees offering shelter from the summer heat.

'I'll be there.'

He looked at her.

'Why don't you come to Isernia with me? You sit at the back and hold the basket. It will be easier for me.'

Nina hesitated. How tempting it would be to sit behind Nicolò on his scooter, arms curled around his waist, as they whizzed through the dusty country lanes lined with vineyards, orchards and olive groves. But she had promised Ambra she would see her at four for their typing session. If she said yes to Nicolò, she would disappoint her friend.

Yet, if she said no, she would miss an entire afternoon with Nicolò.

Nicolò placed his finger under her chin and lifted it. 'Nina, look at me. What do you think?'

The touch of his fingers felt like a tender caress. 'At the usual place?' There was a trembling to his voice.

Nina allowed her feelings to decide.

'At the usual place,' she repeated, a smile playing on her lips.

*

Ambra was filling shelves with stamps and reams of paper when Nina opened the Post Office door.

'You're early today. We're not typing together until later this afternoon.'

Nina leaned on the granite counter, gripping the edge. She felt spots of red heat creeping up from her neck to her jaw. 'I won't be able to make it this afternoon; that's why I've come here now. To let you know.'

'Why can't you make the typing lesson? What happened?' Ambra asked, her breath laboured. Nina could sense Ambra's disappointment. She hated to let her friend down and had never lied to her before. She hesitated, her stomach churning as she struggled to find the right words, a valid excuse. She couldn't possibly tell Ambra the truth. 'Our secret,' Nicolò had insisted. The image of Nicolò's trusting gaze and her promise to him forced her to speak quickly, as if to obscure the lie behind the speed of her words. 'I have to help Gino. It's time to harvest the potatoes. The flowers have already withered and died.'

'Can't you say no to Gino? Surely these hours we put into typing are more important than dirty potatoes. It's for our future.' Nina could hear the thread of anger in Ambra's voice.

'I'll be here tomorrow afternoon, I promise.' Nina placed a reassuring palm over Ambra's hand and patted it, hoping this would end the conversation.

'You're leaving me to practise alone. Watch out, I might overtake you.' Ambra winked. For a moment Nina felt the urge to confide in her friend, to make her swear to keep her secret, perhaps even share what she felt for Nicolò. The knots in their handkerchiefs were the reminders of their pact. Nina knew that their friendship didn't deserve this betrayal, but . . . again Nicolò's passion, the importance of their mission obliterated everything else. Nina kissed her friend—a quick, furtive kiss on the cheek—before leaving the Post Office and gliding over the paving stones towards the arch leading to the farm.

Chapter Eleven

The whirring of the engine on the cobblestones outside the Post Office made Ambra jump. Her father was already back from Campobasso and he would be furious if he found her typing in the storeroom, even if she were alone without Nina. She jumped up, gathered together the sheets of paper lined with her afternoon's typing exercises and hurried into the Post Office, locking the door behind her and placing the key like her father had done on the lintel. Her father crossed the threshold, his shoulders hunched under the weight of a sack full of parcels and letters to be delivered the following morning.

'Many censored letters today for the internees at the camps.' His leathered cheeks appeared more furrowed than usual and flecks of worry shadowed his grey eyes.

'You look tired; you must be hungry. I'll go and heat up the rice.'

'Let's arrange the mail first, so it's ready for the morning delivery. Any letters for me, put to one side and I'll deal with them later.' Ivo flung the heavy jute postal bag onto the counter and began to remove the contents and place them in piles: Villa Sansone, Don Simone, Bar Renzo, the various Bastiani households and last, a selection of censored postcards for the internees in the Vinchiaturo and Agnone internment camps.

'Why do family members even bother to send missives to those internees? What good does it do? They will never see their families again. Better to forget their past, isn't it?'

'How can you, the daughter of a postman, say such things? Remember, Ambra, our duty is to ensure everyone gets their mail, and that includes these unfortunate internees. Do you not understand that these letters are not just paper and ink? They help the internees cope with the severe conditions they're forced to live under. Letters build a bridge between life before the war and their future life at the end of the conflict.' Ivo's voice fizzed with anger.

Ambra's father had never preached to her before. She flicked through the postcards, running her fingers along the inked-out lines. 'Well, the censors don't agree, *papà*. There are many words they didn't approve of today.'

'Well, Ambra. There are two things I don't approve of.' Ivo leaned towards her, chin on his hand, eyes stern and cold. 'First, you don't go into the storeroom without my permission. With or without Nina. This key'—he retrieved the key from above the storeroom door—'will remain in my pocket. And second, since when are you receiving packages from Germans?'

'Packages? From Germans?'

He removed a small rolled-up packet wrapped in tissue paper from the leather satchel slung across his chest. He handed it to Ambra, his face taut. 'A German officer gave it to me today and asked me to hand the gift to my daughter. He seemed to know exactly who I was and who you were.'

'It's just a bit of fun.' Ambra's voice pierced through the Post Office as she shrugged off her father's scowl.

'You're playing with fire, meddling with that lot, Ambra. They are not our friends.' Ivo's bushy eyebrows met in the middle, casting dark shadows on his eyelids.

'But think, *papà*, I'll be the only girl in the village to own a real pair of silk stockings.'

A flash of indignation crossed Ivo's face, the grey of his eyes hard and shiny. 'What is happening to you girls? Even your friend Nina is hanging around with the Sansones' son. Haven't we taught you anything? Pietruzzo saw her with Nicolò on his motorbike on the road to Isernia. That's not part of her job in the household! What is she thinking of, meddling with a Fascist family, considering what her own father did fighting for freedom? Doesn't she realise people gossip here in Bastiani? This isn't the time to be cavorting with Italian Fascists or Germans. The Allies have started their ascent. Things will change once they get here.'

Her father's words of warning washed over Ambra, transformed into the vague mutterings of a frenzied elderly father, obsessed with the consequences of war. Instead, Ambra's brain tingled with the refrain, 'Nina, Nicolò! Nicolò's motorbike! Nina, Nicolò on the road to Isernia?'

'What do you mean Nina and Nicolò together? She told me she was harvesting potatoes with Gino.' Ambra's throat clenched. Was Nina, her best friend, lying to her?

'That's not what Pietruzzo saw. You must warn her to be careful. And you, Ambra, no more gifts from Germans. Do you understand?'

*

The rice they ate for dinner tasted like sawdust. It lay on Ambra's stomach like a rock. If it wasn't for her father begging her to go out that evening—'Esther and Mariolina will be here this evening. I'd prefer if you're not here'—she would have spent the evening in bed, cursing her treasured friendship pact with Nina and the friendship handkerchief stored in the top drawer of her dressing table, underneath her underwear.

Instead, she ran upstairs, the package from the German officer clasped under her armpit. In the silence of her bedroom she unwrapped the soft tissue paper, her fingertips caressing the smooth silk of the stockings. They would look good on her shapely legs, her mother's favourite shoes on her feet. She applied a scant layer of red lipstick to her lips, wondering how long her mother's pre-war makeup would last. She would have to plead for more from her new German friend, Werner Schuster, and hide his gifts from her father from now on.

Ambra crossed the square. Her high heels clicked on the cobblestones, fusing with voices and music floating on the evening breeze from Bar Renzo. With each tap of a heel, the image of Nina's sweet, heart-shaped face, lips searching for words to weave her lie, haunted Ambra.

Inside the bar, Nicolò was chatting in the corner, his eyes glued to the entrance. The tendons of Ambra's neck tensed. Was he waiting for Nina?

She greeted him with a nod of her head.

'Nina's not with you this evening?' Nicolò's lips stretched into a soft smile, the trace of a dimple on his cheek. 'You're always together, you two.'

She longed to say, *I've just heard, it's you two who are always together,* but instead answered, 'Not always, Nicolò. Buy me a cold drink for this hot evening.'

She hoped her deep, husky voice sounded alluring. She wet her lips with the tip of her tongue. The notes from the traditional Italian bagpipes, the *zampogna*, filled the air with a rich velvety sound. Ambra swayed her shoulders in time with the melody as Nicolò handed her a glass of sparkling Pecorino wine.

'*Cin, cin*.' Ambra raised her glass and clinked it against Nicolò's. Their fingers touched momentarily. Ambra entwined her hand through his arm. Flirting came more naturally to her than licking stamps in her father's Post Office. Without Nina, she suddenly felt freer. *Two can play at your game, Nina*, she decided.

Celestina's deep, mournful voice accompanied Renzo on the accordion. Aurelio the *zampognaro* from Castelnuovo al Volturno was playing the *zampogna* alongside them. He was known to be one of the best in the region. Sometimes Ambra and Nina would accompany Ivo and Gino to Castelnuovo to listen to him play. Stirred by the intensity of the notes and the lyrics full of longing, Ambra grasped Nicolò's hand and drew him close. She pressed her body closer to his. She could feel his cheek at her temple like a warm heartbeat.

After a while he stepped back from her. The candlelight cast shadows across his handsome face, his strong jaw.

'I'm going home now, Ambra.'

His words jarred in her ears. A cold frisson swept through her despite the stifling heat. She panicked. Not yet. She didn't want him to leave her. Somehow the closeness of Nicolò's body helped assuage the pain of Nina lying to her. A bud of hope sprouted in her heart. Perhaps Nicolò could be hers?

She widened her eyes. 'Please help me slip off my shoes. They were my mother's and they're too tight for me. But it always feels good to wear them.'

Too polite to refuse, Nicolò bent down towards her knees and took hold of her ankles. As she leaned on him she touched his curly hair; a stolen caress.

'How can I get home? I can't walk. Will you walk me home, Nicolò?'

A blanket of stars glittered in the night sky. Bats dipped and dived around the bell tower of the Santa Croce church, slicing black silhouettes across the silver-grey moon.

Her hand cradling Nicolò's arm, Ambra shifted the fullness of her weight onto him. They crossed the square, her shoes still in his hand.

'Thank you for a lovely evening, Nicolò,' she purred when they reached the Post Office. She thrust her cheek forward, her lips brushing against his. None of the other boys she had kissed had lips as soft as his. He pulled himself free, too fast for Ambra to taste his mouth.

'Good night, Ambra.' He sounded firm. Yet the gentle squeeze of his hand made her smile. She still had a chance after all to cultivate his feelings for her.

The yellow hue of the streetlamps hit the cobblestones of the piazza. Ambra followed Nicolò with her gaze. Hands in his pockets he kicked the dusty pebbles with the toe of his shoe. He approached the villa, but instead of pushing open the gate, he turned and headed towards the arch at the village entrance.

The alcohol was swirling around Ambra's head. The path he trod led to the Caruso farm. She felt a heaviness inside as if a large stone had been planted close to her heart. She decided to follow him. Barefoot, her steps were silent.

She recalled Nicolò's face, his eyes that smiled even when his lips were in a straight line; mouth soft and swollen, just ripe to be kissed. When she saw him enter the Carusos' farm, she stamped her bare foot on the gritty earth. 'You bloody liars, scheming behind my back!' She cursed between clenched teeth and retraced her steps back to the main square.

She pushed open the door and entered the darkened Post Office. From the storeroom on her right, a blade of light streaked the wooden floor. The familiar voices of her father and Nina's brother Gino were muffled by the clicking of the typewriter and the heavily accented voice she knew belonged to Esther. Esther and her sister-in-law Mariolina seemed to spend a lot of time in the storeroom with her father. The smell of cheap tobacco mingled with the tangy aroma of *poncio* liquor, the local drink her father brewed each summer.

Whatever they were doing didn't concern Ambra and she ran up to her bedroom and pulled open the top drawer of her chest of drawers. She rummaged amongst her cotton underwear, searching for the braided handkerchief she'd shared with Nina years ago.

She pulled it out. She stroked the green and white flowers, nostalgic for the companionship that had supported her since the day her mother had died. Didn't they scream aloud their grief, wiping the tears from each other's cheeks? Instead of their lives falling apart, hadn't they looked after each other? Nina had joined Ambra as she trod the cobblestones of Bastiani, delivering letters and parcels to the inhabitants, whilst her father sobbed, perched on a stool in the kitchen; Ambra had helped Nina to collect potatoes and olives from the fields, their backs bent against the heat of the Bastiani summer.

Together, they had learnt how to survive their losses, heads held high with pride, emotions turned to stone in order not to suffer. But now all that was dissolving into the balmy night air.

How could Nina have chosen Nicolò over her? And how could Nicolò have chosen Nina instead of her, to ride on his *motorino* to Isernia?

The muscles under her rib cage tightened. Images tinged with both rage and nostalgia floated across Ambra's mind:

Nina's red cheeks as she spouted her lie; Nicolò approaching the Caruso farm at night. And to think that only a few days ago they were tapping the keys of the typewriter, sharing the same dreams. She picked up a pair of scissors from her makeup bag. She raised an arm and brought the scissors close to the fabric of the braided handkerchief. Then she stopped abruptly and sank down to her knees, crouching on her heels. How could she sever this link with Nina, this friendship pact that had been a lifeline to Ambra for so long? It would feel like cutting off a limb. She placed the scissors back in her makeup bag but didn't return the handkerchief to its usual place. She left it on the floor. She would decide what to do with it in the morning.

Chapter Twelve

The night air wafted through the half-opened window, carrying the remaining heat of the day. Nina lay on her bed staring at the ceiling, reliving the memories of that afternoon spent with Nicolò outside the camp in Isernia. Her thoughts returned again and again to Tonino; torn shirt hanging from bony shoulders, lifeless eyes, skeletal frame. Nina's heart tugged. Nobody in Bastiani looked as bedraggled and starved, despite the scarcity of food, the rationing and lack of grain during wartime.

Tonino's vacant gaze had drifted from the verdant mountain tops and settled on the basket of food Nina was holding. Something had flickered across his face as his hands stretched out to retrieve the food.

'*Grazie*. You are our saviours. This means so much.' He grabbed the basket of food and wedged the cheese and coffee inside his shirt and stuffed the apples in his pocket. 'I can trade the coffee in the camp for some meat in my soup.' He squeezed their hands with his scrawny fingers before fleeing to the camp.

What went on in those camps dotted so close to Bastiani had never really occurred to Nina. So many internees crammed into one room, fed on little food and living in fear of Morra, the irascible camp director. And to think Tonino's only sin was to disagree with the regime. The power the regime had frightened her. It could be Gino in there, interned for his anti-Fascist views. Or Ivo, Esther and Mariolina, or any of the Bastiani villagers who had the courage to stand up to Mussolini and his Fascist supporters. And wasn't Esther at risk of being sent to one of the camps? She was not only an anti-Fascist but also a Jew.

A sound like the crackling of rain made her jump. Nina sat up. Stones showered against the pane of glass. She walked towards the window. The night sky swirled with twinkling stars; the moon's face shimmering bright and clear shone on a male figure, kneeling down to gather pebbles from the ground. He stood up to take aim but jumped back when he saw her standing there. The stones slid between his open fingers like silver sand. In the moonlight his face seemed pale. Heart fluttering, she opened the window wider and leaned out.

'Nicolò, has something happened?' She blinked in the semi-darkness.

'I was hoping to see you at Bar Renzo,' he whispered.

'I arrived home too late from Isernia. My mother punished me. She wouldn't let me out.'

Nicolò reached his arms towards her. 'I have something to tell you. It's about one of the other camps. Let me come up. I won't make a noise.'

'No, no.' She panicked, afraid they would be caught. 'I'll come down. Give me five seconds.'

Nina peeled off her nightdress and pulled on a shirt and the skirt folded on her chair. She dressed with haste then swung her left leg out of the window. She scaled down the drainpipe with the agility of the stray cats scampering around the village streets. She jumped to the ground with ease and stood next to him.

'I'm impressed.'

'It's all that practice from climbing trees and pinching fruit when we were younger.'

Nicolò took her hand and squeezed it. The warmth of his touch sent a shiver down her spine. She could feel his body, strong and muscular close to hers, a comforting presence that made her heart race.

'Let's go down to the river,' he said. 'Nobody will be there at this time of night; we can talk freely there. And it is our special place after all.'

Nina glanced back at the house. Inky dark shadows stretched across the roof onto the silent farmyard. Her mother was in bed asleep, and Gino was probably still at Bar Renzo or with Ivo in the Post Office. They wouldn't notice she wasn't in her room. She nodded at him, and they ran hand in hand, jumping over stones and fighting back stray plants until they reached their special spot by the hazelnut bush. The excitement of their shared escape filled Nina with a blend of joy and anxiety.

Sitting side by side on the pebbled beach, Nicolò began to relate what his father had revealed earlier that evening.

'My father left promptly after dinner. An internee from the Vinchiaturo internment camp had tried to escape. She jumped out of a window and was badly injured.'

'Vinchiaturo?'

'Yes, the women-only internment camp, set up in a private building, owned by the Di Nonno family, in via Libertà. The internees are foreigners the regime doesn't trust: Jews, Yugoslavs, Polish, Russians, some Italian anti-Fascists and I think a few Sintis. Living conditions must be harsh. I overheard my father saying the internee was so malnourished she broke several bones and may not survive. Nina, the situation in the camps in Molise is deteriorating. We must do something, we can't stop with Isernia.'

Clouds drifting across the moon cast shadows over Nicolò's tall forehead. His voice, a mixture of pain and anger, made the recounting of the event seem even more sinister.

Nina pictured a skinny young girl with bones jutting from her shoulders, just like Tonino, throwing herself out of a window and shattering her body. She shuddered and placed a hand on Nicolò's bare arm.

'Nicolò, let's smuggle food in there too.'

A silence descended between them, broken by the hooting of an owl and the gurgling of the river.

'Nina, that's what I was hoping you'd say.' His lips stretched into a deep smile.

'I can easily fill the basket when my mother isn't looking, and your mother never checks. But how do we get the food inside Palazzo Nonno?'

'*Maestra* Anna Martinucci is the director. Wasn't she your teacher at the Bastiani school?'

'Yes, she was. She was very kind to me when my father died. She even came to visit me and brought my homework and sweet almonds.'

'Do you think she will help us?'

'*Maestra* Martinucci?' Nina pondered. 'I'm not sure. She always seemed to be a follower of the regime. She made us salute *il Duce*'s image every time we passed by. When she retired, we gave her a parchment with all the Fascist symbols printed on it.'

'Everyone has to pretend to follow the regime, even if they don't believe in it. Otherwise, they will be arrested.'

'Come to think of it, I remember how she frowned when she opened our gift and thanked the class with a forced smile.'

'You see, we assume everyone is a Fascist. We don't know what they really believe. At home, I'm a Fascist, but that's not my true self. Sometimes I feel like running away.' His words hung in the air, heavy with unspoken truths.

She noticed the sadness brimming in his eyes, revealing his struggle between his outward appearance and inner beliefs. Maybe it was harder to be a Sansone, part of a prominent Fascist family, than she had realised. Carmela was a cold, closed person. She spoke with a hiss as if permanently gritting her teeth. Her perfect outfits and pristine hairstyles matched her tight composed ways as if every muscle in her face was under her control. She was an intimidating woman, a convinced Fascist, intolerant of any other political view. And there was *Avvocato* Sansone, supervisor of all these camps, who greeted the Bastiani villagers with the Roman salute and waved his *Tessera del Fascismo*, the Fascist membership card, to everyone he met. Perhaps living in that imposing house with its Fascist flags and photographs of Mussolini staring down at you was enough to make Nicolò long for freedom.

'I believe we must help these people imprisoned in the camps around here. Like Tonino. Did you see how his eyes, so dead and lifeless, lit up when we handed him the basket?'

Nicolò leaned towards Nina, his breath cool against her skin, like a fresh breeze in the sultry night. The bubbling sound of the Fastino river flowing downstream fused with Nicolò's throaty voice.

'Would you come with me tomorrow afternoon to talk to *Maestra* Martinucci?' He reached forward and stroked her cheek with his thumb. Her heart skipped a beat.

She hesitated. She'd promised Ambra she would meet her in the Post Office to catch up on the typing she had missed. Nina closed her eyes and when she opened them Nicolò's gaze was fixed tenderly on her face. It was as if they were children again, planning their games, whispering secrets, trusting each other. Nina exhaled deeply; the decision was easy.

'I'll come with you.'

'Thank you, Nina.'

He kissed her on the tip of her nose. Without realising she parted her lips. When he lowered his head, her hand reached up to stroke the nape of his neck. They moved closer, their breath rising and descending in perfect accord, shadows and light blending in the expanse of the night littered with stars. She took a sharp inhale as he showered her face with hot kisses. She didn't want to lose his warmth. She needed him. And she knew he needed her too. Nina whispered his name. It made waves in the air like birdsong.

She was in love with him.

She had been all her life.

When Nicolò left her at the entrance to the farm, the house was in deep silence. Nina tiptoed past her mother's bedroom, comforted by the rattling sounds of her snores. She stopped outside Gino's door and listened.

Silence.

She opened the door ajar and peeked through at the untouched bed. He was still out; a tight squeeze of her heart. Where was he? The last thing she wanted was for Gino to end up in a camp like Isernia.

Back in her room, Nina undressed and slipped under the sheets. She tossed and turned in the sweltering heat of the night, the names of the camps swirling around her brain like the refrain of a malevolent chant: Agnone, Vinchiaturo, Boiano, Casacalenda, Isernia. No longer were they simply the villages of her childhood that she knew so well, but detention centres holding those deemed unacceptable to *il Duce*, the man the country was meant to admire and obey.

Outside the moon clung to the sky, casting silvery shadows across Nina's bed. Her thoughts switched to the comfort of Nicolò. She could hear his voice, gentle and passionate, taste his tongue swirling on her lips, inside and outside the mouth he had made his own. Lulled by the sensation of their embrace she closed her eyes, hoping sleep would bring peace.

Chapter Thirteen

The door and windows of the Post Office were wide open. The air was thick with the scent of scorched earth, wild fennel and sun-ripened wheat. Beyond the piazza the hills of Molise loomed above the horizon, their edges blurred in the heat.

Ambra sat at the counter, strumming two fingers on the granite top, face pensive, jaw clenched. The brass bell over the Post Office door jingled. Ambra raised her gaze to see Nina, framed by the resplendent golden light of late afternoon, standing awkwardly in the doorway. Behind her, Bastiani sweltered beneath the weight of summer, rooftops shimmering like beaten copper.

Ambra stiffened and forced her lips into a smile.

Nina looked different. There was something that was smoother, clearer. Less of an edge about her. Ambra squeezed her eyelids together. It was confidence, Ambra decided. She swung back on the rear legs of the chair and contemplated her friend. Nina's loose, raven hair trailed down to her waist and shone like deep velvet; the colour of her almond eyes was deeper, more intense. The skin of her face was smooth and bronzed from the summer sunshine. She appeared even more beautiful than usual.

'There's an air about you.' Ambra sniffed the air like a dog. 'A smell of something . . .'

'Don't be silly.' Nina flicked Ambra's arm with her thumb and first finger.

Nina leaned in towards Ambra, her head close. Ambra could smell the scent of camomile Nina used to wash her hair. 'I need to talk to you.' Nina's voice was barely a whisper.

Ambra felt a melting inside, a sense of both floating and spinning like she was flying away. Finally, an opening. Perhaps now Nina would confide in her, share the secret she was concealing. They would be friends again. She would promise never to lie to her best friend and Ambra would skip upstairs to her bedroom, kiss the *fazzoletto,* their friendship handkerchief, and return it to its special place in the drawer underneath her underwear.

'Is it Nicolò? Has something happened you can't tell me?' Ambra suggested, in the attempt to make it easier for Nina to open up.

'Of course not.' Nina flinched; her cheeks flooded with a crimson hue. 'Nothing to do with Nicolò.' She paused, a shimmer of sweat clinging to her skin.

'I have to stop typing with you, that's all. I don't have the time anymore to devote to the lessons.'

That's all! Stop typing with you. Excuses dropped like pebbles on Ambra's heart. She paused and then the words flew brittle from her lips. 'What do you mean? Stop typing? But why? What about our pact to leave the village, once the war is over?'

Nina leaned forward and reached for Ambra's hand, but it was coiled into a deep fist. 'Look, Ambra. I have so much more work to do these days. With the Sansones now permanently in Bastiani, there is more dusting and ironing, and I have to help my mother prepare meals in the kitchen. I'm busy all day long. And on top of that, I have Gino who is always breathing down my neck, forcing me to help him.'

'Like the other afternoon? When you helped him pick potatoes?'

Nina's mouth twitched. She lowered her eyelids. Mesmerised, Ambra's eyes were glued to a pulse thumping against the delicate, pale skin of Nina's temples. 'Exactly. I just don't have time anymore for typing. I'm sorry, Ambra.'

Another lie! The walls of the Post Office pressed inward as if the building itself could sense the thudding and hammering in Ambra's chest. Before she could stop herself, her fingers closed around Nina's wrist pressing tight, too tight.

'Ouch! You're hurting me.' Nina flicked Ambra's fingers away. She rubbed the red marks the grip had sealed on Nina's skin.

'Do as you wish,' Ambra grunted. She rose from her stool and stumbled towards the door. She opened it wide and gave a slight nod. 'You can leave now. I'll continue typing on my own. Without you.'

Nina remained rooted by the counter. 'We're still friends, aren't we? We have our pact, our knotted handkerchiefs . . . Mine is still under my mattress at home. This doesn't change anything between us, does it?'

A thick cloud descended on Ambra, damp and cold against her skin. Memories flooded back; their shared pact by the *lavatoio;* stained fingertips from autumn porcini hunts; and the weightless joy of splashing in the river beneath an endless summer sky. Of course it changed everything. Nina was tearing their friendship apart. It clearly meant nothing to Nina if she could lie so easily, her cheeks crimson, her lips quivering.

'I think you should leave now.' Ambra nodded towards the open door and with a trembling hand pushed Nina through. She turned the notice hanging on the door to '*CHIUSO*' and slammed it shut, the windowpanes rattling with the force. With her back against the cracked wall, she exhaled in short, angry bursts.

'So much for our friendship pact,' she muttered to the empty room. 'You're lying to me. Again. To me.'

Something inside Ambra hardened. She ran up the stairs to her bedroom and snatched the scissors and the knotted friendship handkerchief. This time she didn't stop. She snipped away and with angry movements of her fingers cut the braided handkerchief into pieces. One by one she watched the shreds of their friendship float to the floor.

'Nina, this is our war now.'

The scent of dust and lemons drifted through the open window. Somewhere, a dog barked, and the crickets groaned in the trees outside in the piazza. Ambra bent down to gather the strips of fabric. She placed them in a battered tin box in the top drawer of her chest of drawers, underneath a moth-eaten cardigan. For some reason she couldn't explain even to herself, she wasn't ready to dispose of them completely, despite Nina's lies, despite her betrayal.

*

It was Tuesday, the day of the week she ran errands to Campobasso for her father. She pulled on a pleated cotton skirt with a tight, white top that emphasised her breasts, hoping Werner would buy her an *aperitivo* at one of the fashionable bars off the main square, as he had promised when they last met. She dabbed a blob of red lipstick onto her index finger and smeared it along her cheekbones. With renewed confidence, she popped her head around the Post Office door.

'*Papà,* what shall I collect from the *Ufficio della Censura Fascista*, the Fascist censorship office in Campobasso?'

'Take the jute sack and fill it with the censored and stamped postcards for the internment camps of the area. The sooner the internees hear from their loved ones, the better they will feel.' His back was bent over the counter, his shoulders hunched.

'You were up late last night, *papà*. What were you doing?'

He turned and faced her, red-rimmed eyes boring into her. 'Ambra, sometimes secrets must be kept. I'm trying to protect you.' With a terse nod of his head, he thrust a small pile of postcards into two large brown envelopes. 'These are from our people in Bastiani.' He placed the second envelope in Ambra's hand. 'And these are postcards from the internment camps for the censorship office, please hand them over as soon as you arrive in Campobasso. It's vital the families know the internees are safe.'

Ambra placed her arms around her father's waist and teased him. 'Sometimes I wonder whether the inmates of the camps are more important than your own daughter?'

He kissed her on the nose, his voice soft. 'Off you go, you silly one. You'll miss the bus. And make sure you don't spend time cavorting with German officers. Remember which side this family is on.'

Chapter Fourteen

Ambra sat on the bench under the linden tree by Bar Renzo. She waited for the *corriera* to Campobasso; the River Fastino shimmered in the distance. With her back to the river, she had a clear view of Villa Sansone beyond the wrought-iron gate and the oak tree with its dense cloud of green leaves. The door opened. Could it be Nicolò? She stretched onto her toes and craned her neck. It was only his mother. Her blue eyes vibrant against the whiteness of her suit and blonde hair, she nodded at Ambra and waited a few paces apart. Carmela Sansone was wearing a white linen skirt with a matching jacket. Her hand was gloved, a cream, lace glove, buttoned on one side of the wrist.

When the *corriera* arrived, Signora Sansone swayed down the aisle towards the back. A man wearing the buttoned black shirt, broad-shouldered jacket and high black boots of the *squadristi* movement, Mussolini's Blackshirts, jumped down and gave Signora Sansone a Roman salute and bowed his head in deference to the wife of the *avvocato*.

Ambra indicated the empty space next to her. 'May I, Signora Sansone?' Smiling at the Blackshirt, she lowered herself into the seat, careful not to crease the signora's suit.

Signora Sansone clicked her handbag open and drew out a long glimmering pink lipstick to retouch her lips. A twang of envy flashed through Ambra as she thought of her own lipstick, a mere stub of red. How she wished she had money to buy such luxuries. She glanced at her own flimsy cotton skirt. Didn't she deserve luxuries like Signora Carmela? The German officer understood that. Whatever her father thought about him and his politics, Werner made her feel important, seen, treasured. And in times of war, surely there were more ways than one to accrue possessions, money, trinkets. The heat on the bus thickened. When would she have another chance to sit next to Carmela, alone? An idea hatched in Ambra's mind. She must seize the opportunity now.

Ambra weighed her words with care. 'Your son is quite friendly with my friend Nina, isn't he? I suppose all those years playing together has made them close.'

Carmela blinked once, twice, three times. A nervous laugh escaped from her throat. 'I know my son. He belongs to an important Fascist family. He doesn't mix with the *contadini*.' Carmela shot Ambra a cold stare.

'I wouldn't be so sure, Signora. He even went to see her, late at night,' Ambra added, surprised at her own impudence. A vein pulsated on the left side of Carmela's temple just below her fine eyebrow.

'I'm sure you're wrong, Ambra, and I trust you're not spreading rumours.' Signora Sansone offered Ambra a smile with long tight lips, the corners of her mouth curled upwards. Ambra didn't reply. Silence was her weapon.

The bus approached the outskirts of Campobasso. The crenellated walls of Castello Monforte perched on the hilly rock appeared silhouetted against the sapphire-blue sky. The bus stopped at the corner of the main square, opposite the town hall. The Italian flag with the Savoia crown nestled in the centre was motionless in the dense heat of the day.

Ambra crossed over to the fountain in the middle of the piazza and sat on its concrete edge. She dipped her fingers into the cool water, dabbed her temples and smiled. What a fortuitous bus journey that was.

*

Walking from the *Prefettura* to the bar where many of the German soldiers congregated, Ambra wished she owned a fine pair of brand-new heels to show off her shapely calves, not merely her dead mother's pre-war shoes. The pavement outside Gran Caffè Lupacchioli in Piazza Pepe was lined with round tables and metal chairs. On white tablecloths lay empty espresso cups and ashtrays piled with cigarette stubs. Soldiers in greeny-grey uniforms gulped down shots of *poncio* and mingled with Italian Blackshirts. Laughter, intertwined with smatterings of German and Italian, rose into the air.

Ambra lengthened her neck to gaze amongst the crowd. There he was. He waved at her, his dainty white teeth flashed below his wiry moustache. He sprang out of his chair, saluting her, his arm at an angle in the Nazi fashion. She wondered whether to salute him back. Her father would not approve. In Bastiani the formal Roman salute was used in official events, not for compatriots. But she was in Campobasso. Nobody in Bastiani could see or hear her. She lifted her arm straight up to the sky, as Mussolini had prescribed and mouthed the words, '*Viva il Duce*.'

Uttering the words here felt easier than she expected, as if she were merely shouting to spur on one of the Bastiani mules. She settled herself at a table whilst Werner brought her a slice of milk-pan cake covered in hazelnut cream. A luxury. In Bastiani she could only dream of such delicacies.

He sat down beside her, eyes fixed on Ambra's mouth as she licked the cream off her lips with the tip of her tongue.

'I hope you received the silk stockings.' He reached for her hand.

'Thank you, I did. They fit beautifully.' She smiled and took a mouthful of cake. 'But please don't ask my father to be your messenger. Next time give them to me directly.' Ambra batted her eyelashes in what she hoped was a seductive gesture. 'Because there will be a next time, won't there?'

Werner offered Ambra a wry smile and took a long drag of his cigarette before stubbing it out on the pavement. '*Fräulein* Ambra, there will be many more luxuries, I promise.'

'Lipstick?' How she would love to apply a new pink lipstick, like the one Carmela Sansone had pressed to her lips.

'Lipstick, perfume, a silk scarf. Whatever you like if . . .'

The forkful of cake suspended in midair, Ambra tilted her head. Excitement and expectation mixed with the unknown surged through her.

'If what?'

He leaned forward and whispered into her ear. 'I need your eyes and ears. The Allies are approaching from the south. Any sleeping village can hide enemies of the regime. We can't trust anyone. You and I are on the same side, remember?'

Ambra didn't think of herself on any side except her own. Fascist, anti-Fascist: what did it matter? Couldn't she pretend to be on Werner's side without betraying her village? At least this way she could be more than the Post Office girl, attempting to type her way to a better future. She was right to think she could profit from this war. She turned her gaze to Werner. He was not an overly handsome man. His shirt pulled across his stomach and Ambra wondered whether his buttons would pop open. His eyes were small and bulged slightly from their sockets, but they were soft and reassuring. He had money and power, and he made her feel valued.

Ambra replaced the fork on the plate and pushed it to one side. 'I'll be here in two weeks. Bring me a pink lipstick and a bottle of perfume and I'll see what I can find out for you.'

She crossed her arms over her chest and leaned back on her chair, a sly smile playing on her lips. Satisfaction welled up inside her knowing she had both Werner and Signora Sansone exactly where she wanted. A small victory, but in these uncertain times every win counted.

Chapter Fifteen

After sorting through the afternoon post, Ambra decided to go down to the river to calm the turmoil tossing inside her. She sat down close to the shore under the shade of a hazelnut bush. Gathering a pile of pebbles, she cast them one by one into the river, her worry abating at each throw. Mesmerised, she watched the ripples as the sunlight cast golden flickers on the surface of the water.

The whirring of an engine alerted her. She squinted through the branches, bobbing her head through the gaps of the foliage. It was Nicolò Sansone. She was about to leap forward to surprise him, when a crunching of footsteps on the shingle and a soft velvety voice reached her ears.

'Nicolò, I've got lots of food for the camp.' Nina was clasping a wicker basket between her arms. Nicolò took it from her and placed it beside the motorbike, before pulling her towards him, his lips seeking Nina's and sealing them in a long kiss, the tips of his fingers caressing the long strands of her hair.

Ambra's heart quickened; her mouth tasted of ash. She remained still and listened, her ears strained towards them. She didn't want to miss a single syllable.

'It's time we leave, Nicolò, if we want to get to the Vinchiaturo internment camp.'

Ambra sat back on her heels. She forged a gap through the foliage of the hazelnut bush and peeked through. Nina and Nicolò, two figures huddled together, whizzing along the road enveloped in a cloud of dust. In her ears, the drone of the *motorino* speeding away, a hum fading in the distance.

Ambra bent down and picked up two shiny pebbles from the shingly riverbank. She didn't usually think of herself as a lucky person, an ambitious person yes, but not a lucky one. A lucky person wouldn't lose a mother at twelve years of age, have her own youth stolen by years of war, with only one pair of high-heeled shoes and a single stub of red lipstick. Would a lucky person have a best friend who kept secrets and told lies to her?

But that afternoon when she had least expected to see Nina and Nicolò kissing and talking of Vinchiaturo, she knew she was lucky indeed.

She kissed one of the pebbles and threw it in the air. It hit the water with a clean splash. She watched it drift downstream as she whispered aloud.

'Werner, I have something you will be very interested in. Just wait and see.' She pressed the second stone to her heart, feeling its warmth against her skin. 'And you, Signora Sansone, you will find a way to thank me for what I'm about to reveal.'

Her plan was thickening, moulding into something sharper, richer, more defined. And she would put that plan into action, soon. Very soon.

*

Ambra walked up the gravel path to Villa Sansone and pulled the cord outside the double-doored entrance. The sound of the brass bell reverberated on the stone steps. Ambra shifted her weight from foot to foot. Marta appeared on the threshold, wiping her fingers on her apron, droplets of sweat beading her hairline.

'If you're looking for Nina, she's not here. You should know not to use the front entrance.' Marta pushed the door closed.

Ambra wedged her arm in between the door and Marta. 'Wait, I've come to talk to Signora Sansone.'

Signora Sansone appeared in the hall, a crisp silhouette behind Marta's scrawny frame. A silk flag with the House of Savoy crown in the middle of the *tricolore* was pinned flat to the wall above them.

'What brings you here, Ambra? Is there something to sign?' she asked, lips painted red and drawn into a thin line.

'Signora Carmela, I need to talk to you.' Ambra glanced at Marta, still standing in the hall, a puzzled expression etched on her face. 'In private.'

A strange silence fell between them, broken by Carmela's acid tone. 'Follow me.'

This was the first time Ambra had stepped into the drawing room of the Sansones' villa. The walls were lined with large antique furniture that smelled of wax and wood. In front of two velvet sofas stood a coffee table. Porcelain figures and silver frames with photos of the Sansones were displayed on the windowsill. Ambra's eyes drifted to the black and white photograph of *Avvocato* Sansone shaking hands with Mussolini.

'Has the *Avvocato* met *il Duce*?' Her eyes widened, as she spun round to face Carmela, a mixture of surprise and awe printed on her face.

Carmela motioned to Ambra to sit down. 'Only once, when *il Duce* appointed him supervisor of the internment camps of the Molise region. It was a great opportunity for him and our family to further serve the regime.'

Ambra paused. Blood rushed to her face. If only Signora Sansone knew what Ambra had just heard at the river. But this information she would keep for Werner.

'I've seen them.'

A nerve quivered on Signora Sansone's eyelid. 'Ambra, I've warned you. Don't spread rumours.'

Ambra leaned against the back of the sofa, her fingers tracing the flowers embroidered on the velvet material.

'They were at the river, kissing, hidden away from prying eyes. It was unfortunate for them that I happened to be there, behind the hazelnut bush.'

Carmela sprang up from the sofa, opened the door and shouted at the top of her voice, 'Riccardo, please join me in the drawing room. It's important.'

When *Avvocato* Riccardo entered the room, Ambra's eyes captured the flicker of silver in his well-trimmed moustache and slick chestnut hair. *Avvocato* Sansone was a handsome man, taller than Carmela. With a hint of a smile and a swift movement, he raised his arm and stretched it upward, palm to the ceiling to greet Ambra. Dazzled by him, she jumped up and returned the salute, surprised how comfortable and easy it felt. Here, in this room, she could almost taste what it felt like to be a Fascist.

'Riccardo, Ambra claims she has seen our son with Marta's daughter.'

'And what's wrong with that, *cara?*'

'Riccardo, they were kissing at the river.' Carmela's voice, a high-pitched squeal, resonated around the room. She grabbed a silver cigarette box from the coffee table, plucked out a cigarette and snapped it shut with force.

Avvocato Sansone spoke gently but firmly to his wife, 'They have known each other all their lives. Even if they kiss . . . Well, what's so terrible about that?'

'What are you saying, Riccardo?' Carmela lit a cigarette and took a long, angry drag.

'Carmela, it's gone on for centuries. Nicolò is looking for distraction with our housekeeper's daughter. As long as he's discreet, what does it matter? Look at what our *Duce* gets up to.'

Carmela shot her husband a look of disapproval, stubbed the cigarette out in the silver ashtray on the coffee table in front of her. 'What does it matter?' Her puzzled expression caused her eyebrows, plucked into two half-moons, to meet in a perfectly curved bridge. 'You, of all people! You know perfectly well the rumours swirling around Gino's political leanings. Your reputation is at stake if your son cavorts with Gino's sister. Remember, you have an official role. And to compare what *il Duce* gets up to with our son . . .' Carmela's voice trailed off.

'Carmela, as you well know from the wireless bulletins, things are changing politically day by day. One never knows what will happen next.'

Ambra listened in silence. She turned her head from Carmela to Riccardo, wondering if they had forgotten she was in the room. She cleared her throat.

'Excuse me, *Signori*. Why don't I keep an eye on them both?'

'That is not necessary,' Riccardo Sansone barked.

Before Ambra could reply, Carmela hooked her hand under Ambra's elbow and accompanied her through the hall, past the Fascist flags to the front door. She delved into the pocket of her navy-blue cotton dress and pressed a piece of paper into Ambra's palm. 'This is for you. Don't listen to my husband. Report to me.'

Ambra knew it was money, her fingertips stroked it as if it were velvet.

She skipped down the steps of the villa, savouring the sharp scent of the lemon trees flanking the front entrance. Barely containing her excitement, she turned the note over in her hands. The printed image of King Vittorio Emanuele on the front and the wing-splayed eagle on the back beckoned to her. She touched the note to her lips and kissed the wrinkled paper.

*

In the piazza, her father was sitting outside Bar Renzo under the awning with a group of friends. He waved at Ambra and lifted his glass, motioning for her to join them. Ambra smiled and mouthed back the word 'later'.

She strolled to the other side of the square and sat on the bench overlooking the River Fastino, glinting under a violet-blue twilight sky. She uncurled her fist in slow motion and stared at the money resting in the centre of her outstretched palm. Her father would not be proud of her; of that, she was sure. She shook her head and quickly dismissed the worries of her father's disapproval and rebukes. Instead, she allowed herself to dream. She shut her eyes to savour the moment. She imagined herself shopping in Campobasso; she might even buy a new pair of high-heeled shoes.

If Carmela was prepared to reward her with a five-*lire* note, she couldn't wait to see how Werner Schuster would respond to what she was about to tell him. The smell of jasmine and rose wafted past her. When she opened her eyes, the sun was dipping behind the mountains, turning them a deep magenta. A slice of pale moon appeared above the octagonal steeple of the church. It was time to return to the Post Office to prepare the potato and onion soup for her father's evening meal.

Chapter Sixteen

Nina sat behind Nicolò on his *motorino*. A hot afternoon wind blew strands of hair around them. They sped past villages with russet-tiled houses clinging to the rock. The mountains, a patchwork of rust, green and white, jutted against the blazing blue sky. Blankets of thick velvet trees swayed in the light breeze. They passed crumbling shacks, stone churches and corn fields.

They approached Vinchiaturo, leaving behind the woods and dust-filled roads. The village perched on a hill glowed in the sunlight imbuing the terracotta roofs of the stone houses with an enchanted aura. Nicolò parked his *motorino* under the shade of an oak tree in via della Libertà. He pointed to the building opposite.

'This is Palazzo Nonno, an unusual place to house internees, I know. But the government uses whatever structure they can get hold of; Agnone, a former convent of San Bernardino of Siena; Boiano, the old tobacco factory; school buildings in Casacalenda; and a Benedictine convent in Isernia, *Antico Distretto*.'

Nina hopped off the *motorino* and stared up at the imposing facade; a wrought-iron semi-circular fanlight framed the wooden front door. Four balconies, with railings fashioned in the same cast iron, dotted the pale green walls. Leaning over the balcony of the next-door house was a small girl in pigtails. A jagged fringe framed her eyes. She waved at Nina, her mouth stretching into a toothless grin. Nina was about to wave back when the front door of Palazzo Nonno opened. Two *carabinieri*, caps perched on their heads, stepped out of the building. The buttons of their uniforms glistened in the sunlight. The long-legged *carabiniere* beckoned towards the door, his square jaw and moustached upper lip set in a stern expression exuding authority and intransigence. The short younger one with a pockmarked face and sad-looking eyes ushered out a line of young women: tall, small, thin, hair colour ranging from red to blonde to midnight black, eyes cast down, shoulders hunched, feet shuffling onto the pavement.

A loud shout and whistling caused Nina to turn. A group of Vinchiaturo youths materialised out of nowhere as if a magician had waved his wand.

'Hey *tu rossa*, red-haired one, look at me. I love you,' a lanky lad, fists dug deep into his trousers pockets, shouted at the woman with copper hair.

Nina winced as more insults followed.

'*Biancaneve,* take off your white shawl and show me the whiteness of your breasts.'

'And you, beautiful *principessa,* I am waiting for you tonight.'

Nina's cheeks flushed hot pink at the insolence of the young men's obscenities, almost as if the affront was aimed at her. The women lowered their heads in shame, their mouths hardened into thin lines. She wished she had the courage to stop these youths mouthing such humiliating remarks. A profound sadness overcame her.

A tear streaked the cheek of the beautiful woman the men called *Biancaneve,* Snow White. Nina longed to hug her and wipe away the tear. The woman's watery emerald eyes met Nina's. It was like falling into a deep sea, wondering what lay concealed at the bottom. Despite the presence of the *carabinieri* Nina couldn't stop herself from stepping forward to squeeze the woman's hand in the hope she would feel comfort from a stranger.

'My name is Malka Schwartz. I've done nothing wrong. My only fault is, I am a Jew, *un'Ebrea*. I need help.' Her voice was a whisper, but Nina heard the desperation in the accented Italian phrases. 'It's desperate here. We are alone, letters are censored, we don't know what's happened to our families. We are kept totally in the dark. Hygiene is poor and there is very little food.' She spoke fast, words spilling out in one great rush.

A celestial melody rose through the air. The boys scampered away. The chins of the *carabinieri* lifted towards the girl with pigtails, singing as if she were in a church choir. Nina seized the opportunity of this distraction to whisper back to Malka, her words muffled by the angelic notes of the hymn, 'We are here to help.' Nina pointed to Nicolò, a figure under the shade of the oak tree, hands clutching the handle of the basket.

'More food and uncensored letters. That's what we need.'

Maestra Anna's appearance froze the words on Malka's lips.

'Nina, what are you doing here in Vinchiaturo? If the *carabinieri* catch you talking to the internees, we'll all be in trouble. You must leave now.' With a frantic gesture she motioned to Nina to leave.

Nina's eyes sought out Malka's pleading stare, heavy with desperation. The lack of hope in Malka's eyes, the musty smell, her frail voice, all shook Nina. *I can leave*, she thought, *they can't*. She felt a squeeze in her heart, wondering if her father had suffered from the same desperation and lack of hope in that foreign country, so far away from Bastiani and his family. Nina realised she had never allowed herself to imagine him fighting in the fields, hungry, hurt, in need of aid. Perhaps he had also been interned in a camp, alone, just like these women.

With a fearlessness unknown even to herself, Nina said, 'I'm not leaving, *Maestra Anna*, I've brought food for them.'

'Not now.' The *maestra* glanced at the *carabinieri*, their eyes still fixed on the little girl singing in the pink house. 'Leave it behind the oak tree. I'll collect it later.'

Nina nodded. The line of women trudging along the gravelly road reminded her of emaciated and exhausted mules returning to Bastiani after a gruelling day's work in the fields. How could she abandon Malka, the *Biancaneve* of Vinchiaturo, and the other sad women like *La Rossa*, the red-haired one? The weight of their struggles made her heart heavy. The pleading in their eyes anchored her decision. Something switched on inside her, a newfound determination. She would be there for the internees, no matter the cost.

Riding back to Bastiani behind Nicolò on the *motorino*, the warm July evening air caressed Nina's cheeks. Her arms wrapped tightly around his waist, she could feel the tautness of his body through the thin cotton of his shirt. For a fleeting moment, her yearning for him waned as Malka's voice echoed in her mind, 'More food and uncensored letters. That's what we need.'

Nina squeezed Nicolò's waist, leaned closer, allowing her voice to blend with the wind and carry her words to his ears. 'Nicolò, those women are hungry and lonely in Palazzo Nonno. We brought them food, but they also need letters from their loved ones; real letters, not merely those censored scripts they already receive. The food nourishes their bodies, but letters feed their spirit. Nicolò, we must help them in every way we can.'

Chapter Seventeen

It was Tuesday afternoon, the day when Ambra left for Campobasso to run her father's errands. Nina was helping her mother at the Villa Sansone, reassured she could keep her eyes on the Post Office from the kitchen window. She needed to be sure Ambra had already departed before she made her way to visit Ivo that afternoon.

The noise of the *corriera* approaching the square alerted her. She craned her neck, watching as Ambra ran to catch the bus. 'That's Ambra, typical Ambra,' Nina muttered and smiled inwardly, noticing that despite the heat of the day, Ambra had sheathed her legs in a pair of silk stockings. Nina imagined a faint trace of French perfume trailing behind her, mingling with the exhaust of the *corriera*.

Nina slipped out of the villa, her movements soundless against the hushed backdrop of the afternoon. As she stepped out of the kitchen's cool sanctuary, the piazza's heat enveloped her like a smothering blanket. The sun's rays pressed on her skin; beads of sweat traced her upper lip, and she dabbed them with the back of her hand. Apprehension and the weather made her pulse quicken. Nicolò's doubts echoed in her mind: *are you sure it's okay to reveal our plan to the postmaster?*

But Nina had been adamant. This was their only option. They had to trust Ivo if they wanted to deliver uncensored letters to Vinchiaturo and Isernia. 'He's close to my brother. They share the same beliefs.'

'There's a difference between sharing anti-Fascist beliefs and compromising his official position.'

'Let me try,' she'd insisted, her voice firm as she rose on her tiptoes to kiss him on the mouth, savouring the freshness of his lips.

Ivo was at the counter, engrossed in preparing a postal order for Antonio, the carpenter. He raised his head, his dark bushy eyebrows lifting. 'Nina, *ciao*. You've just missed Ambra.'

'I know, but I need to speak to you, Signor Ivo.'

Nina greeted Antonio and waited patiently until he left the Post Office.

'How can I help you, Nina?' Ivo's stern, professional tone froze her for a moment. She hesitated. 'Is it about the Sansones' mail, or are you waiting for anything in particular?' Ivo asked, leaning against the counter. A broad smile spread across his face, lifting his cheeks in an expression of warmth. A nervous cough tickled Nina's throat. How could she explain? She turned her head to check no other customers were approaching from outside. The blood drained from her cheeks. Was she doing the right thing? Should she have listened to Nicolò? But the image of Malka pleading for help had shaken her to the core. She half-closed her eyes and imagined Malka and the other internees, eyes shining as Nina placed letters devoid of thick black-ink censored lines, in their hands.

'It's about letters for the internees,' she replied, her eyes fixed on Ivo's face.

'Has the *avvocato* sent you here to check on me?' Ivo frowned; the grey of his eyes deepened with worry. 'You can tell him I know the rules and I can recite them to him by heart if he wishes,' he shouted into the stifling Post Office, his cheeks purpling. 'One.' He raised his thumb to indicate the number. 'One', he repeated with a forceful voice. 'The Post Office must counter any possible attempt by the internees to evade censorship. Two,' he continued. 'Only one letter is permitted per week, not exceeding twenty-four lines. Three,' he ended his speech with three fingers in the air and a furious dip of his head. 'Only one postcard per week.'

Nina fixed her gaze on him and moved so close that she could clearly see the stubble shadowing his jaw.

'What if these rules are broken . . .' Nina hesitated, her voice hoarse.

Ivo raised a hand to stop her from continuing. He walked to the door, spun the '*APERTO*' door sign to '*CHIUSO*' and said, 'Nina, follow me. We'd better go and talk in here.'

From his trouser pocket he extracted a long key and inserted it into the keyhole of the storeroom door. Nina followed him, noticing that it was no longer hidden on the lintel above the red door.

She hadn't been in the room since that day in early June when Ambra had shown her the new Olivetti portable typewriter. In the dim light the metallic outline of the heavy safe stood out amongst the shelves and filing cabinets. A musty smell of *poncio* liquor mixed with a whiff of white wine impregnated the air. It seemed just like any other room. Was this where Gino met with other members of his anti-Fascist cell printing the propaganda leaflets he often left scattered around the farm, to her mother's despair?

Ivo locked the door behind him and gestured to Nina to sit down. 'Tell me more.'

Nina cleared her throat. 'Signor Ivo, what if we arrange for the letters to be addressed to those of us willing to receive them? By doing this, the internees could receive uncensored letters and more than one letter a week, contrary to the rules.'

The more she spoke, the steadier her voice became. 'It will ease their loneliness and break the monotony of their lives.'

'Nina, you are right,' Ivo said. 'These internees, the Roma, the anti-Fascists, the poor Jews: they need our help. As if the regime's Racial Laws, thrust upon us five years ago, weren't enough of an insult. "A pure Italy", they call it. A disgrace, I call it. Nina, you are truly your father's daughter, your brother's sister.' Ivo stretched his arm across the table and shook her hand. Nina felt a surge of pride swell in her chest. It was as if her heart expanded in joy.

'But Nina, this is risky,' Ivo continued. 'If *Avvocato* Sansone or *Carabiniere* Palotta find out, they'll close the Post Office down and imprison us all.'

Nina shuddered at the thought. 'But isn't risk necessary at a time like this? How else can they maintain family bonds during wartime if we don't take that risk?'

'I'll keep it a secret from everyone but the others in the storeroom. Gino can keep an eye out so you are safe. I'll organise what needs to be done. I can have letters addressed to me too. It will be easy for me working here.'

'I'll take the letters for Palazzo Nonno in Vinchiaturo; Nicolò can take the ones for Isernia.'

'The *avvocato*'s son?'

'Yes, he is on our side. I have taken food to Isernia and Vinchiaturo with him. He's committed to helping the internees.'

'I believe you. But come here alone. Ask for me, not for Ambra or anyone else, and I'll hand over the post for you and Nicolò.'

When Nina left the Post Office, a sense of achievement washed through her. Her plan with Nicolò was in place. And now that Ivo knew, it felt lighter on her shoulders. She knew the risks, but the vision of the internees receiving letters, free from the regime's oppressive gaze, heightened her determination.

Swallows soared and glided around the octagonal bell tower of the Santa Croce church in the sweltering July heat. The sun's rays turned the piazza's cobblestones incandescent. The River Fastino's water shimmered silvery gold. Nina was excited to share Ivo's words with Nicolò. Together they would carry a small flame of hope in these unsettling times.

Chapter Eighteen

Ambra was at the crossroads outside Bastiani where a large blackberry bush rose majestically, its ripe fruit coated with a white film of dust from the unsurfaced road. Werner wasn't there when she arrived at three in the afternoon. Ambra waited, the whirring of the crickets jumping around her, as impatient as she was.

She was excited to see what surprise Werner would bestow on her this time. She pulled out a compact mirror from her bag and retouched her lips with the pink lipstick Werner had given her along with the perfume the previous Tuesday in Campobasso. His soft kind eyes had exuded not only passion but also admiration and excitement when Ambra shared with him the discovery of food parcels smuggled into the internment camps, although she remained cautious not to mention any names despite his constant pressing. Just a few kisses and that was enough for Werner to invite her to a surprise trip at the Rio Vivo beach on the Termoli coastline.

With a screeching of brakes, a black Volkswagen pulled up beside Ambra, scattering clouds of dust in her face. She sneezed and brushed the powdery film off her pink dress.

'For a moment I thought you weren't coming.' Ambra unbuttoned the front of her sundress to reveal the deep brown furrow between her breasts.

Werner took her hand and helped her into the passenger seat. 'I love the Italian seaside.' His slightly accented voice sang with excitement. 'I'm taking you to the beach where the sand forms small dunes covered with wild fennel. They smell like liquorice.'

He bent down and blew her a small kiss. 'And I have a surprise for you.'

Ambra had visited the seaside once, shortly after her mother became ill. It was her father's idea, a lunch in a restaurant by the sea, eating fish with olive oil and fat red tomatoes that smelled of the Adriatic waters and the heat of the hills of Molise. He'd hoped it would lift his ailing wife's spirits.

Ambra inhaled the air; Werner was right, the plants did smell of liquorice. Children were making castles of grainy brown sand and close by their mothers lay on deckchairs. Men and women, Germans and Italians smoked and chatted in small groups, dipping their toes in the frothy waves. A blending of languages hovered in the breeze, the harshness of the German consonants almost swallowing the melodic Italian vowels.

It was hard to imagine there was a war raging in the distance, death blotting the Italian landscape, an unsettling future looming on the horizon. The lapping of the sea, its soft murmur silenced Ambra's musings. She allowed Werner to kiss her neck, slip her sandals off and lead her to the water's edge.

When he spread out a towel on the sandy beach and indicated to her to sit down, Ambra wondered whether this was the moment he would give her the surprise he'd promised. Would it be a perfume? More stockings? Or perhaps even a ring? Whatever it was, she would have to find a way to hide it from her father's judgemental gaze.

'Shut your eyes and give me your hand.' Werner's voice was authoritative and sensual at the same time. Ambra's stomach flipped with expectation as she squeezed her eyes shut. He placed a square metallic object into her open palm. It felt heavy, cold. Under her fingertips the surface felt uneven, granular and metallic at the same time. This was clearly not a box of sweet-smelling perfume or a precious ring. Her eyes sprang open.

'It's a Wehrmacht Leica. I'm giving it to you.'

'Why? I can't wear it.'

'That's right, but with this you could acquire more: silk blouses, valuable jewellery, anything you fancy.'

'How?'

'This will be your third eye. I want you to record everything you witness. Every single image is currency, a reward for a new gift. But I must teach you how to use it.'

'I'm a quick learner. I'll hold the camera, you put your arms around me and show me how it works.'

The buttons of his shirt pressed against her bare skin, exposed at the back by the deep V scoop of her sundress.

Click, click, click.

Together their fingers pressed the shutter button. Through the lens Ambra conjured up images of the afternoon: the sparkling waves of the sea, the idling sunbathers, Werner's pointed nose shadowing his moustache, golden in the sunlight, the leather holster, a glint of a gun strapped to his portly waist.

Click, click, click.

'Now, you pose for me.' With his thick fingers and short clipped nails, Werner turned the camera to face her. 'Turn your face towards the sea and let me take a profile photo.'

He leaned forward. The smell of salty sweat mixed with cedar aftershave reached her nostrils. Ambra swivelled her body around and arranged herself into a seductive pose.

'You're a natural model, Ambra. Let's see if you can become a natural photographer.'

The thought of a new challenge thrilled Ambra. Perhaps now she could give up typing. Without Nina it wasn't the same. It had become boring. And after all, she would be the only one in Bastiani to own a camera.

She allowed Werner's fingers to fondle the sides of her breasts and made him promise to send her the photos, a reminder of their perfect day together.

She flung her arms around his neck and pulled him towards her. They kissed. The sea whispered in their ears, its crushing waves sweeping away the seeds of doubt planted by her father's words: '*Don't spend time cavorting with German officers. Remember which side this family is on.*'

Post Office

Ivo has been in the storeroom with Gino, Esther and Mariolina all evening, heads close together, ears pressed against the radio. Sweat trickles from forehead to neck. Their backs must ache from crouching over the wireless as night falls. A half-empty bottle of Pecorino wine lies on the table. Shadows dance on the walls. Ambra sleeps in her bedroom, unaware of the political discussions downstairs, directly beneath her.

It's 11 p.m. The cold impersonal voice of the EIAR Italian state radio broadcaster mingles with the heavy and rhythmic tolling of the church bells.

'*Attenzione, Attenzione*.'

Chairs fall backwards as the group in the storeroom jumps at the urgency of the announcement.

'*The King has accepted the resignation from the office of the Head of Government, Prime Minister and State Secretary, tendered by His Excellency Cavaliere Benito Mussolini, and the King has appointed as Head of Government, Prime Minister and State Secretary, His Excellency Cavaliere Marshal of Italy Pietro Badoglio*.'

Ivo grabs hold of Gino, shaking his shoulders. 'It's the end . . . the end of Fascism, Gino. Mussolini is gone, Badoglio is now the *Capo del Governo*.'

'Twenty-one years of dictatorship is over; it's a celebration.' There is a freedom to Gino's voice that I haven't heard for years.

The solemn cadence of military music from the wireless fills the room.

Esther's voice trembles. 'Listen! For the first time in more than two decades we don't have to hear the thumping notes of "*Giovinezza*" at the end of the evening news.'

The national anthem of the Kingdom of Italy, '*Marcia Reale*', fills the room.

'*Viva il re*,' Ivo shouts.

'We might be free to cover the walls with big painted letters: *LA FINE DEL FASCISMO, LA GUERRA È FINITA, VIVA LA LIBERTÀ*—THE END OF FASCISM, THE END OF WAR, LONG LIVE FREEDOM,' Gino enthuses. A sheen of excitement crosses his light brown eyes.

'I'm not sure.' Mariolina picks up one of the fallen chairs and slumps into it, her head in her hands. 'We could be in even more trouble. And don't I know it. Remember when I was imprisoned years ago for attaching anti-Fascist posters to these walls?'

I recall Mariolina gluing anti-Fascist posters to my wall in the darkness of the night. It was 1927, Agostina was still alive and Ambra was merely a baby. Ivo and Agostina had to scrub my walls clean and pure, a bucket of soapy water and brushes with hard bristles in their hands. I shook from the violence of their movements delivered in haste. But I understood. They were worried the *carabinieri* would incarcerate them in the prison in Trivento just as they had imprisoned Mariolina and her tiny baby girl. Agostina had sobbed for days hugging little Ambra to her chest, hearing the news of the death in prison of baby Sovietina—a name I struggled to understand. It wasn't a name I observed on letters or telegrams, or the name of a saint, displayed on the leaves of the calendar. In those days every single customer walked into my space with teary eyes, commenting on the tragic news of Sovietina's death. This name I had never heard of suddenly appeared on everyone's lips reverberating from my walls to the piazza, hovering over the church steeple, slithering under tables outside Bar Renzo.

'Can we trust our king and Badoglio?' Ivo's voice quivers with doubts. Despite Mariolina's fear and Ivo's worries, I share Gino's enthusiasm.

Esther frowns, a pink hue tinting her cheeks. 'Does this mean the Racial Laws don't apply anymore? Will I finally get my job back in the school in Castelnuovo?'

Ivo places a hand on her shoulder. 'But what happens if the Germans don't react well to this change of plan?'

Outside a small crowd gathers in the piazza. In the distance the River Fastino glimmers under the starry sky. A sliver of moonlight hovers above the dark mass of mountains surrounding Bastiani, their tips silver as if covered by unseasonal frost. From the cobbled alleyways, a trickle of villagers reach the square.

Voices shout: *Viva il re*; *Viva Badoglio*; *Abbasso il Duce*—Long live the king; Long live Badoglio; Down with *il Duce*. Santino slaps Renzo on the back. Celestina hugs Pietruzzo. Tommaso the ricotta maker twirls his wife Rita around, her clogs barely reaching the ground.

The commotion shakes my foundations. The news of Mussolini's resignation has sent shockwaves from the rivers to the mountains, the fields to the roads, the streets to the square. Only Villa Sansone's windows remain shrouded in darkness. The news of the king's announcement had come like a storm.

Woken by the clamour, Ambra runs downstairs, naked feet stamping the floorboards, her cotton nightie brushing against her bare calves. '*Papà*, what is this commotion about?' she asks, eyes still heavy with sleep.

'Mussolini has gone. Fascism is over. We're free,' Gino shouts, joy threading his words, eyes brimming with hope.

Ambra's black eyes are wide open. Could it be astonishment or fear?

The leaf of the calendar twirls.

It is the 25th July, 1943, Saint Christopher's feast day.

Today is the end of *il Duce*, the beginning of hope for a brighter, freer future.

Chapter Nineteen

In the Post Office the morning sun spilled onto the brass scales, the large till and the smooth granite counter. It cast a glow that sent particles of golden dust floating around the room. The scent of basil leaves sweetened the air infused with the bitterness of the chicory coffee, a reminder of her father's morning ritual.

His broad, confident smile greeted Ambra as she stepped into the room. 'It's the first morning we wake up and *il Duce* is gone.' Ivo breathed out with a sense of cheerfulness. Ambra responded to her father's enthusiasm with a nod, her brows knitted together in concern.

The July heat was already building up. Stifling, humid air pressed in on the Post Office. Yet, to Ambra the room felt colder. Her thoughts were consumed by Werner. What would he do now? Would he leave? Surely the Germans would fight back. All night she had tossed and turned in her bed, having ensured the Leica was concealed under her mattress. Now she had to be extra cautious. The camera must remain well and truly hidden.

Ivo spread the morning paper on the counter, smoothing its creases with calloused hands. The clock on the wall facing Ambra ticked on as usual, marking the time, as if indifferent to the turmoil inside her mind—and in the outside world.

'What happened last night will be here in black and white for everyone to see.' With a bony finger, her father tapped the front page of *La Stampa*. Then he stopped, fingers in midair. 'No, no, it's not possible.' Ivo's lips puckered, his freshly shaven cheeks reddened, his voice trembled. Ambra leant over him and skimmed the morning headlines.

The words of the king were still there, spelling in bold capital letters Mussolini's defeat: '*LE DIMISSIONI DI MUSSOLINI ACCETTATE DAL RE*.' But following below in smaller font was the proclamation of *Maresciallo* Badoglio: '*I am taking command of the military government with full powers. The war continues. Anyone who disturbs public order will be relentlessly pursued.*'

The war continues. Ambra read the words over and over. It was as if a miracle had answered her silent wishes and prayers. *Werner will be so relieved*, she found herself thinking. Did she truly care for him or was she purely thinking of the gifts he gave her? A smile was budding on her lips. She concealed it with a light cough.

'The fireworks of joy were short-lived,' Ivo muttered, more to himself than to Ambra, his voice tinged with bitterness. 'The war is now edging closer to us.'

He sighed, his shoulders tight. It was as if the weight of Badoglio's inflammatory words caused him to stoop, even more than when he carried heavy bags of mail. Ambra wished she could console him but she found it difficult to align herself with his desperation.

She looked out of the window. Above the verdant foliage of the oak tree, she caught a glimpse of the Fascist flag still hoisted on the balcony of the villa. It reassured her that victory could still be on the side of the Fascists. Her father should listen to the *avvocato* rather than to Nina's brother Gino.

As if conjured up by her thoughts, Gino entered the Post Office, shadows circling his eyes, hair uncombed, unruly.

'We were duped, Ivo,' he panted. 'Our happiness lasted only a few hours. The Germans aren't leaving, and the war hasn't stopped.' He gasped for air as if the news had struck him in the middle of his chest.

Her father rose to his feet and encircled Gino in his arms. It was as if he was hugging a brother, Ambra thought, with a sensation of wonder and embarrassment.

She listened to her father's cries. 'They promised us an end. And all we've got is more war.' Ivo hid his face against Gino's shoulders. Was her father sobbing? It pained Ambra to see him hurt and vulnerable.

The villagers were soon piling into the Post Office, full of questions, riddled with angst. Celestina and Rita pummelled the counter and shook Ambra by the wrist, begging for news of Giovannino fighting in Albania and Greece. 'Is he safe? What will happen to all our Molise boys at the front? Will they fight for the king or the Allies? Or Hitler?'

She felt sorry for them. She understood their pain, their worries. In their desperate eyes she saw the same fear and anguish she had experienced at her mother's deathbed. She chewed the inside of her cheek to transfer the ache touching her heart into something physical, more controllable.

She looked at her father and at Gino. Their dismay was palpable in the slowness of their movements. Lost for words they shook their heads, compassion veiling their gaze.

Antonio stormed in, forcing the door open with an angry shove. It scared Ambra to witness such violence in the usual calm of the Post Office. Antonio, with his shock of white hair and face carved with wrinkles, normally so calm, was wringing his hands, his fingernails blackened and bitten to the quick. 'What about our village?' he pleaded. 'Will we be safe in Bastiani?'

When Don Simone arrived with his sister Teresa visiting from Castelnuovo, Antonio, Celestina and Rita reached for his hand. '*Padre*, tell us, will the Lord protect us?'

Ambra shifted her gaze from one to the other, her forehead etched with concern. She wanted Bastiani to be safe too.

Suddenly, the chatter waned. Silence simmered amidst the peeling walls of the Post Office. Ambra scanned the room. She saw him and sighed with relief. The tall frame of *Carabiniere* Palotta in his grey-green uniform, the black tricorn hat on his head making him resemble a crow perched on a tree, was visible at the entrance, blocking out the rays of sunlight and casting a long shadow on the dusty floor. Now order would be re-established, Ambra hoped.

'Do not panic,' he commanded. He stamped his foot and raised his arm in the Roman salute. The villagers shuffled, a flicker of discomfort. Ambra was the first to salute him back.

'Only Ambra? Come on, villagers, my people. Aren't you saluting the prescribed way?' he barked.

Ambra watched, as one by one the villagers lifted their arms. She could read fear and resignation in the crumpled features of their faces.

Rita coughed, Teresa sighed and Don Simone muttered a prayer, his eyes heavenward. Ambra wondered why it was so difficult to believe in the *carabiniere*'s words.

'The war continues. The war continues.' By evening these words echoed from everyone's lips like the refrain of a funeral litany. Ambra heard it at Bar Renzo, at the baker, at church, until it became a distant hum by night-time.

When she went to bed, she slid her hand under the mattress. Werner's Leica was still there. She stroked it, passing her fingertips over its smooth lens, the cold metal of its body. Her eyelids grew heavier. She shut her eyes. 'Don't spend time cavorting with German officers. Remember which side this family is on.'

Her father's warning rang in her ears, fading as she drifted to sleep, unaware that the morning's news would test her loyalties and reshape her world.

Chapter Twenty

A breathlessness filled Nina's days. The frenzied delivery of letters and food parcels to the internees occupied most of August. When she wasn't accompanying Nicolò on his motorbike, she borrowed his bicycle and cycled up the hills, along winding roads, pushing her feet firmly down on the pedals, her skirt billowing behind her. The hot wind in her hair and the determination in her heart carried her through each arduous journey.

The news that the Allies were approaching from the south, together with Mussolini's incarceration in Gran Sasso at Campo Imperatore in the north of the region, gave her hope that the end of Fascism was close. Shreds of information of German losses gathered from Esther's translations from the radio in the storeroom contributed to her hopes.

Night and day, her thoughts were consumed by assembling food, collecting letters from Ivo and delivering them to Isernia and Vinchiaturo, always alert, always careful not to be discovered. She was grateful to *Maestra* Anna who managed to sneak her into Palazzo Nonno to offer Malka a listening heart. What would happen to the internees? How long would they have to stay cramped in those dormitories, lonely and forlorn? The uncertain future combined with the overwhelming emotions of her daily missions tore at Nina's heart.

Her respite came under the starry evening sky when she met Nicolò at the River Fastino. The damp smell of earth, the fresh water of the river, the shelter of the hazelnut bushes provided not only a secret location to plot their next move, but also a private residence for their love.

That evening, Nicolò was already at the riverbank, his curls shining under the moonlight. She felt a rush of tenderness towards him. They embraced with a warmth that was deeper than passion and sweeter than desire. Nina remembered the first taste of him that afternoon in mid-July at the football match, when she had sealed her lips against his knee. It was the beginning of their story. Or maybe their story had started well before, when they were still children.

Wrapped in Nicolò's strong arms, her head leaning on his shoulder, Nina felt safe, the perils of the day melting away. She lifted her head towards him and reached for his lower lip.

'*Ti amo,*' she sighed. She bit him softly and in the wetness of her mouth he whispered back, '*Ti amo.* I love you too, Nina,' he repeated in English. She loved hearing him speak to her in that foreign language that Esther also spoke. How many times had he been unable to play with her as a child when his mother had insisted he read to her in English instead.

How special she felt. She flung her arms around his neck and pulled him towards her. A fish plopped in the river, creating ringlets on the surface of the waters. They kissed, bodies entwined, hearts merging. The hot earth held them, the ferns and fronds nestled against their calves. A soft breeze ruffled Nina's hair and smoothed her cheek as Nicolò held her closer and closer, his breath caressing her skin, white pearls of perspiration beading his forehead.

Nina closed her eyes. She was happy. She hadn't been as happy since . . . since she first became friends with Ambra, she realised, but that moment was a happiness tinged with sadness from the loss of her father. This was pure happiness, a joy derived not only from her love for Nicolò, but from their commitment to helping the internees.

Soothed by the stillness of the night, nourished by the stars, they drifted into a sweet slumber.

In the distance church bells chimed. It was midnight.

'I must leave, Nicolò. I'll be in trouble with Gino and my mother.'

He pulled her back down towards their bed of leaves. 'Don't go. Stay with me a while longer. We are safe here, you and I, together.'

They left when soft light shimmered through the branches and shadows appeared across the water, smearing the liquid surface of the Fastino. As they reached the main road, sporadic blasts of artillery fire from Campobasso echoed in the air, shattering the peace of their night.

'Who knows what's coming next,' Nicolò whispered and squeezed Nina close. 'But at least we are doing what we can to alleviate the struggles and hardship faced by the internees. Ours is a small contribution to the injustice of the world.'

Chapter Twenty-One

The air in the Post Office was stifling, making Ambra's hair damp and lank at the back of her neck. She ran one hand through her locks, planning to style it afresh before her next encounter with Werner.

From the window she could see her father sitting at a table outside Bar Renzo deep in conversation with Don Simone; before them two full glasses of white Pecorino wine glistened in the August morning sunlight. With the tips of her shoes, she knocked against the bulky jute bag of mail placed under the counter. Alone in the Post Office, she wondered whether to take the opportunity to find something that might interest Werner. She dragged the mailbag out, untied it and with both hands delved into it. As she picked up a parcel for Bar Renzo, two letters fell onto her lap. She turned them in her hands. The letters were addressed to Nina. 'To Nina?' Ambra mouthed into the quiet calm of the Post Office.

No matter how much she tried, she couldn't recall Nina ever receiving personal letters, not even when Nina's father was away fighting in Spain or when Gino was in the sanatorium in the north of Italy, recovering from the tuberculosis that had prevented him from being called to war.

The envelopes in her hands felt light and heavy at the same time; curiosity gnawed within her. She shuffled them from one hand to the other, ruminating on the best way to open them without her father and Nina knowing. She ran to the kitchen, placed a saucepan of water on the stove and waited until small bubbles broke the surface and a warm steam arose. Then she glided one of the envelopes over the steady cloud of steam until the paper turned damp like her hair. Little by little the sealed flap lifted, the gum melted. Ambra slid a finger underneath the paper to pry the letter open, heart racing, hands trembling with the fear of what she might discover. She leant against the stove and began to read.

Mia cara *Malka,*

I hope you receive this note through your kind friend Nina; it brings me relief to hear you are still alive. Herbert Kappler, head of the German police under the command of Generalfeldmarschall *Kesselring, is now in charge of SIPO in Rome. The Germans know where the Jews live, and there are rumours of imminent roundups, arrests and deportation en masse.*

My beloved city is turning into a theatre of hatred and crime. I believe you are safer in the internment camp where you are. I hope you find comfort and solace from your painting during this difficult time.

La Vostra affezionata professoressa,

Elisa Cavalli

She grasped the second letter and held it over the steam. Lips twitching, her eyes quickly scanned the words.

Caro *Tonino*, fratello mio,

Your last letter brought us all much joy. We are happy you are safe, despite the appalling conditions you write about in your camp. We are grateful for the kind man who sends and receives letters on your behalf. I'm writing to give you our important news. You have a nephew. Your sister Donata has just given birth to a healthy baby boy. We christened him Antonio in your honour. We pray every day for your safe return and for baby Tonino to grow up in an Italy free of Fascism.

Ti abbraccio,
Tuo fratello *Domenico*

Mystified, Ambra collapsed onto the kitchen chair. She twirled a lock of her hair between two fingers. She regretted being too absorbed with Werner to notice the happenings under her nose. Yet Werner had told her, 'We need eyes.' He even presented her with that precious little Leica to record what she saw.

Ambra smacked her lips. 'So, this is also what you are keeping from me, Nina. You are not only delivering food to the internees but receiving letters for them in order to avoid censorship.' Ambra's clenched teeth clicked like old bones and echoed around the kitchen. Her cheeks flushed. So that's why her father recently insisted he was the only one to sort the mail. They were all keeping things from her. It was as if she was an outsider, unworthy of being included in their plans. Nobody trusted her enough to ask for her help—only Werner. She bit her lip. Anger and discontent swirled within her.

She couldn't waste any more time. She rushed back into the Post Office. From the window she saw her father leave Don Simone at Bar Renzo and walk towards her.

Trying to control the shaking of her hands, Ambra reached for the pot of *Coccoina* glue on the counter and opened it. Its familiar fragrance of marzipan wafted through the air. She dipped the tiny brush into the white paste, dabbed the brush on the flaps of the two envelopes to reseal them. She placed the letters back with the rest of the mail and returned to the typing she had started earlier, as if nothing had happened, just as her father walked in. He picked up the jute bag of mail and with a warm smile took it with him into the storeroom.

The bell jingled and the front door swung open. A shaft of apricot sunlight spilled into the Post Office. Sitting at the counter, Ambra lifted her head from the typewriter. Her eyebrows, knotted into a 'v' from the effort of concentration, briefly unfurled before arching high in astonishment.

'What are you doing here?' Ambra scowled at Nina. 'You don't type with me anymore. We don't do anything together anymore.'

Nina's skin paled, she bit her lips and seemed at a loss for words. Between them the air was charged with tension. Ambra's mouth stretched into a tight smile, relishing her friend's hesitance, her palpable fear. Nina's almond-shaped eyes darted from the typewriter to the storeroom's red door; anxious, wary, their brown depths shadowed with unease.

'I have something to collect for my mother,' she mumbled.

The storeroom door creaked open, and Ambra turned. Her father stood tall on the threshold, a bundle of letters clasped in his hands.

'I'll deal with Nina, don't you worry, Ambra.'

A tempest of emotions churned within her; the muscles of her stomach stiffened. Anger? Jealousy? Who was she angry with? Her father or Nina? Ambra couldn't be sure. She gripped the countertop, her knuckles white from the pressure. She jolted her head, directing her gaze at the letters her father held. She squinted. Nina Caruso. Nina Caruso, Nina Caruso. More letters, all addressed to Nina, like the ones she had just found.

Just you wait, Nina. You've given me enough to secure yet another reward from Werner, Ambra cursed inwardly. The tattered remnants of the friendship pact handkerchief came to her mind. She wished she could fling those frayed shreds in Nina's face.

Ambra returned to the counter. Seated at the typewriter, her fingers flew swiftly over the keys, but her eyes followed Nina as she crossed the piazza, the bundle of letters clutched under her arm. Only then did Ambra spot Nicolò Sansone slumped on the bench beneath the oak tree, his golden-brown hair catching the sunlight in soft waves. His long legs stretched out before him, and he shielded his eyes from the sun's glare with his large hands. Nina reached the bench and took a seat beside him. They remained silent as if they were strangers, their gaze fixed on the expanse of wheat fields heavy with ripening grain, on the olive groves with rows of ancient trees, their gnarled trunks twisting out of the dry earth. Nina lowered her arm and let the bundle drop onto the bench in between them. Ambra would have missed it if she hadn't been watching them like a stalking fox. Nicolò hesitated, slid one arm down, then furtively picked it up and placed it on his other side.

A flash of realisation; Ambra's cheeks reddened. Of course! Nina and Nicolò, with her father's collaboration, were aiding the internees by addressing their mail to themselves and delivering it clandestinely, uncensored, to the camps.

The sense of exclusion from her friend's life since Nicolò Sansone had returned to Bastiani and Nina had stopped typing with her vexed Ambra. She cursed herself for not having kept those two letters she'd read. She needed proof for Werner; her words wouldn't be enough. Yet, what irked Ambra most was the complicity revealed by the closeness of Nina and Nicolò's bodies, the way they moved together almost as if one.

The storeroom door was closed; her father had locked himself in. It was safe for Ambra to retrieve the camera. She rose to her feet and dashed upstairs. The Leica was under her mattress. She grabbed it and hurried back downstairs, hoping to secretly capture what they were doing. Not only would she present Werner with photos of people smuggling food into the camps, but also photos of the uncensored letters for the internees.

But they were gone. Now, only *Avvocato* Sansone sat on the bench smoking his pipe, the fragrance of his luxury tobacco reaching her through the open window. Santino walked past and greeted him with the prescribed Roman salute. There was nothing suspicious to catch on camera. Ambra's face twisted with frustration and self-reproach, her hands clenched into fists at her sides. A twinge of frustration gnawed at her. If only she'd had the camera with her, she could have captured the evidence of their illegal act.

The storeroom door opened. She fumbled with the camera and slid it under her blouse to hide it from her father's eyes.

'I've managed to find you the latest issue of your favourite magazine, *Mani di fata*.' His grey eyes were soft and warm when he handed the glossy journal to her. 'Hope you like it.' He winked at her, considerate, affectionate, before disappearing again into the storeroom.

Ambra's heart lurched with a sudden surge of relief. She had missed the chance to expose any wrongdoings but if she'd succeeded, the photographs would have incriminated not only Nina and Nicolò but also her father. He was the person in charge of the Post Office. He would be the main culprit. She feared for him. She needed to protect him. If something happened to her father, she would be all alone in the world. If Werner knew what was going on in the Post Office, her father would be arrested, even shot. With all her ambitions and dreams of the future, she would never reveal this to Werner.

She climbed up to her room, placed the camera back under the mattress and sank onto her bed, the pages of the unopened magazine rustling against her side.

Chapter Twenty-Two

Werner dropped the developed photos onto Ambra's lap with a sigh of exasperation.

'These are not helpful to me. I can't see any faces clearly. The only thing apparent is that food is being smuggled in, somewhere, by someone. Who knows whom, who knows where.'

Werner's lips were forced into a thin line, the muscles of his neck twitched and tensed. Ambra placed a hand on his arm, smiling inwardly with relief.

'Ambra, I need names, locations. Otherwise I have nothing to report. These photos are fuzzy, out of focus. You must remember to keep the camera still when you click. And you have taken so many of yourself! Not that I mind under normal circumstances, but remember, your *Duce* was shamefully dismissed only a few weeks ago and the situation is much more complicated now.' Werner twiddled with the medals on his uniform jacket. 'Do you want my superiors to laugh at me? You were on a mission.'

Ambra jumped and looked around the Gran Caffè Lupacchioli, wondering if the other customers had heard their conversation. She fiddled with a strand of hair. If Werner only knew which photos she had failed to capture—the storeroom, the meetings between her father, Gino, Esther and Mariolina, the discovery of her father breaking rules, evading censorship—they would be rounded up and shot in the village square. She complimented herself on the photos of baskets of food, of Nina and Nicolò's backs, impossible to recognise unless you knew them well. Despite her outrage and resentment at Nina's lies and secrets, her intention was never to lead her and Nicolò to harm. But the last thing she wanted was to anger Werner. She had to think quickly and find a way to pacify him. She leant forward to kiss him, her breasts almost knocking their drinks over. 'You're right to be cross with me, but it's my first attempt.'

Werner lowered his voice, hissing between his teeth. 'Ambra, you work for us now. We need photos of anti-Fascists and deserters. Our Führer doesn't trust the Badoglio government. Hitler will never abandon Mussolini. There are rumours of a plan to kidnap him from Campo Imperatore and bring him to safety.'

Werner's words hammered in her head. 'Working for them?' Did Werner think of her as a spy working for the regime? She was working for herself, to create her own future, to better herself. Sides and politics were insignificant to Ambra. It didn't matter which flag she raised as long as she was the one to win.

'Next time I'll be more careful and vigilant,' she said, hoping to mollify Werner's temper. She swallowed hard; her stomach flipped. She knew she was treading on dangerous ground. She didn't want to lose the gifts, the delicacies and expensive lunches Werner bestowed on her.

The printed photos spread across her skirt like a fan. Reaching for them, they slipped through her fingers one by one like a silent movie. She knew which ones she needed to keep, not for Werner's mission, but for her own.

*

That day she worked in the Post Office in a merry mood, as if the war were merely a grey cloud on the Matese mountains.

Her father even asked her if she had been drinking during her visit to Campobasso.

Ambra knew the Sansones managed to retain the Campobasso custom of drinking a Martini *aperitivo* on the terrace throughout the war years. At six o'clock, after arranging stamps in the correct folder, she informed her father she would be back in time to heat up the *minestra* she had prepared that morning and set out to reach Villa Sansone across the piazza.

Marta led Ambra onto a large terrace with potted lemon and orange trees displayed at regular intervals along the marble balustrade. The rays of the end-of-August sun tinged the sky with red and purple streaks. The Sansones were sitting at a low table on two comfortable chairs with floral cushion covers. Ice cubes floated in glasses on the tray in front of them, a slice of lemon the only colour.

How detached they are from the way the rest of us live in Bastiani, Ambra thought with a sense of admiration and envy. *Not like us with local homebrewed* poncio.

'*Signori* Sansone, I'm sorry to disturb you,' Marta said, wiping her hands on her apron. 'Ambra insists on speaking to you.'

With a wave of her hand, Signora Carmela indicated to Marta to leave.

'I have something that may interest you.' Ambra pulled a small wad of printed images out of her handbag. *Avvocato* Sansone reached across the table, and one by one passed them to Carmela as if he were dealing a small deck of cards. She placed them in front of her spectacles, thin, round and rimmed in gold. Silence thickened the air around them.

Ambra, fists clenched, waited for the Sansones to praise her and reward her for being a good Italian Fascist.

Flicking through the photos, Carmela pursed her lips and deep furrows etched her forehead. When she saw the photograph of her son with Nina, arms entwined, lips glued together, in a deep embrace, her cheeks whitened. She lifted her chin and stared at Ambra. 'Where on earth did you get these photos from?'

'I took them, myself. A German officer, a friend of mine, gave me a camera to record unusual activities in the area.'

'It's a good thing, Ambra, to remain patriotic to *il Duce*—to the Italian cause—and not be misled by propaganda and the events of the moment.' *Avvocato* Sansone twiddled with the wedding band on his fourth finger. 'The Allies may be on their way, even gaining some victories, but the Axis will defeat them, you mark my words. The Badoglio government won't survive.' He smacked his lips under his moustache threaded with grey streaks. 'I trust you haven't shown these photos to anyone else. They incriminate our son.'

'Of course not.' Ambra hoped her flushed cheeks did not reveal her lie.

'Look at this one, Riccardo,' Carmela's voice trembled. *Avvocato* Sansone brought the photo closer to his face. He squinted as if trying to make sense of it.

'It looks like they are delivering food to the Vinchiaturo internment camp. It's blurry but I recognise those walls of Palazzo Nonno with the wrought-iron balconies and semi-circular fanlight.'

'I did tell you, *Avvocato* Sansone,' Ambra interjected, pointing at the photograph. 'It's serious.' She kept the delivery of the letters to herself.

'You must sort this out, Riccardo.' Carmela's ice-blue eyes were firmly fixed on her husband's.

When *Avvocato* Sansone accompanied Ambra to the door, he placed a piece of paper into her hand. More money. Her fingers tingled at the crisp rustle of the lira note. Her fingertips stroked it as if it were velvet.

Chapter Twenty-Three

They agreed to meet after lunch to bring food and letters to Vinchiaturo. Nina arrived first, letters folded under the waistband of her skirt. The sun scalded her face. She sat by the edge of the river and dipped her toes into the water, her face raised towards the golden afternoon sun. It was early September, yet the blazing summer heat still lingered.

A rustling in the bushes. She turned her head and gasped. Nicolò was pushing a rusty bicycle, his large hands grasping the handlebars, knuckles white from the pressure.

'Where is your *motorino*?'

His eyes were drained of their sparkling blue colour. All Nina could see was the dull grey of his irises full of distress and fear.

'What has happened, Nicolò?'

'We've been discovered. My parents have threatened to send me to Campobasso if I don't stop seeing you and visiting the camps. They have seen photos of us delivering food to the camps.'

'Do you mean someone is spying on us?'

'I have been wracking my brains, thinking about who it could be. Could it be Renzo or *Carabiniere* Palotta? Whoever it is, we can't go to the camps anymore.'

'But we must continue, Nicolò. Malka and Tonino rely on us. I have just collected more letters for them and their fellow internees.' She tapped the side of her skirt. 'Ivo handed them to me.' Her eyes pricked with tears of frustration and disappointment. 'We can't let them down.'

'Look, Nina.' Nicolò's voice shook. 'They tried to forbid me to leave the house, but I sneaked out through the back door so I could warn you. And you are banned from entering the kitchen.'

'I'll find food my own way. Tommaso and Rita will give me cheese, Celestina will offer bread and Ivo and Gino will help too, I'm sure.'

'Don't trust Renzo; I'm not sure which side he is on.'

'Don't worry, I know what to do.'

'Nina, remember, it's dangerous. Now that Mussolini is being held not far from here, nobody knows which side Italy is on. You can't trust anyone. We are all under surveillance. We are all being watched.'

Nina lifted her eyes towards the mountains soaring above them. The image of Mussolini imprisoned on a mountain close to Bastiani and the five internment camps sent shivers down her spine. For two months, she and Nicolò had been delivering food and letters to the internees of the camps; listening to their tales of displacement; offering her ears and heart.

'Nicolò, I can't stop now. I'll continue for both of us.'

He folded her into his arms, his lips brushing the top of her hair.

'Take my bicycle and remember: if you are stopped you are taking food to the church. And Nina, please be careful.'

*

After safely delivering the letters for Isernia into Tonino's grateful hands, Nina climbed back onto her bike, her feet pressing on the pedals, her forehead beaded with sweat.

She had many more kilometres to cover, cycling up steep hills in the sweltering heat to reach Vinchiaturo. As she cycled past rows of silver birch trees her mind jumped to Nicolò's words. *You can't trust anyone*, whirled and spun around her head in time with the movement of the wheels. Would she lose Nicolò? Would he be sent away?

When she reached Vinchiaturo, Nina leaned Nicolò's bicycle against the oak tree opposite Palazzo Nonno. Breathless from the strenuous ride uphill to reach via della Libertà, Nina waited until she saw *Maestra* Anna's curly head peeking through the half-opened door beckoning her inside.

As usual, the smell hit Nina as soon as she crossed the threshold, a mixture of cooked cabbage, sewage and sweat. No matter how many times Nina visited Palazzo Nonno, she never accustomed herself to the stench.

The reflection of rays of sunlight through the window picked up auburn strands on the tall woman with the copper hair, the one the *carabiniere* had nicknamed *La Rossa* and who Nina now knew as Leanda, one of the three Sinti internees in Palazzo Nonno. Despite documents allowing them to be in Italy, these three women had been snatched from their villages, separated from their families and interned in Vinchiaturo. Ivo and Gino had explained to her that many members of the Sinti community were scattered in camps all over Molise. Since the 1938 Racial Laws it had been perilous for those who were not considered pure Italians.

Next to Leanda stood Malka clutching her white shawl to her chest, despite the suffocating heat in the corridor.

'*Vieni, vieni,* hurry,' *Maestra* Anna whispered to Nina shuffling the three women into a tiny room off the corridor. 'You are late today. The *carabinieri* Russo and Pinzi will soon be here, you have no time to chat. Be quick.'

Nina pulled five letters from under her waistband and waved the ripped-open envelopes in front of Malka. Malka's eyes reminded Nina of Molise mountain streams, a mixture of pale blue and jade green. Her nose was small and straight, dotted with freckles the size of the breadcrumbs she used to store with Nicolò in a metal tin to feed the birds in the garden of the Villa Sansone at a time of peace. Slim and tall, Malka was a dainty creature apart from the thick, fleshy lips highlighting the triangular shape of her face.

Every time Nina handed over the letters, she reminded herself she wasn't prying when she tore open the envelope to discover who the recipient was. It was for a good cause, yet she remained relieved she couldn't always understand the uncensored content. They were written in foreign tongues, Polish for Malka, German for the Sinti women.

'I'm sorry, only letters today. No food,' Nina said.

Malka grabbed the two letters from Nina's hand with a hunger that surprised her.

At a time when food was scarce all over Molise, Nina marvelled at how the treat of a letter had more value to Malka than sugar.

A high-pitched scream from Malka's lips broke the silence. She slumped to the terracotta tiled floor, the letter limp on her lap.

'They have taken my parents,' she whispered between sobs, clutching the white shawl she always wore draped around her shoulders.

'My cousin has written to me. They've gone. I'll never see them again!'

Nina crouched down next to Malka, the cold tiles against her sweaty shins bringing some relief from the baking air inside the *palazzo*. She slipped an arm around Malka's shoulders, the coarse wool of the shawl rubbing against the skin of Nina's arms. The touch of the wool reminded her of Malka's drawings of her mother knitting the garment before Malka left for Rome, for the Bel Paese, to escape the trappings of anti-Semitism in Warsaw and further her studies in fine arts. It was the one item that had kept her warm when she lost her right to continue her studies and her part-time job as an art teacher after the Racial Laws were announced. No matter the season, the white woollen shawl accompanied Malka from one camp to another until she arrived in Vinchiaturo. Malka was not only an alien but also a Jew and this double affliction lost her the right to work or to return to her native Poland.

She thought of Esther. At least she was safe in Bastiani and not in one of the internment camps like these Jewish and Sinti women.

'Where have they gone?'

'My cousin thinks they boarded a train east when the Warsaw ghetto was liberated. He doesn't know where but there is no trace of them. Rumours circulate that many in the ghetto have been taken to Majdanek or Treblinka. For the time being my cousin is safe but doesn't know for how long.'

Crouching down on the other side of Malka, Leanda stroked her cheek. 'That's what we all have in common here. My people, the Sinti, know what it's like not to be trusted and to be shunted from place to place. We are a blend of minorities with no country.'

Nina wondered what it must be like to feel you don't belong. She had Bastiani; hers were the sparkling waters of the River Fastino; hers were the imposing Matese mountains, custodians of the surrounding villages. But today after Nicolò's disclosure, her Bastiani was marred with a veil of suspicion and distrust.

Post Office

It is a mellow September evening, wisps of clouds, pinky-orange, dot the sky. The shrill chirping of birds from nests in the trees surrounding the piazza welcomes the twilight. The bells of Santa Croce chime rhythmically.

The women in the village waddle towards the church gates, arms laden with flowers freshly picked from the fields, to honour the birth of the Madonna. Celestina dips her face into the bunch of daisies she is holding, relishing its sweet fragrance.

Marta and Signora Sansone leave the villa, hurrying across the square to join the congregation inside the church. They nod at *Carabiniere* Palotta, on duty patrolling the square, his thick moustache concealing his smiling mouth. He lifts his cap to them and bows with deference.

The soft notes of the pipe organ and the melodious voices of the congregation rise through the rafters of the building. They flow past the tiled roofs towards the mountains above, rippling in waves through the square. The bells toll across the valley, from Castelnuovo, Vinchiaturo, Isernia. I sense the clanging of church bells from Boiano and Casacalenda. A cacophony of sound.

The clicking of the typewriter inside the storeroom halts abruptly. The sound of the radio booms and the door bangs against my wall. Ivo's feet stamp the floorboards as he darts into the square, shouting at the top of his voice,

'Badoglio has surrendered to the Allies. The Armistice has been signed.'

A river of villagers pours out of the church, arms swinging white handkerchiefs above their heads. '*La guerra è finita.* The war is over.'

'What will happen to our *Duce*?' Renzo shouts.

'What will happen to us?' Tommaso and Rita exclaim in unison, wringing their red-raw hands in worry.

'What will happen to our soldiers, my Giovannino? Will he finally come home from Albania?' cries Celestina.

A dissonance of voices; relief, joy, astonishment, fear weave a tapestry of confusion into the purple rays of the setting sun.

Don Simone follows them, his brightly embroidered chasuble flapping in the evening breeze. 'Don't ring the bells to celebrate because death will come from this.' His voice is sombre, his words of admonishment chill the air. Villagers shiver. What if he is right?

Gino, overalls rolled up to the elbows, a cigarette dangling from pinched lips, rushes through the arch towards Ivo. Forehead creased, he grabs his arm and pulls him into the Post Office. With a clang Gino switches the '*APERTO*' sign to '*CHIUSO*'.

'You know this is not the end, but just the beginning.' He shakes Ivo's shoulder and stubs out his cigarette. 'The war with England and the United States may well be over, but the Germans are now not only the enemy of us anti-Fascists but also of our entire country.' He hesitates. 'It's a call for action.' He taps his chest with the palm of his hand. Eyes gleaming with fervour and determination, he continues: 'I'll assemble the anti-Fascists from Bastiani and Castelnuovo. We'll hide in caves in the Matese mountains and fight in any way we can against the Germans. But we'll need your help from here.'

Ivo pulls Gino close. 'You can count on us. We'll continue our work from the storeroom. But we have to keep Esther safe. Remember, she's a Polish Jew and she speaks German as well as English.'

'She could be in grave danger.' Gino steps forward and thrust his chin towards the storeroom. 'You know where to hide her.'

Outside the sky is deep crimson and swallows dance in the evening shadows.

The leaf of my calendar dangles askew.

It is the 8th September, 1943, the Birth of the Blessed Virgin's feast day.

Today is Armistice Day, the day of surrender.

Chapter Twenty-Four

It was market day. They parked the *motorino* at the edge of the piazza, not far from the Fortuna fountain. Nina felt a quiet relief that Nicolò had managed to slip away from his parents, who'd been summoned to Campobasso for further orders. The internment camps in the region had been freed after the Armistice, yet the silence they left behind was louder than ever.

The structures were abandoned, left empty and vacant, but nobody knew what had happened to the internees. The bench where they usually met Tonino was empty. They had to try and locate him, discover what had happened to him.

The villagers of Isernia, tired of hatred and violence and desperate for peace, were performing their customary daily tasks in a jovial atmosphere. Nina's heart lifted at the sight. The semblance of peace, however fragile, was something to hold onto.

Nina and Nicolò walked past the market stalls; the chatter of bargaining voices reached their ears. Then came a sound—a faint whirring at first, then a distant hum that rose in pitch. Nina stopped, her gaze snapping upwards. Planes buzzed above their heads, whining and whirring in the air. She pointed to the sky. 'What is happening, Nicolò?' she asked, her voice edged with unease.

'These are not German planes. They are American: look at the blue circle with the white five-pointed star,' Nicolò replied, his voice dimmed by the noise of the engines.

The words barely reached her ears before the air split open.

The first bomb struck.

The earth trembled beneath Nina's feet.

A chorus of screams rose, sharp and piercing, as if the town itself was crying out in agony. Another explosion, and another. The sky unleashed its fury, and chaos consumed the piazza.

'Nina, take my *motorino.* Quick. Go!' Nicolò shouted, pulling at her arm. But her feet hesitated. She turned, her eyes drinking in the devastation.

Minutes was all it took for the *centro storico* to crumble into dust, for the bridges to collapse into the rivers they once spanned, for the cathedral to stand scarred and trembling against the skyline.

'Come with me,' Nina shouted above the turmoil.

'No, I must stay and help.' Nicolò pulled her toward the *motorino,* his voice frantic. She could barely hear him over the echo of the planes. Their hum reverberated in her chest, shaking her as much as the ground beneath her feet.

She climbed onto Nicolò's motorbike, turned the key and pumped the gas. Before she sped away, she glanced back one last time. Smoke curled into the sky, blotting out the sun. Isernia, fractured, bleeding, was no longer the town she had stepped into moments ago.

Peace after the Armistice? What an illusion. Don Simone had been right. The bombing of Isernia was the sad proof. And whose fault was that? Only the vital and strategic position of Molise, their region squeezed in between the Tyrrhenian and Adriatic seas where the Germans were retreating. The coveted peace was slipping away like flowing water through fingers, and her heart was shrinking.

Her chest tightened as her thoughts turned to Bastiani. Who could reassure them that Bastiani wouldn't be next?

Sitting beside the river in Bastiani waiting for Nicolò to return, Nina, white pearls of perspiration beading her forehead, closed her eyes and wondered how, despite the blood that now stained the soil of Molise, the waters still flowed clear and fresh amongst the silvery pebbles of the riverbed.

In the distance, church bells chimed.

'Where are you?' she uttered, her insides plunging with apprehension. The warm September sun scalded Nina's face. A soft breeze ruffled her hair and smoothed her cheeks. But the gentleness of the weather wasn't enough to soften her battered and bruised soul.

A rustling in the bushes. Her stomach somersaulted in fear and anticipation. His face appeared in front of her but not the face she knew. Dust, mud, blood covered his head, his neck, his arms. Shirt torn at the waist, thick golden-brown hair matted with chunks of rubble.

'Nicolò.' She pulled him to her, holding his limp body.

'Isernia is a cemetery . . . I managed to get a lift on a truck.'

She could feel his muscles tense against her chest; his laboured breathing filled the space between them. After a moment he took a deep inhale and continued. 'The Allies dropped bomb after bomb on Isernia. Bodies drenched in blood line the streets. People are buried alive in the rubble. You hear their howls everywhere. I managed to drag a child from under mounds of stones and lift him to safety. Death and suffering is everywhere. Nina, it's no longer the Isernia we know.'

Depleted by the retelling of what he had witnessed, Nicolò leant his head against her shoulder. She held him close trying hard not to imagine the horrors he had seen.

'And the camp? Tonino?'

'The *carabinieri* went to the camp yesterday and freed the internees.'

'Tonino?' Nina repeated, her voice more insistent, her eyes searching Nicolò's face for a swift answer.

Nicolò paused, his gaze dropping to the ground. Nina's brow furrowed in concern.

'I heard he was captured by the Germans. They are using the anti-Fascist prisoners to dig anti-tank ditches and lay mines. The Jewish ones have been deported to camps in the east.'

The recollection of what happened to Malka's parents flooded back to her. Despite the heat Nina shivered, her tongue dry and chalky, salty tears pricked her eyes. A droning sound filled the air. Dark shadows loomed around them. Nina tilted her head. A formation of American warplanes dipped and dived across the azure sky. Were they getting closer to Bastiani?

'Nicolò, why are the Allies doing this to us? Aren't we now on the same side?'

'Fascism is not over yet, Nina. Mussolini has been freed by German paratroopers. Operation Oak, they call it, organised by Hitler and Goebbels. Ten military gliders approached Gran Sasso from the air and rescued him from Campo Imperatore.' A rush of words flew from Nicolò's mouth as if his lungs were gasping for air; a stream of sentences that Nina struggled to keep up with.

'Mussolini's back, Nina. Our Italian soldiers are deserting the army in droves. The Germans are capturing them, shooting them or deporting them if they refuse to fight. It's mayhem. The Resistance movement is taking shape; many people have joined the partisans, just like your brother Gino. Don't you see Nina? We are in an unthinkable situation.'

'What do we do, Nicolò? I'm scared. What is going to happen to Bastiani, to all of us?'

'The previous regime with the help of Hitler plans to create a new Fascist state with the collaboration of the Germans, with Mussolini at its head in Salò. I believe my father will be part of that. The Fascists are sending him to the north of Italy. For them, *Fascismo* is definitely not dead.' Nicolò's eyes shone, feverish and glassy as he continued to talk, faster and faster. 'It's time, Nina. Don't you see it's time to act now? Look at your courageous brother, Gino. He's formed *una banda partigiana,* a band of partisans, and they are hiding in the Matese mountains, risking their lives, fighting in secrecy to save our country.'

He reached for her hand and drew her close to him. 'I've decided to join the Allies. I speak English, remember? I can translate for them. My father wants me with him in the north of Italy but I refuse to be part of another Fascist dictatorship.'

'But Nicolò, I don't understand . . . Why are you thinking of joining the Allies? They're bombing us to liberate us from the bombing of the Germans? It doesn't make sense.' Her voice was mixed with confusion and sorrow.

He drew a long, exhausted sigh. 'Sometimes you have to do bad things to get the results you want. We have to clear our country of the invaders. I've made up my mind; I'm leaving tonight.'

A blend of admiration, anger and fear coursed through Nina. Gino and Nicolò, the two men she loved most in the world, were willing to put their lives at risk, to fight as *partigiani,* to help the Allies. What about her?

'Let me come with you!' She flung her arms around his neck.

'No, Nina. You stay here in Bastiani.'

'You can't expect me to stay here, do nothing and just pray to the Madonna for peace and freedom.'

'You have a role here. Gino's *Banda* needs couriers. The *Banda* has plans: ambushes of German soldiers, procuring forged documents, getting maps of the area to the Allies, along with weapons. They need all the help they can get from trustworthy partisans like us. You have experience, you've been working for the Resistance these past few months, delivering food and letters. Stay and help the *Banda* with Ivo, Mariolina and Esther.'

Nina sighed. 'But what will happen to us, Nicolò? I might lose you.' Nina nestled her head against his chest.

'You'll never lose me, Nina.'

He moved a step away from her. With a shaky hand, Nicolò patted his shirt pocket and unclipped a black and forest-green fountain pen with a semi-circular gold tip. 'It's still here, a miracle I didn't lose it amidst the chaos of Isernia.' Relief crisscrossed his eyes. 'I received it for my eighteenth birthday. My initials are inscribed here. I want you to have it. Think of me every day.'

Nicolò released his clenched fist and with his free hand, pointed to the letters N.S. The gold of the fountain pen glimmered, a heroic survivor in the middle of his palm streaked with blood and dirt. Nicolò placed the pen onto her palm and curled her fingers around it.

Nina pulled Nicolò towards her, searching for his mouth. She kissed him deeply, hoping to find support and consolation in the closeness of his body.

His mouth tasted of dust and gunpowder. More planes streaked across the sky. A howitzer blasted. Germans? The Allies? Who was the enemy now? Her thoughts turned to Vinchiaturo.

'And Malka, Leanda? Now that the camps have been opened up, what happened to them? Will I still find them waiting for me in Palazzo Nonno?'

'Your job now is to work together with the *Banda* and keep them safe. Go and tell Ivo you're ready.'

'But Nicolò, how will I know you're safe?'

'I will find a way of contacting you. Trust me. I'll write from the Winter Line. And I'll send you a letter via the Post Office whenever I can.'

'The Winter Line?'

'It's the web of defensive lines the Germans are creating from the Adriatic to the Tyrrhenian to stop the Allies crossing the Apennines. There are several different lines, and I want to be there to help the Americans and Canadians liberate Molise, our Italy.'

Nina pulled him close and searched for his mouth. Between sobs she kissed and bit his lips at the same time, afraid to let him go, desperate at the thought that she would be alone without him. He would be somewhere on this wretched Winter Line fighting for a freedom that felt so far from her grasp. But she would make him proud, she would work with the *Banda* and become their *staffetta*, their courier.

Chapter Twenty-Five

Nina waited until her mother's snores seeped through the bedroom door, rattling and uneven. With a gentle tread she tiptoed downstairs, slipping through the kitchen towards the back door, careful not to wake Marta, who had always been a light sleeper. Since Gino had fled to hide in the forest with the *Banda*, her sleep had become even more restless, agitated by worry.

Nina closed the door and stepped outside. There was a chill in the night air. It pressed against her bare legs and crept through the gap between her shirt collar and her skin. She shivered. As she made her way through the slate-grey arch to the piazza, the sky above throbbed with stars, their light pulsating like a heartbeat.

Bastiani lay shrouded in darkness, but the star-spangled sky pointed her the way with a calm quiet. Ivo was expecting her. Earlier that afternoon, he had told her to come to the Post Office storeroom whilst the village slept. Nina glanced up at Ambra's bedroom window. Was Ambra asleep, too? A candle flickered on the sill, its flame casting restless shadows onto the piazza. The Post Office door was locked. She knocked three times, following Ivo's precise instructions, then turned toward Celestina and Pietruzzo's bakery.

'There's a narrow gap between the bakery and the Post Office,' he'd explained earlier. 'Slip through and walk until you reach a black door, half hidden by ivy. When you find it, cough twice and say the code words, "*oggi piove*".'

Oggi piove! Today it's raining. She had not expected such intrigue, but she followed Ivo's instructions, pressing herself through the gap, the scent of yeast and flour mingling with damp ivy. At the black door, she cleared her throat and whispered the code.

The door creaked open. Mariolina stood before her, hair plaited and wound into a tight bun, light grey wisps escaping and curling around her ears. A lone hair sprouted from her nose. The lines on her face had deepened, the skin beneath her eyes was bruised with blue-veined shadows, giving her a defeated, tired look. Yet there was an energy, a vigour in her smile and in the way she squeezed Nina's hand.

Without a word, she led her down a dim corridor to a small opening no bigger than a large window and no higher than Nina's waist.

'Bend down and climb through,' Mariolina ordered. 'This is a secret passage to the storeroom; it's safer than using the main Post Office door. There is a tiny cubbyhole where we're hiding Esther.'

'Hiding Esther?' Nina's voice was barely a whisper. 'Why?'

'If the Gestapo finds her, she'll be killed.'

'But she's been safe in Bastiani for the entire war. Everyone knows she's an anti-Fascist, a socialist, but no one cares. Not even *Carabiniere* Palotta. Or *Avvocato* Sansone.'

'Well, they care now. She's a Jew and that's all the Germans need to know. If they find her, she'll be arrested, possibly tortured. Even shot. And us too for hiding her and for the work we do with the *Banda*.' Mariolina's voice was steady but piercing, carrying the weight of the horror Esther was facing. They were all facing.

Nina thought of the document hammered on the exterior walls of the Post Office all those years ago, stating Jews could no longer hold public office. She had been too young then to understand why Esther had stopped working as a teacher in the school in nearby Castelnuovo.

'Being a *staffetta* is not for the faint-hearted. Are you ready for this?' Mariolina's eyes bored into Nina with an intensity that made Nina tremble. Her throat tightened. Fear like a living being curled in her bones, wrapping around her ribs, her skin, her skull. Was she ready to be a courier for the *Banda*?

A silence swelled between them.

Then Nina gave a single, firm nod.

Mariolina clicked her tongue against the roof of her mouth and with a softer tone, she added, 'You're brave, and we need you. You have youth on your side. The Nazis and Fascists don't expect young girls to be working for the *partigiani*. Esther and I will train you; we'll guide you.' Her lips split into a wide smile and then she pulled Nina close. 'Nicolò and Gino both said you are reliable. Unlike Ambra.'

Nina flinched.

'We can't trust her,' Mariolina continued, her voice low. 'You must keep this from her, you understand. Ivo is worried but she is his daughter. He's torn.' She pried open the wooden hatch, the beams battered and splintered. With a flick of her fingers, she signalled for Nina to crawl through.

Nina lifted the hem of her skirt, crouched down and squeezed through the gap. She tumbled into a tiny concrete, windowless room the size of a *cantina*, a small cellar. Shelves lined the walls, stacked with green bottles of Ivo's homemade wine and *poncio*. Pale and bulbous pairs of *caciocavallo* cheese hung from the ceiling.

On a mattress on the floor sat Esther and Ivo. They jumped up and wrapped their arms around Nina's small frame. Nina pulled back and stared at the bare concrete walls.

'Where are we? Is this the Post Office storeroom?'

Ivo pointed to a hole in the wall. 'Yes, this secret hiding place is behind the safe. It's where we keep Esther, away from prying eyes. If the *Fascisti* or the Gestapo come searching, they will never find her here.'

Esther studied Nina carefully. 'This work is full of risk, Nina. Especially now.' Her voice was quiet but firm. She blinked several times. Her eyes were round and as black as a starless sky. Her hair was thinning and sprinkled with silver. Ivo had told Nina that Esther met her late husband Rodolfo in America. She had come from an impoverished *shtetl* near Lvov and he from a tiny hamlet near Bastiani with its ramshackle buildings and destitute *contadini*. She had fallen for the Italian man with skin like burnt hazelnuts and eyes that shone with a vigour and youthfulness she had rarely seen in her native Poland. They were united by a love of politics and interest in the new Soviet Union and shared a determination to improve the lot of peasants. Esther gave up her job as a teacher and followed Rodolfo to Bastiani, both determined to fight against the Fascist decrees of Mussolini in whatever way they could. After Rodolfo's death from tuberculosis, Esther had moved in with Mariolina, Rodolfo's sister, united in their political fight.

'The Germans will be on our backs, the Blackshirts too. You can't trust anyone,' Ivo said, then whispered into her ear, 'Not even Ambra.'

Ambra!

Ivo's daughter, her close friend. The friendship handkerchief they had entwined together still lay under Nina's mattress, although she rarely looked at it now. There was a time when she would lift up her mattress each night and check it was still there. Then she would touch it, even kiss it sometimes. It had been their bond. How had their friendship changed so much? How could it be that not even Ambra's own father trusted her?

'We must help Gino and our men hidden in the mountains,' Esther said slowly. 'They need us. If I could be there by your side, I would be, you know that. But I will support you from my hiding place here behind the storeroom. Are you ready to take on this demanding role working for the *Banda*?'

She thought of Nicolò, of how he had left the comforts of his villa to join the Allies. Of Gino, hiding in the mountains with barely enough food to survive. She thought of her father, of the fire that had always burnt in his chest for justice. She was strong; she was healthy and determined. She could do this. And within her she carried Nicolò's love.

'I am.' She took a deep, jagged inhale.

'Are you certain?' Ivo raised his eyebrows. They were no longer peppery but pure white like the patch of hair on his head. The skin of his face was thin and lined like brittle parchment. Was it the clandestine work they were undertaking or the uncertainty of his daughter's loyalties? Nina couldn't imagine which weighed more heavily on Ivo's heart. But one thing was certain, worry had aged him. Yet there was still a resoluteness to his grey-green eyes, a steeliness. Standing before him Nina felt stronger too. Nicolò and Gino were no longer there to protect her, but she had Ivo, Mariolina and Esther.

'I am,' she repeated. 'I'm ready to join the Bastiani *Banda*, to help the cause.'

Ivo picked up a candleholder from the floor. Mariolina and Esther poured three tumblers of wine.

'This is your initiation ceremony, Nina. We name you *staffetta* Luisa. "*Oggi piove*" will be the code to enter the storeroom from the door in the passageway.'

Luisa! A pretty name. A strong name.

'It means famous warrior,' Mariolina said, handing her a tumbler of wine.

Ivo placed a hand on her shoulder. 'You're young. You won't rouse suspicion. Not like Mariolina, whose anti-Fascist views are well known.'

'You are fighting for freedom, Nina.' Esther grasped Nina's hand and planted a kiss on her palm.

Ivo raised his glass. 'To *staffetta* Luisa.'

'To *staffetta* Luisa,' they echoed, and clinked glasses, their voices laced with hope and defiance.

Esther kissed Nina's forehead. 'Luisa is your name when you are on missions. Never use your real name. Never utter it unless you are working for the Bastiani *Banda*.'

Ivo handed her a thin folder. 'This is your first mission: take these forged documents to Gino and his men. They are hiding internees who have escaped from the camps, in a shack between Vinchiaturo and Castelnuovo.'

Nina swallowed hard. 'What if the Germans or Fascists find them?'

'They'll be shot.'

'Or transported to camps in Germany,' Esther said with a sigh. 'We have to protect them.'

*

Outside the Post Office, the night air was thick with the scent of damp earth and distant smoke. Nina scanned the piazza, her gaze resting briefly on the Sansone villa, the church, Bar Renzo.

Everything was the same.

But she had changed. She was no longer Nina Caruso, ferrying food and letters from family and friends to the internees—quiet reassurances that life outside the internment camps still existed. She was *staffetta* Luisa and the documents she carried, hidden inside the waistband of her skirt, were more than forged names on paper. They were lifelines. If she was caught, the best she could hope for was imprisonment, the worst was unthinkable. And what would happen to Malka and Leanda if she was unable to reach them? Danger now lurked in the shadowed alleyways, the forested mountains, the nearby villages. The world had changed and so had she.

Chapter Twenty-Six

It was a tattered and soiled envelope. The paper stamp at the corner was missing, and in its place the words *'a mano'*, by hand, were highlighted in capital letters. That's why it didn't go into the mail jute bag, into her father's hands, Ambra thought. Who was sending such a missive to an internee?

With curiosity she opened the letter and began to read the words:

Mia amata *Nina,*

I miss you and I long to hold you in my arms once more.

Ambra's heart quickened. Her hand shook as she scanned the words written by Nicolò.

I have joined the Allies in Salerno. I am translating and interpreting for them. I am glad the English novels my mother made me read have a purpose. It's my contribution to the freedom of our country. Don't worry about me. I am well and content to be doing something useful. I will keep you posted.

You are in my thoughts every day, my love, and as soon as this war is over, we will be together, no matter what my family thinks.

Tuo *Nicolò*

Ambra closed her eyes, fingers clutching Nicolò's letter. She sank down onto a stool and reread it. A stabbing pain in her chest deepened with each sentence. She slammed the letter on the kitchen table and reached for the packet of Sturm cigarettes Werner had given her, hidden in a secret compartment in the kitchen. She lit one, inhaled deeply, the swirls of smoke spinning with her thoughts.

A realisation struck her as an idea fizzed in her mind. What if Nina never received this letter? She stubbed out her cigarette, the letter clenched in her hands, her fingers stroking it. The tattered envelope between her fingers had the scent of money. It felt like the five-*lire* note Signora Sansone had given her so unexpectedly.

Ambra stared into the humid air, eyes glazing. Like a coin dropped into the fountain in Campobasso, another idea plopped into her mind. She now knew she had a special delivery to make before her father returned.

*

Ambra darted across the piazza, her hand protecting the newly found treasure in her pocket. She waved at her father and Don Simone, who lifted his black biretta and nodded a warm greeting. She rang the doorbell, her hands shaking with excitement.

It was Nina who opened the door. Suddenly, the letter felt heavy in Ambra's pocket.

'I didn't know you were still working at the villa.' She lowered her face to hide her eyes, afraid they would betray her.

'Now that Nicolò has left, I am allowed back to help my mother.' Nina's tone was curt, unfriendly.

In the old days of their friendship, Ambra and Nina would have hugged and chatted happily. In some ways, Ambra wished they could still share their typing sessions together, or enjoy meeting on the terrace outside Bar Renzo. Ambra bit her lip to stop these nostalgic reminiscences. She must not allow herself to be trapped by cheap sentimentalism. Since that morning when her mother's body had lain on the kitchen table surrounded by candles and her father couldn't stop crying, Ambra had come to the conclusion that it was wiser not to live a life led by emotions. And it had worked. Wasn't that exactly how she behaved with Werner?

Ambra tilted her chin and looked directly at Nina.

'I have a letter for *la signora*.'

'I'll get her for you.'

When Ambra entered the room, Signora Carmela did not look up from the book she was reading. Ambra narrowed her eyes. She couldn't read the title, but the name of the author was clear. Gabriele D'Annunzio. Even Ambra knew about him, a fighter pilot in the Great War, a poet, a playwright, a journalist and a womaniser. At school they'd learnt his poems imbued with his convictions of Italy's greatness. Ambra cleared her throat. Her heels made a scraping noise on the marble floor as she shifted from foot to foot.

Carmela lifted her gaze, and her spectacles slipped to the tip of her nose. A string of pearls hung around her neck. Her eyebrows were plucked to form two perfect half-moons over shimmering blue eyes. Carmela jumped to her feet and stepped closer to Ambra. She was more than a head taller than her. Ambra could smell the powdery scent of rose mixed with the tang of musk.

'Have you news of my son?' A grunting sound, like a lioness defending her cubs rose from Carmela's throat.

Ambra stepped back and held Nicolò's correspondence to Nina close to her chest. 'Yes, in fact I do.' She waved the letter in front of Carmela's eyes. 'I intercepted a letter from Nicolò to Nina that might interest you.'

Carmela stiffened. 'Give it to me.'

Slowly and with deliberation, Ambra placed the letter in Carmela's outstretched palm.

As she read Nicolò's words, Carmela's jaw dropped, her cheeks paled. The tiny muscles at the sides of her mouth quivered and contracted, as if she no longer had control over them.

'Soon I am going to join my husband in Salò. It would kill him if he knew his son had switched sides. And it kills me to know my son is in danger. Nicolò thinks he is a hero, translating for the Allies. And if he thinks he's going to spend the rest of his life with Nina, he can forget it.'

Ambra fixed her gaze on Carmela's face. Her raised eyebrows gave her a serene expression, so contrary to her burst of emotion. Her curled lips revealed pearl-white teeth.

'Nobody can see this note, do you understand me, Ambra? Nobody. I cannot allow this letter to fall into the wrong hands. My son will be regarded a traitor.'

'My silence is not free, Signora Sansone.' Ambra waited.

Carmela Sansone reached for her purse on the sideboard behind her and pulled out two five-*lire* notes. 'This is for you.' She stretched her arm across the coffee table and picked up the silver cigarette box Ambra had admired on her first visit. She handed it to Ambra.

'And this is a further token for your collaboration. I am relying on you. Make sure any future letters to Nina from my son disappear.'

Their hands touched. Ambra grasped the cold, shiny box and held it to her chest. 'It's a deal, Signora. Our deal.'

'You will not regret it, Ambra. You are not only saving Nicolò, but our country, our *Patria.*'

'You won't regret it either, Signora Sansone.'

Chapter Twenty-Seven

Werner's hotel room smelt of stale air, in the unseasonal early October heat. It created a dampness that weighed on the bed sheets. Light flooded the room through the tall window opening onto a tiny balcony cluttered with blood-red geraniums in flowerpots. A large brass bed covered with a midnight-blue satin quilt took up most of the room.

Out of the window in the distance, the white walls of the neighbouring palazzo glittered in yellow sunlight. The roofs of the surrounding buildings, a jigsaw of terracotta hues, absorbed the copper rays of the sun.

Werner was unbuttoning Ambra's blouse. Then slowly, he lifted her skirt and peeled off her stockings. As his hands cupped her breasts, she looked up. Her eyes met the pattern of the wallpaper, the small blue flowers of a cornfield. After months of stolen encounters in bars, at the beach, and in restaurants, she had agreed to meet him at his hotel. He winked as he ruffled her hair and bit her lip with affection, the mist of their breath mingling in the air. Their bodies met with passion, arms intertwined like the twisted branches of the trees in the piazza. He smelled of cloves and she liked it.

In Werner's arms, Ambra was no longer the Post Office girl, in a region devastated by bombs. She was in Campobasso amidst bars and restaurants with food and drink flowing, a glimpse of a world without war, far removed from Bastiani and the surrounding villages. It was the freedom she yearned for.

Legs entwined, they rolled onto the quilt, Ambra's hair spread behind her, like an open fan. He caressed her face with his lips. He was no longer the military man she had first encountered, shouting orders and seducing her with gifts. He was a delicate, attentive lover, treating her with kindness.

Entangled in the sheets after making love, cigarettes in their mouths, lips pouting over the thin yellow filter, Ambra tossed her head back and laughed at Werner's attempt to recite poetry in Italian. He talked of his childhood in a big house above the Rhine close to Köln, of his father, a musicologist who taught him arias and the beauty of the Italian language. His eyes filled with tears when he spoke of the concerts he attended with his family, whom he hadn't seen for several years. It was an intimacy she hadn't expected him to share with her. She stroked his cheek and lowered her lips onto the bristles of his moustache. He drew back from her, swung his legs off the side of the bed and pulled on his trousers.

Silently, Werner wiped dust off the wine glasses arranged in a row on the chest of drawers opposite the bed. He popped open the half-bottle of white wine and poured two glasses.

'I need to tell you something, Ambra.' His face solemn, his eyes heavy, he handed her a glass. A whisper of a warning glinted at the edge of her heart. Ambra feared he might ask her for a roll of film, of photos she had not yet taken with the Leica. Instead, he sat down in the armchair, opposite the bed, his gaze flicking around the room.

She took a sip of wine. The cool, fruity taste soothed Ambra's nerves.

'We have been ordered to raid villages all over Molise and to get Italian soldiers—any man in fact—to join us.

The German army wants to punish your country. It's part of our scorched-earth policy. It's going to get nasty. They will be after your livestock, your crops, your houses. You need to warn your people in Bastiani to be alert and ready.'

Ambra bolted upright, a sheet covering her breast. 'Why are you telling me this now?'

'Tomorrow my regiment is transferring me from Campobasso to Berlin. You won't see me again.' Werner hesitated, his eyes staring into the empty glass of wine. 'The British and Canadian forces are planning an attack. I'm telling you all of this at great risk to myself. Let it be my last gift to you: I've grown fond of you. You remind me of a girl I knew at school in my hometown. Strong-minded and sensuous.'

Ambra's thoughts swirled in her head, making her dizzy. She thought of her father in the Post Office, of Nina's farm, of Celestina kneading bread in the bakery, of poor Don Simone, of Tommaso and Rita and their sweet sheepdog, Fido. These were her people. This was where she belonged. Her heart clanged in her chest. She threw off the sheet and reached for her skirt and blouse.

'But we still have our *Duce* in command.'

Werner shrugged his shoulders; shadows darkened his eyes.

'Your region is vital to us: the rivers, the mountains. Molise is the narrowest part of Italy. The aim is to stop *die Allierten*, the Allies, from conquering the region. Italy has betrayed Germany; it will have to pay the consequences. We will all suffer now.'

'So is it the end? For our country? For us?'

'Ambra, I am tired. Of war. Of killing. Of stealing. I want to go home.'

Ambra hadn't expected Werner to reveal this mournful and pensive part of his soul. When she first met him, he'd been a confident soldier, sure of himself and proud of his country. And now here he was, tired, disillusioned, fearful. She wondered if she could exploit this new mellow Werner and use it to her advantage for the very last time.

'And the Leica?' She clambered onto his lap and snuggled close to him, her bare breasts rubbing against his shirt. 'Let me keep it; it's the only thing I have to remember you by.'

His lips clasped hers; his arms held her in a tight embrace.

Was his answer yes?

Chapter Twenty-Eight

The bus rattled on the country roads between Campobasso and Bastiani, snaking through rose-blushed mountains, past olive groves and vineyards. Ambra smiled to herself and held her bag tightly to her chest. Hidden inside was the Leica and several rolls of film. How clever she had been to persuade Werner to let her keep them. What did he have to lose? He was leaving for Germany; nobody would ever know. Yet she had to keep the Leica and the spare rolls of film hidden: it was still forbidden to possess a camera unless you were working for the Germans. Who was she working for now? she wondered. Herself of course.

On the outskirts of Bastiani, Ambra jumped off the bus. She decided to walk the last kilometre up to the piazza and compose herself before she arrived back at the Post Office.

The evening sunlight shimmered on the tops of the olive trees, the burnt orange sky streaked with wisps of clouds. The air smelled of freshly turned earth, pungent and warm. The roaring of military motorcycles and their sidecars zoomed past her, khaki brown monsters shattering the peace. As they passed by, the soldiers wolf-whistled and lengthened their arms in the Nazi salute.

'*Ciao, bella. Schöne Fräulein*,' they chortled above the droning of the engines. She kept her eyes lowered to the path but smiled inside, marvelling at how her ears had become accustomed to the sound of German.

As the clamour of the engines faded, Ambra became aware of a high-pitched whimpering. Was it Fido? The ricotta makers' white sheep dog often yelped when herding the goats back to the *baita*, their hut, from the nearby fields. Whenever she delivered the mail to Tommaso, Fido would bark warning yelps of protection until he recognised her scent. As soon as he realised it was only Ambra, the Post Office girl, Fido would wag his tail and Ambra would stroke the rough fur at his neck and tickle him under the chin the way she knew he liked. Then Tommaso, with a dimpled smile, would invite her to dip a clean finger into the barrel and taste the fresh ricotta.

But these cries were different. Not the urgent warnings of a dog protecting its owners. These were, drawn-out, plaintive wails, the kind that scraped at the heart and lodged under the skin. They reminded her of her father's lamenting sobs the night her mother died.

She quickened her step and turned the corner. Fido was circling in distress, his yelps even more frantic. Nearby, Rita and Tommaso's mule whimpered, ears pointing upwards. It was a strange, broken sound, not quite the full-throated braying of a donkey nor a mere whinny, but something in between. A sound of grief.

'What on earth has happened?' she murmured, her own voice hollow in the cool evening air. The sunlight shimmered on the mountains as the sun sank lower in the sky, an orange-red hue. Evening sunlight splintered through the trees casting golden strobes on the fur of the dog, the twitching ears of the mule.

And then she saw them.

Two bodies swung from the oak tree outside the *baita*, where they made cheese for the village.

Tommaso. Rita.

Their arms dangled, lifeless. Their legs swayed, limp as puppets. Lips tinged a cyanotic shade of bluish-purple.

The shifting light dappled the bodies creating a golden glow like a halo over their slumped heads. It was as if the sun itself mourned them. Shadows stretched on the ground as the sunlight waned.

Ambra tried to make sense of the image. It reached her but it was as if her mind was emptied of all reason, as if she was disconnected from her body as she tried to fathom the scene in front of her eyes: Tommaso and Rita, wrists slack, fingers curled, the rope biting deep into their throats.

Her eyes brimmed. Dark pools spilled down her cheeks. Her shoulders hunched with rage. She could feel her neck tight as ropes, her cheeks blotched scarlet with shock. A hot rush of fury burnt under her skin, an anger she knew she would never extinguish.

Two pairs of wooden clogs rested in the dirt beneath the dead bodies, as if waiting for Rita and Tommaso to slip their feet back inside. Something about those forlorn, empty clogs, so small against the cruelty of the hanging, sent a sharp pain coursing through Ambra's chest. Her choked scream echoed through the silent evening air: 'Not them. Not Tommaso and Rita.'

She felt lightheaded and crushed at the same time as if every speck of air was being pumped out of her body, gasp by painful gasp.

Ambra snapped her eyes shut, hoping to erase the haunting image. But it was still there . . . She knew then it would never leave her. It would follow her into sleep, haunt the dark corners of her mind.

Her stomach twisted. Bile rose sharp and bitter in her throat. She retched. An acid taste burnt her mouth, her throat, her heart. She doubled over. A yellowish stream of vomit splattered onto the dusty path, curling at her feet like one of the vipers that lurked around the foothills of Molise.

It was then she felt the metal camera pressing against her ribs from the inside of her bag. She remembered Werner's words when he first pressed the Leica into her willing hands, months ago.

'Every single image is currency.'

She was too late to save Tommaso and Rita.

But not too late to capture the horror.

Hands trembling, she pulled the camera from her bag. What if there were still German soldiers nearby? She scanned the horizon but all she saw was the blue shadow of the mountains, the brown stubble of the fields, the empty *baita* and the bodies still swaying in the twilight.

She lifted the camera to her eye.

The legs, stiff with death.

Click.

The bruising, the raw lacerations around Rita's neck.

Click.

Tommaso's face, sunken, yellow.

Click.

They had always been part of her life, part of Bastiani. After Agostina's death, it was Rita who had fed her and Ivo, spooning *zuppa di pallotte* into their empty stomachs, ensuring the soup with ricotta cheese balls nourished the two mourners. The soup had tasted of warmth, of care, of something close to love. She had eaten it with Nina, a mourner too, by her side, their friendship handkerchiefs lying next to the bowls as they whispered secrets between spoonfuls.

How different things had been then. How much simpler. Before war had chipped away at friendship, at loyalties, at ideals.

Ambra clicked faster, as if those ideals she had carried within her bones—the blind devotion, the fragile dreams of a better future—were slipping away with each snap of the shutter like wisps of early morning mist.

Then a feeling akin to shame coiled within her; shame at her eagerness to believe in the promises of a rotten regime. Shame for the photos she had taken of Nina and Nicolò, smuggling food and letters to the internees, even if it had only been their backs.

She would feel shame no longer.

Italy had changed sides. And so had she.

Chapter Twenty-Nine

Legs petrified by shock, thoughts a tumult of anguish mixed with a strange sense of pride and resolve, Ambra slipped the camera back into her bag and continued along the winding path to Bastiani. Tommaso and Rita's lifeless faces, their necks limp and tilted to one side, bloodshot eyes now blind to the hills and fields they'd loved so dearly, were printed not only into her mind, but recorded forever on the film inside the camera.

A soft pitter-patter made her turn. Her eyes brimmed with tears, her heart ached. Fido was trailing behind her at a distance. His head tilted, the pink tip of his tongue poking out, a soulful look in his cast-down brown eyes, he seemed to be imploring, 'I am lost, take me with you.'

She ran towards him and knelt beside him. He nestled his head in her lap, and she stroked him gently, her touch slow and reassuring. A small groan of contentment escaped from his mouth, a subtle vibration she felt through her hand.

'Fido, don't worry,' she murmured. 'Justice will be done in the end. Come, let's return to Bastiani. There is much to be said and done.'

She stood up and sauntered along the dusty road, Fido's panting marking a rhythm to her steps.

The sun sank behind the mountains, tinging the sky a solid violet hue. The air had picked up in freshness. Ambra shivered and quickened her pace. At the edges of the road, the hazelnut bushes still held a few clusters of caramel-brown nuts, enclosed by their leafy green husks. The very last of their summer yield before autumn turned it yellow and stripped of leaves.

Ambra's thoughts drifted to her relationship with Werner. It had been a dangerous gamble, one that could have cost her dearly. But it hadn't. The Leica was still with her.

Fido trotted beside her, brushing his muzzle against her calves. The coolness of his snout was a comforting sensation amidst the agitation burning within her. He whined softly. Was he hungry, thirsty, still mourning the loss of his owners? Ambra lowered her arm and stroked his head, feeling its white fur matted with mud beneath her fingers. His whining ceased, and he wagged his tail, giving her two short, quick yaps as if to express thanks.

In Bastiani, twilight bathed the main piazza. The bell tower of Santa Croce church, Bar Renzo, the Post Office walls were all shrouded in the deep, velvety blue of the approaching night. The Post Office door was ajar; she pushed it open and, heart pounding in her chest and throat, she drifted inside like a shadow. Nina emerged first from the storeroom, followed closely by Ivo and Mariolina. 'Ambra, what are you doing with Tommaso and Rita's dog?' they exclaimed in unison. For a moment their disbelief cut through the air spreading a sense of annoyance that unsettled Ambra.

Sobs shook Ambra's shoulders. Her lips trembled as she blinked back the tears welling in her eyes. It took several attempts from Ivo, Mariolina and Nina to piece together Ambra's broken words and sniffles: Tommaso and Rita had been brutally murdered by the Germans, who had ransacked their pantry and stolen their goats. Ambra's words, punctuated by Fido's whimpering, stirred the air.

Nina covered her eyes with a shaking hand; Mariolina stifled a gasp, covering her mouth with the corner of her black apron. Ivo rubbed his face with both hands as if to erase the harrowing images his daughter was describing. The more Ambra conveyed the haunting details of the execution, the more she felt as if she had been struck by a lightning bolt, forcing her to confront her own naivety and recklessness, along with the harsh realities of the world.

'I have seen too much; I feel too much pain and rage.' Ambra dropped her face into her trembling hands. 'I'm ashamed. I was blinded. Forgive me, *papà*. Everyone, forgive me.' More sobs muffled her words.

Ivo, sunk in a chair, muttered in a broken voice, 'This is what war does to you, my child. It blows you over, Ambra.'

Without another word, Ambra steadied her shaking hands, and opened the satchel.

The square, metallic Leica gleamed faintly in the dim light of the Post Office. She thrust it towards her father, Nina and Mariolina.

'This will be my weapon, our weapon,' she declared.

'Where did you get that?' Ivo whispered, his voice barely audible.

'It doesn't matter,' Ambra said firmly. 'But I will use it to our advantage. Wheat fields scattered with mines; bridges blown to dust; roads hollowed into chasms, people murdered—these disasters that plague our region won't go unrecorded. We don't know who the culprits are. Germans? Or even the Allies? All I know is that we are the victims, and we must not give up fighting for our freedom.' Ambra stood taller, determination flashing in her eyes. 'And I've already started by capturing images of our dear Tommaso and Rita.'

As Ambra spoke, a sense of togetherness surged in the Post Office, melting away any initial tension. It warmed the humid autumn evening air.

'But first, I want to inform Don Simone. He must give them a proper dignified burial, before they fall prey to animals or the mockery of the Blackshirts.'

Her father's embrace felt like a cleansing rain after weeks of drought. Nina's hand stroking her cheek reminded her of their friendship pact handkerchief, made so long ago. Death had cemented their friendship; another death might restore their trust in each other. Mariolina clapped her on the back with a hearty thump in a sign of camaraderie. Ambra stroked Fido. 'Now you are alone. I'll take you to Don Simone. I am sure he will find the right home for you.'

Post Office

Huddled in the storeroom, under the glare of an oil lamp, backs bent, foreheads nearly touching, Ivo, Mariolina and Ambra listen to Radio Londra's broadcast. The announcement crackles through the air.

'The Allied forces landed in Termoli yesterday: *Operazione* Devon.' Lightness and hope rolls through Ivo's words.

A different noise echoes amongst my walls, cutting through the radio broadcast and Ivo's words. Three heads jerk in unison. The clandestine telegraph device Mariolina had built several weeks ago by welding copper coils clicks fast and slow. Pen in hand, Ivo translates the electrical impulses of the machine onto a piece of paper. Mariolina sits still, her wrinkled features as hard as the stone of the Matese mountains. Nina storms into the room, her coat dripping with rain, the acrid smell of burnt autumn leaves clinging to her. The air shifts.

'There has been an execution at Fornelli, just a few miles from here,' Nina utters. 'Ordered by the 26th Panzer Division.' Nina's voice catches in her throat.

Ambra barely stirs, her face a mask of controlled emotion.

'The news is coming through now, here . . .' Ivo's tone is sharp with dread; the telegraph needle moves fast. He reads what is transcribing aloud; his voice carries the metallic pitch of a mechanical device.

'*In the main piazza of Fornelli, after reading aloud the death sentence of the six citizens guilty of posing resistance to the German troops and responsible for the death of a German soldier, the village inhabitants were evacuated, houses burnt to the ground.'*

Mariolina slams her fist on the old kitchen table and the telegraph device rattles, the typewriter wobbles.

'I know what triggered it,' she shrills. 'The other morning three German soldiers were raiding cattle in the Castello district of Fornelli and one of our young defecting soldiers threw hand grenades at them, wounding two. After his brave gesture he managed to escape and reach Gino's *Banda*. But the unharmed soldier transported the two wounded Germans to the hospital where one died.' She draws a long breath. 'That was the beginning of the reprisal.' Air whistles through her nostrils. It is rage I hear.

Nina is the first to speak; her voice falters. 'A public hanging to teach the village and us all what happens if you oppose the Wehrmacht.'

Ivo shakes his head, his lips drained of blood. I am amazed he manages to continue reading his transcript.

Laurelli Giuseppe, *avvocato* and *podestà*, 54 years old
Castaldi Vincenzo, landowner, 64 years old
Castaldi Giuseppe, *contadino*, 53 years old
Lancellotta Domenico, *contadino*, 52 years old
Lancellotta Celestino, *contadino*, 74 years old
Petrarca Michele, *contadino*, 44 years old

The names of the victims leave his lips, one by one, like the tolling of the bell Don Simone pulls when someone dies in Bastiani. Ivo stops to swallow the tears welling up.

'A gramophone was stolen from a nearby house and played music as the six bodies were left to dangle as a warning to the population.'

I see horror in my people's widened eyes, in the contortions of their faces.

'Macabre,' Nina whispers.

'Brutal,' Mariolina spits out the word with a fiery intonation.

Ambra lifts her head slightly, her vacant expression flickering at the edges. 'Innocent victims like Tommaso and Rita.' Her voice is calm, but her cheeks and neck are deep crimson. Eyebrows arched, she listens with intent to her father's words.

'A hero. *Podestà* Laurelli is a hero,' she repeats. 'He gave himself up. If not, they would have hanged four other innocent men.'

'You're right, Ambra.' Nina places a hand on Ambra's shoulder, her voice trembling. 'The rule is clear, ten Italian civilians must be executed for the killing of each German soldier.'

The silence that follows hangs in the air as if they are all picturing the six men dangling under the scorching sun, birds pecking at their skin.

'I must send telegrams to Castelnuovo, Vinchiaturo and all the other villages around Bastiani and alert them,' Ivo says. 'Is there no end to the repression and crimes that the Germans are committing in our country?' he mutters half to himself, his voice a mixture of despair and disbelief.

Ambra straightens in her chair. Her eyebrows curl; her lips part. 'And to think I was warned this would happen. This is just the beginning. It's part of the German scorched-earth policy. Now it's Fornelli. Next time it could be Bastiani.'

She rises and hurries into her bedroom, her steps heavy on the staircase. When she returns her satchel bulges. She taps it and says, 'Our weapon.'

Outside rain falls in relentless sheets, carving the wheat fields into jagged scars of mud.

The top left-hand corner of my calendar leaf curls faintly, frayed by the damp air.

It is the 4th October, 1943, Saint Francis of Assisi's feast day.

Today is the day of despair for the region.

Today marks the change for my Post Office girl.

Chapter Thirty

Pedalling under a light rain, Nina noticed flashing lights in the distance, silhouettes of grey-green uniforms and army jeeps. Her heart stopped. It was an important mission as *staffetta* Luisa and she didn't want it to go wrong. She was taking forged identity documents to Malka and Leanda, who had come to mean so much to her over the past months. Gino's *Banda* had finally found them hiding in caves in the Matese mountains. Now they were safe in the shack used by the *Banda*.

What if the Germans searched her and found the fake documents? The outcome would be the end not only for herself, but also for Malka, Leanda and the Bastiani *Banda*. They would all be arrested, shot on the spot or hanged like Tommaso and Rita and the men in Fornelli.

But after all, this was the risk and peril of being a *staffetta*. Mariolina had warned her when she had offered her services to the *Banda* after Nicolò disappeared from Bastiani. The thought of Nicolò flashed across her mind. Had he encountered similar roadblocks or even been arrested? If only she had received news from him as he had promised. But there had been nothing, and her heart ached for him.

Now she had to banish thoughts of Nicolò from her mind and think of herself. One thing she knew from Mariolina and Esther's teachings about being a *staffetta* was never to show fear, no matter what. That would make her vulnerable, easy prey. She pedalled towards the roadblock with a forced confidence, aware that all their lives were in her hands.

'Halt!' An arm stretched out in front of her forcing her to stop. '*Dokumenten*!'

Nina thought of how Ambra behaved in a flirtatious way, tilting her head, batting her eyelids and pouting. It had always worked for Ambra. She flashed a warm, engaging smile and elegantly swung her legs to dismount the bike.

'What's in your basket?' the officer said in almost perfect Italian.

'The Sansone family in Bastiani asked me to take provisions for their son's old *maestra*,' she bluffed, hoping they were unaware the Sansones had moved to Salò. 'She lives in Vinchiaturo, on the opposite side of the railway.' She spoke slowly in a rasping voice, hoping she sounded seductive enough to soften him and get him on her side.

'You mean *Avvocato* Riccardo Sansone?' His voice became less stern, his gait more relaxed.

'Yes.' She batted her eyelashes. Ambra's technique was working.

A second officer arrived, peeked inside the basket and said, 'I am sure the Sansones would be glad to hand the food to us, we who are protecting your country from the invaders.' He snatched the wicker basket from the handlebars of Nina's bicycle.

Nina hid her disappointment at losing the food she had obtained from Renzo who, had changed sides and now offered his services to the *Banda*.

Nina tried another of Ambra's tactics. 'Of course, *signori*,' she purred sweetly, relieved the papers were safely hidden in the fake-bottomed satchel Mariolina had fashioned for her to conceal documents and other items the partisans might need.

The first soldier motioned to Nina to continue her journey. 'Be careful, the next bridge is in ruins. We have just blown it up. You will have to push your bike across. *Tchuss, signorina.*'

She waved, copying Ambra's walk, seductive enough to protect herself and the documents but not enough to give the wrong impression. She'd heard horror stories of girls in nearby villages being taken advantage of, even raped.

As she approached the damaged bridge, she pushed the wheels of the bike through rubble and debris. *Am I safe now?* she wondered. She turned her head to glance at the soldiers. They were rummaging through the basket and were no longer interested in her. Instead of her usual path towards Palazzo Nonno in via della Libertà, she swivelled her bike in the direction that Ivo and Mariolina had indicated to her to reach Malka and Leanda's hiding place.

*

It was easier to find the shack used by the *Banda* to hide Malka and Leanda than she had imagined. The walls of the barn were blackened with smoke. A carpet of straw lined the concrete floor. The wooden beams of the ceiling were pockmarked with tiny holes. Nina blinked to accustom her eyes to the dim and gloomy interior.

'It's me.'

A pale face peered from behind a haystack, eyes bloodshot and hollowed.

'I thought you'd forgotten me,' Malka said, wrapping herself inside her shawl, now no longer white but grimy with dirt. The *carabinieri* of Vinchiaturo would no longer call her *Biancaneve* if they saw her now.

'We had to organise false papers for you and Leanda . . .' Nina hesitated and scanned the room. 'But wait a minute. Where is Leanda?'

Malka's face collapsed. She whispered, 'She left. She wanted to find her Sinti family. She wasn't happy hiding here with me. She prefers to run the risk of being caught out in the woods rather than here in this shack. She is a free spirit.' Malka's greeny-blue eyes, hollowed with hunger, searched Nina's face. Her paper-thin skin was tightly stretched over her cheekbones. 'I'm so hungry, Nina. The last time I ate was three days ago when *Maestra* Anna managed to smuggle in some bread and scamorza cheese.'

'I'm sorry, Malka. I had some food for you, but I was stopped at a roadblock. They confiscated my basket, but here, I have an apple in my pocket. Take it.'

Malka's hands grabbed the apple. 'But, good news is I have your false documents.' Nina rummaged under the fake bottom of the satchel and slipped the papers out. She watched in astonishment as Malka's lips devoured the fruit in seconds, surprised the primal instinct to satisfy hunger prevailed over Malka's interest in the false document and the chance of escape.

Nina sat down beside Malka. With authority, she outlined the meticulous plan the *Banda* had prepared to transfer Malka to the south of Puglia. 'You will go to a transit camp in Santa Maria al Bagno. There, the mild weather, the sea and the kindness of the people will help you recover. You'll become a new person, Malka. Be ready tonight. Gino will come and bring a warm coat and shoes for you. He will whistle four times. You come out. And remember from then on you will be Anna Rossi.'

It struck Nina that she too had become a new person: Luisa, the *staffetta* of Bastiani. She had begun to change since Nicolò had introduced her to the internees; since she had become a *staffetta* to help Gino and the Bastiani *Banda*; since Nicolò had left her.

She touched the fountain pen Nicolò had given her, hidden in the pocket of her skirt, fingertips caressing the etched N.S. He had helped her to change, but most of all she owed that change to herself. She had become stronger, wiser and courageous. She hugged Malka, close to her. 'Write to me at the Bastiani Post Office; let me know when you arrive. Good luck, *Biancaneve*.'

Chapter Thirty-One

Three knocks.

'Is that you, Nina?' Ambra's voice seeped through the wooden door of the Post Office.

'Yes,' Nina whispered.

Ambra unbolted the lock and pulled Nina inside, checking nobody in the square had seen her. The piazza was empty; all that remained were Bar Renzo's tables and chairs dripping from the evening downpour. Puddles of water glistened in the moonlight, the first fallen autumn leaves dotted the cobblestones of the piazza.

Ambra hugged Nina. 'You are shaking. Are you okay?'

'I was stopped by Germans at a roadblock. I copied your tactics, and it worked.'

She pulled away from Nina and held her at arm's length. Nina had changed. War had changed her. She had become more confident, more daring. There was an intensity about her, a passion that radiated through her every movement. She seemed to glow with a sense of purpose, a belief that what she was doing truly mattered. Yet, the signs of war were still there. Fine lines etched the corners of her eyes, and her face bore the slight hollowness of someone who had seen too much. But these marks only added to her strength, giving her a timeless, resilient beauty. Ambra admired how the hardship had not dimmed Nina's spirit but had instead honed it, making her more determined and steadfast. A twist of jealousy gnawed somewhere inside her. Was Nina overtaking her? What about herself? She too had seen the horrors of war firsthand.

The hanging bodies of the cheesemakers Rita and Tommaso and the six men from Fornelli had been a grim reminder of the consequences of trust misplaced in a regime that was no longer victorious. Just to think that only a few weeks ago she was with Werner in his hotel room in Campobasso. She would have been captured as a collaborator, turned over to the Allies with Werner. The change within her was profound, even if not entirely by choice. The sight of their hanging bodies had been a reminder of the consequences of misplaced trust.

With a hand on her shoulder, Ambra nudged Nina into the dimly lit storeroom. The crackling voice from Radio Londra filled the air.

Two heads were bent low over the radio. Mariolina's long hair twisted into a braid brushed the bald patch of skin on the top of Ivo's head.

'I delivered the papers to Malka, but Leanda had left. It's the Sinti spirit in her; she is used to roaming free.' Nina flicked her thick plait across her shoulder and handed Ivo the papers intended for Leanda. 'Malka is there, waiting for Gino to arrange her transfer.'

'At least we managed to save Malka. We can use Leanda's false documents for someone else. We'll just glue a different photo onto it,' Ivo said. 'I'll alert the *Banda* to keep their eyes out in case they spot Leanda through the woods. Well done, Nina. Now sit down. Mariolina will update you on what the Germans have done in Campobasso.'

Mariolina lifted her head and turned towards Nina. She spoke above the crackling noise of the radio, her voice jagged and full of anger. 'The city hall and the cathedral have been attacked by the Germans with artillery and grenades. Thirty-eight civilians were killed in the action. Poor Bishop Secondo Bologna: he didn't stand a chance.' Almost choking on the words, Mariolina wrung her hands, veined and withered. 'He was praying when the roof of the cathedral was hit by a grenade and a wooden beam from the ceiling fell on him. It killed him instantly. May God bless his soul.'

'That's the ugliness of war.' Ivo's voice shook with emotion and rage. 'Our men too are risking their lives, hidden in the cold, rugged Matese mountains.'

Mariolina waved a red handkerchief in the air as if sending courage and support.

'Look, we must continue our fight.' Ivo gripped the edge of the table. 'Once the Wehrmacht cross the River Biferno and break through the mountains, they'll reach Bastiani. We must stop them. We need to draft routes for the *Banda* to deliver to the Allies to help them navigate the roads.' Ivo placed a hand on Ambra's shoulder. 'Take the Olivetti into the main Post Office and type the routes with Nina.'

He turned to Nina, his eyes shining with admiration. 'You have done a remarkable job today, Nina. I'm proud of you. Since you started working as our *staffetta* Luisa, you've proved to be invaluable to the *Banda*. We all trust you.'

Ambra's eyes narrowed. Her father had never said anything like that to her. For years he kept his mission against the Fascists a secret from his own daughter, hiding in the storeroom with Gino, Mariolina and Esther, helping Nina and Nicolò Sansone behind her back, with the delivery of letters to the internees. Did he trust her less because of her liaison with Werner? Did he ever trust her? And did he trust her now, his own daughter? With a tightening of her heart Ambra lifted the Olivetti and placed it with a thump on the Post Office counter.

'Do you remember when we first started?' Ambra's voice was a tight whisper as she sat beside Nina at the typewriter. The little worm of jealousy still gnawed at her brain, twisting her thoughts into knots. Side by side on the same mission, Ambra couldn't shake the doubt—could their friendship ever truly be repaired? Her father trusted Nina more than her, the *Banda* admired Nina and even the Germans had been fooled by Nina's clever mimicry of Ambra's flirtatious tactics at the roadblock.

'Only four months ago, but so much has happened. It feels like a lifetime,' Nina said, her fingers stabbing at the keys. 'I'm so slow now; I am out of practice.'

'If you had kept typing, you would be much better at it. But you decided Nicolò was more important,' Ambra snapped, unable to hold back. Her heart burnt with the memory of the lies Nina had spun to conceal her relationship with Nicolò. Lies that hurt her and shattered their friendship pact. Lies that made Nicolò Nina's. And Nina Nicolò's. She glanced at Nina, wondering if she would ever be honest about Nicolò.

'No, Ambra. Not Nicolò: the internees were more important. We were helping your father.'

'Then why didn't you tell me? I work here with my father. I am the Post Office girl.'

'You were seeing that German officer. How could we trust you?'

'And now? Do you trust me now?' Ambra's voice wavered with a mixture of hope and bitterness.

'Witnessing those barbaric murders has changed you.'

Ambra lowered her eyes. 'It did. Events can change your life. I thought the Germans were our friends. I made a mistake and I'm not the only one. Look at Renzo, he's changed sides too. You and I, we are on the same side now, aren't we?'

'Of course.' Nina nodded.

Ambra blinked. Did she hear a flicker of hesitation in Nina's voice? *Let's see how much she really trusts me*, Ambra thought.

'And you and Nicolò?' Ambra asked, vigilant to any change of expression on Nina's face, the slight clenching of the muscles on her jaw.

'I haven't heard from him. Nobody has, not even among the partisans.'

'Feelings, emotions, even sides change during a war. Believe me, Nina, I know. And remember, Nicolò is a Sansone. He will always be a Sansone, a member of a Fascist family. Maybe he isn't even a partisan any longer. Better to forget him.'

Nina stopped typing. 'How dare you say that, Ambra? Nicolò has risked his life feeding the internees and now working with the Allies. You clearly don't know him, you don't understand him as I do.' A landslide of words tumbled from her bloodless lips.

'Do you love him?' Ambra probed.

'Nicolò and I are childhood friends, comrades, fighting on the same side. That's all. There is nothing between us except politics. Love has nothing to do with it, Ambra.'

She's still lying to me! Ambra raised her eyebrow. 'I see.'

'But I am worried about him. He promised to write to me and I haven't heard from him. Have you? Has Ivo?'

'Of course not. I would have told you.' Ambra sighed. A sense of relief washed through her, justifying her actions of keeping Nicolò's letter from Nina. If Nina continued to keep secrets, so could Ambra.

Ambra snapped the lever of the typewriter and slid the paper out of the carriage. The air in the Post Office crackled with tension. Every corner held whispers of distrust. Ambra clenched her hands into fists.

Chapter Thirty-Two

Outside, shadows danced under the flickering lamplight. Nina slammed the Post Office door, the false-bottomed satchel banging against her hip. Hidden deep inside were the rolled-up sheets of paper containing routes still accessible in the surrounding area for the *Banda* to pass on to the Canadians.

She mounted her bicycle and pedalled at a slow pace, overwhelmed with a sudden fatigue. It had been a taxing day; the altercation with the German soldiers, concern about Malka and now here was Ambra again doubting Nicolò's political leanings. Nina didn't believe it for a moment, regardless of the views of the Sansone family. She had witnessed firsthand his passion, helping the internees, his courage leaving the luxury of his home and devoting himself to the Allied cause. Yet there were no letters from him. Could his feelings for her have changed? Was that possible? She thought of the sweet words Nicolò had whispered into her ear at the river and in the hidden recesses of the villa; the forest-green fountain pen he'd gifted her as a token of their love now stored under her mattress together with her friendship handkerchief. Her stomach muscles hardened as if someone had struck her under the ribs. What if he were dead? Killed in action like her father. She shuddered. Would she rather that his feelings for her had changed or that he might be dead?

Nina pedalled faster. She sped towards home, her thoughts quietened by the wind whooshing in her ears. A cold fog hovered over the branches of the oak trees, already shedding their burnt orange leaves. A spangle of stars lit her way along the path towards the Caruso farm.

Nina propped the bike against the wooden gate. The silhouettes of two figures loomed against the light of the oil lamp burning on the kitchen windowsill. Nina's heart banged in her chest. Who was with her mother at this time of night? Had something happened to Gino? She clenched the handlebars with fingertips frozen from the cold night air. The pressure of the bag against her hip reminded her of the important documents hidden inside. She had to protect them. She glanced around the farmyard and her eyes rested on a large trough used to store feed for the hens. She dug a well in the grain and slid the satchel in before covering it with handfuls of grain.

She brushed down her skirt, arranged her hair behind her ears and pushed open the kitchen door. Her mother was sitting at the table with a man wearing the uniform of the *carabiniere*. He rose when she entered the room. Nina recognised him as the long-legged man with a square jaw who had guarded Malka, Leanda and the other internees at Vinchiaturo. Was he there to arrest her for helping Malka? Or had someone informed on her, revealing her role as a *staffetta,* a courier? It couldn't be Ambra. Ambra would never betray her, her own father and the *Banda*. Of that she was sure now. And like so many in the village, when Italy changed sides, so did Ambra.

If the *carabinieri* knew she had carried routes and documents in her bag to help 'the enemy' she would be shot. She sighed with relief that the satchel was safely hidden outside in the trough.

'Nina, *Carabiniere* Russo wants to talk to you.' The purplish shadows circling Marta's eyes seemed more pronounced in the dim lamplight. Since Gino had left to join the *Banda*, her mother's days had been laced with continuous worries and fears. Her sunken orbs made her appear a ghoulish fiend, like the ones that used to frighten Nina when she was a child during the procession of Corpus Christi. Nina swallowed hard, hoping to control the tremor in her voice, dread pressing on her chest.

'*Buona sera, Carabiniere* Russo, how can I help you?' Nina stretched out her palm with a false confidence mustered from somewhere deep within, recalling once again what Mariolina had taught her. The words 'A *staffetta* must remain calm, and not show fear, no matter what,' pummelled through her mind.

She flashed a warm smile hoping it would ingratiate her to him.

'Where is your brother Gino? I've asked your mother, and she doesn't know.' He paused, stared into her eyes and asked, 'Where is he, Nina?'

Nina glanced towards her mother. Marta's eyes dilated with fear, blinked rapidly. With clenched lips she jerked her head, a slight flicker of her chin. Nina knew what she was trying to tell her.

'I don't know where he is. Nor does my mother. We haven't seen Gino for several weeks. Anything could have happened to him. Maybe you have news of him?'

'I have received strict orders from the German commander to arrest Gino Caruso.'

Nina sidled up to her mother and placed a hand on her shoulder, hoping the pressure would stop Marta from trembling. 'Why? What has he been accused of?'

'Your brother Gino is involved in a *Banda*, hiding in the Matese mountains.'

'My son is a grown man with his own political views,' Marta interjected. 'How do you expect us, two helpless women, to keep an eye on him, *Carabiniere*?'

'Your son, *cara* Signora Marta, is sheltering Allied prisoners and helping them escape through secret paths in the mountains.'

'My son, *caro carabiniere*, is neither a partisan nor a Fascist. He is a *contadino* through and through, a man who toils the earth.'

Carabiniere Russo cleared his throat and turned to Nina. 'Your mother may not know what your brother is up to, but you do, Nina.' He pointed a finger at her. The flame from the oil lamp flickered, casting shadows around the room. Silence fell on them.

I am a sister, a daughter and a staffetta, Nina thought. *I would never betray my brother or the* Banda. *This is what I have been fighting for.* Instead of feeling fear, Nina was overcome with a steel-like defiance. Images of all those who had put others first and had not been afraid of the consequences of losing their lives: *Podestà* Laurelli, the Bishop of Campobasso, Nicolò himself who had shown the courage to fight against his family's beliefs. And of course, her father Gaetano. This war had given her the confidence to be true to herself and her ideals just as they had been.

She squared her shoulders, tilted her chin up and gazed directly into the *carabiniere*'s eyes. 'I will never tell you where Gino is. Take *me* instead.'

'No,' Marta jumped out of the chair, her voice echoing across the darkened room. 'Don't you dare lay a finger on my daughter, *Carabiniere*. Take me.'

'*Mamma*, quiet.' Nina circled her arms around her mother's slender waist, feeling the sharp rib bones and gently set her down on the chair. She took Marta's gnarled, cold hand in hers and whispered, 'Don't worry, I know what I am doing.'

She stepped towards the *carabiniere* and placed a hand on his arm. 'Take me. Please take me,' she begged. The sound of Marta's stifled sobs hovered over the room.

Under her fingertips, Nina felt the tension of his clenched muscles. He lowered his head and she saw his lips quiver beneath the bristles of his moustache. A long stream of air escaped from his mouth almost as if something inside him was deflating. Even his uniform with the shiny buttons seemed to hang off him.

She reached for his hand and squeezed it. Was there anything she could do to make him change his mind?

A slight squeeze back of his fingers. Did she have the power to save Gino and herself? She choked back a sob as she whispered, chin lifted with daring determination, 'Campobasso is liberated. Soon the whole of Molise will be free. I am sure that's what you want too. Isn't it?'

'I'm merely obeying orders. You might be a patriot of our country, but you are an enemy of the regime I have the misfortune to represent.'

'So are you going to arrest me?' A shadowy quiet invaded the room.

'In my heart I know it's wrong.'

'So let me go, and let Gino be free too. We are fighting for a new, just and free *Italia* without invaders,' Nina said with a tremor in her voice, determined to make him understand what the *Banda* stood and fought for.

'You are brave, Nina. I remember seeing you take food to the internees in Palazzo Nonno. You thought we didn't know, but I did, and I kept quiet. I felt sorry for those poor women.'

Carabiniere Russo collapsed onto a chair. He looked up, head cushioned in his hands, long legs draped across the tiled floor, a wild expression crossing the walnut hue of his eyes. He raised his hand towards his chest.

'Please, trust me,' he pleaded.

One by one he began to rip the stripes off the jacket of his uniform. The sound of the material tearing made Nina jump.

'*Carabiniere* Russo, what are you doing?' Marta asked. She bent down to retrieve the golden stripes.

'Ladies, your bravery has touched me. I am on your side now.'

'What will you tell the commander if you don't fulfil his orders?' There was a tender strength to Nina's voice, anticipation and hope.

'I am no longer a *carabiniere*; I have no commander to answer to. Allow me to join the *Banda* with your brother Gino. I want to become a *partigiano*.'

Nina glanced at her mother before turning her gaze to *Carabiniere* Russo. 'How can we trust you?'

'You must trust me. I'll show you how. Come with me to the barracks in Vinchiaturo. We have weapons and ammunition there. You can take them to the *Banda*. They will need them.'

Marta's cheeks were stained with tears. 'I only wish there were more men like you, defiant and brave. But you'll need civilian clothes.' She glanced at Nina. 'It's the only way to keep him safe. Fetch your father's winter coat from the trunk at the back of Gino's bedroom.'

'I'll find a pair of Gino's trousers. If they don't fit, I can always alter them.' Nina smiled at the *carabiniere*, hoping someone, somewhere was keeping Nicolò safe too, no matter where he might be, even if his feelings for her had changed.

Chapter Thirty-Three

Bumping along the mountain path at the back of a lorry filled with sheep, pigs and goats, Nina felt an urgent need to vomit. Her stomach churned, bile rose to her throat from the stench of the droppings and the closeness of the animals' bodies. She was used to being close to animals at the farm, and wondered whether the nausea was brought on by the presence of grenades and rifles *Carabiniere* Russo had given her to take to the *Banda*, hidden under the blanket close to her body. The butt of a gun pressed into her calf, the satchel with the list of routes for the *Banda* pressed into her ribs, reminding her of the danger of the mission she was on.

Her teeth chattered with the cold mountain wind. Nina pulled Gino's old winter coat around her to protect herself from the rain pouring into the open van. She moved closer to the sheep, hoping their thick fleece would keep her warm. Ahead she could see the Morgia, the dark, pointed rock silhouetted against the low, blackened clouds. She felt a huge sense of relief when Mariolina pushed her foot on the brakes and came to an abrupt halt at the side of a rocky path.

Nina jumped out, held her stomach with both hands and watched as a trickle of vomit escaped her mouth and mingled with the muddy path.

'Forgive me,' Nina said to Mariolina, wiping her lips and chin with the back of hand. 'I don't know what came over me.'

'It's the fatigue and anxiety of these times.' Mariolina fished in her pocket and pulled out a red handkerchief and passed it to Nina. 'You've been through a lot these past few days, Nina.'

Together they dragged the sack of weapons from under the blanket and balancing it between them stumbled through a wood of oak trees. Their bare branches like ominous shadows stretching towards the starless night, their huge trunks a shield from the outside world.

'Your brother will come out from the cave where the *Banda* is hiding and meet you. Come back to the lorry as soon as you hand them over. I'll wait for you there. Be quick.' There was a strength and confidence in Mariolina's low-pitched yet commanding voice. Nina watched as she disappeared into the darkness like a vanishing ghost. Left alone, the hooting of the owls the only sound, she waited in the depth of the night for Gino to join her.

The last time she had seen him was a week ago. She had been surprised how different he looked. His unshaven, ragged face appeared more hollow than usual, yet his eyes shone with an ardour that left her full of admiration.

A crunching and crackling of the leaves on the ground. A whisper.

'Luisa. Luisa.' Her *staffetta* name sounded like it was coming from the sky above. She turned and there he was, half shielded by a large holly bush. He folded her in a tight embrace whispering in her ear, 'You are a brave *staffetta*. Our father would be proud of you.'

'Of us both.'

She clung to him and felt his heartbeat through his coat. She breathed in the musty, woody scent of him. She longed to ask Gino if he or any of the other *partigiani* were aware of Nicolò's whereabouts, but she knew only too well that this was a risky mission, and she couldn't let sentimentalism get in the way. Instead, she pointed to the sack of weapons on the ground by her feet. 'Here are the weapons from *Carabiniere* Russo.'

'Nina, the *Banda* has gained secret information. Bastiani is the next village on the Germans' scorched-earth policy.'

'Bastiani! Our village. I must go back quickly and warn them.' Nina turned as if to leave, then stopped. She dug her hand into her satchel.

'I almost forgot. Take the routes Ambra and I typed up for you and the *Banda*.'

'Nina, be wary of Ambra. I know you say she's changed and is on our side, but she reminds me of a weathervane, switching directions where the wind blows. Ambra will always do what's good for Ambra!' Gino grabbed the rolled-up routes and tucked them inside his jacket.

She knew Gino meant political matters, but the political and the personal were intertwined for Nina. 'Don't worry, there are still matters I keep from her.'

A pinecone fell to the ground scattering leaves and twigs.

'Nina, go quickly back to the lorry. Warn everyone. Stay safe and remember I love you.'

And with that Gino disappeared into the woods, like a deer bounding away from its hunter. She hadn't even had the time to reach for his hand.

Nina retraced her steps, stumbling over the gnarled roots of ancient oak trees, eager not to fall. She reached the main track, narrowed her eyes and stopped. The muscles in her neck were clenched so tight, she could barely breathe. Where had the truck gone? Where was Mariolina? The fleeting thought Mariolina had betrayed her lasted only a second. Perhaps she, Nina, had taken the wrong path out of the woods? Perhaps they were both in danger? Nina bit the inside of her cheek, the metallic taste of blood filling her mouth. Then she saw it. Mariolina's red handkerchief hung from a branch like a spiderweb, right in front of her. It was the couriers' sign. Now she knew she was in danger. Legs shaking, she debated whether to return to the woods or follow the track. A sudden scraping of boots behind her interrupted her thoughts. A hand clamped onto her shoulder, forced her to turn. A beam of light pierced the night and shone onto her face, almost blinding her. She blinked, then a sharp thud struck the side of her head, sending a jarring pain through her skull. Blood whooshed in her ears as her legs crumpled beneath her. All she could think was, *I'm too late to warn everyone in Bastiani that the Germans are on their way*.

She felt herself falling into a blank, empty space.

Down, down, down.

Chapter Thirty-Four

A barrage of questions struck her like bullets from a gun.

'Why are you alone in the middle of the night?

'What are you doing wandering around the mountains?

'Who are you hiding?'

'A cowardly soldier refusing to fight? Or an Allied prisoner?'

Then came the blows, slaps, beatings. Her cheeks, arms and legs, red raw and stinging from the wooden sticks and rifle butts cracking against her skin. The pain was relentless, each strike thrusting her further into silence.

She shook her head, lips pressed tightly together, the Latin phrase hammering through her mind. '*Etiam si omnes ego non*—even if all others, I will not.'

She had been careful, but she had been caught. And here she was in a sordid cell, arms tied behind her back, head slumped against her shoulder, eyes heavy with fatigue.

With each question, she steeled herself. She would not reveal names, locations or actions to these Italian guards working for the Fascists, no matter what they did to her. She envisaged the faces of Esther and Mariolina, their voices instructing her how to behave when caught. 'Never show fear. You are no different from our brave soldiers going into a battle. This is your battlefield.'

The questions kept coming.

'Which *Banda* are you working for?'

She shook her head. 'No *Banda*.' She whispered with difficulty. Pain was engulfing her bones, her body, her throbbing head.

'Don't lie to us.' The man Nina believed to be the head interrogator leaned over, his face close to hers. The bristles of his beard scratched her skin. She could smell his breath, rancid, bitter. His pockmarked face, the hate in his eyes, the clench of his jaw, his loathing enclosed her.

He reached out and grasped her long mane of hair. He twisted it, yanked it.

'Answer me!' His scream was raucous and wild. It sliced through her as he tugged and tugged at her hair. 'Answer me, you anti-Fascist scum, you whore!'

'No *Banda*,' she whispered again. With ragged words she tried to explain. 'I work at Villa Sansone . . . Bastiani . . . *Avvocato* Sansone was supervisor of the internment camps . . . He works in the new Social Republic. He . . .' The words bled out like a breathless stream.

'Liar.'

Another blow to the side of her head. The room spun. A fuzzy kaleidoscope of colours floated before her. A pang of nausea rose in her throat. Was she going to die here in this cell? Were they going to beat her until she bled to death?

'What were you carrying inside that satchel of yours?'

'Nothing.' She could barely speak.

'Don't lie to us.'

A crack to her chest. Pain ripped through her. *I'm too late to save Bastiani, my beloved village*, was all she could think of. She was falling. Falling down a deep, endless hole.

*

A soft whisper. A gentle voice pulled Nina back from the dark abyss she had entered. She pried open her eyes, blinking, as the grey light of early morning filtered through the small window above her head. She was lying on a mattress in the corner of the cell. Mice scurried along the edges of the walls; yellow flakes of old paint were scattered across the concrete floor. A dark beetle crawled up her arm.

The pain in her jaw was immense. Her bones ached; her arms felt as heavy as the blocks of beechwood Gino hauled to the farm on cold winter mornings. Her mouth tasted of metal, acid, blood.

A man was bending over her, dabbing her forehead with a cloth, his gaze kind and concerned. A stethoscope dangled from his neck. He leaned closer, cradling the back of her head with his hand. He lifted a tin cup close to her lips. As she reached for it, her hand trembled. Bruises were already darkening her wrists where the guards had bound her hands.

Red marks stained the skin of her arms and legs where they had beaten her.

She had heard of other *staffette* in Emilia-Romagna and the north of the country who had been tortured by Germans for refusing to reveal information. Esther and Mariolina had whispered of women who had been beaten, raped, even shot dead.

'Don't be scared. I am a doctor. I work at the police station.'

There was something familiar about him. Was it the mole on his chin? The inflection of his speech carrying the lilting cadence of Molise?

'I won't harm you, I promise.'

A sweet feeling of relief swept over Nina. At least her captors were Italian Fascists. Perhaps she wouldn't be tortured or raped. Maybe she had escaped lightly with the beatings.

'You've got yourself into trouble, signorina. But I can help you. I've told the guards to let you go.'

She grasped his hands. Relief, exhaustion, overwhelmed her.

'No matter what you may have done, they should never have harmed a pregnant woman. Don't worry, the baby is fine. I could hear the heartbeat.'

'Baby?'

Eyes fixed on the crumbling plastered ceiling, Nina tried to make sense of the kind doctor's words. 'What baby? What do you mean?'

'You're pregnant, signorina. Did you not know?'

She shook her head. The pain from her injuries faded with the shock of this revelation.

'I believe you must be four months pregnant.'

'Pregnant? I can't be!'

'But you most definitely are. The guards ordered me to examine you after you passed out. We needed to be sure you weren't hiding anything under your clothes. Consider yourself lucky you were caught here in Molise and not in the far north. There they even torture pregnant women if they refuse to talk.'

The doctor guided her hand and pressed it on the tight flesh of her belly.

'But I can't be,' Nina repeated. Were the heaviness of her breasts, the absence of her monthly bleeding, signs she had ignored? And to think she had believed her aching bones and constant fatigue were due to the endless kilometres of cycling in her work as a *staffetta*.

She thought of Nicolò, their stolen moments by the River Fastino, the warmth of their embrace, sheltered beneath the hazelnut tree, the sun hugging their bodies, the nights whispering their love. And now here she was, imprisoned in a cell, Bastiani in danger, war raging in her beloved Molise. And a new life growing inside her. Tears spilled from her closed eyelids down her face and nestled at the crook of her neck.

The doctor reached for her hand. 'Look, the guards told me you are from Bastiani. I'll drop you outside the village later this afternoon, but from there you'll have to walk. I'm sorry, I can't do more to help you. Try and rest now.'

'But why are you helping me?'

He sighed, his skin puckered with sadness. 'Because we are both from Molise. No matter what is happening around us, we must help each other. Our people's spirit must live on.'

*

Chicken feathers were scattered around the yard. The farm mule had gone; the burnished iron ring Nina used to pass the thick rope through to tie the animal dangled empty from the wall. It looked like an eye. The image scared Nina. Shivers buzzed through her entire body. The rabbits? She turned her gaze to the rabbit cage. The small aluminium mesh door had been torn from its hinges and laid askew. Those animals were supposed to be their livelihood through the winter months. They could barter them for shoes, tobacco, sugar. Not anymore. A piercing pain in the groin made Nina wince. She clutched her lower belly as if protecting the baby from the devastation in front of her.

A strangled sob burnt Nina's throat. And her mother? Where was she? She stumbled forward through the half-open door of the farmhouse and entered warily, her heart throbbing against her chest. '*Mamma? Mamma*?' she called.

Wine was trickling out of Gino's straw *fiasco*—his bottle holder—and dirty glasses were strewn across the kitchen counter, the stove, the floor. An overturned chair with smashed legs lay against the wall. Soiled plates were piled on the wooden table. A mixture of human sweat and the putrid remains of cooked chicken and rabbit meat permeated the air. A bout of nausea overcame her. Nina's legs buckled, and she collapsed on the floor, head in her hands. 'They stole, ate, drank and left.'

Tears of rage, and desperation wet her cheeks. She closed her eyes, wishing everything could revert to the way it had always been. She rose to her feet and went to check the rooms upstairs. '*Mamma? Mamma*?'

Silence. Her mother had no doubt stayed at the villa. Nina sighed. At least she would be safe in that Fascist household. The Germans wouldn't touch it, Nina was sure.

The tall, mirrored wardrobe on the upstairs landing flashed her own reflection. She pulled up her sleeves. The blue bruises were turning purple and yellow. She thought they looked like clouds heralding a storm. Slowly she lifted the hem of her skirt up to her waist. Her belly was small and rounded. Perhaps her stomach hadn't grown because she ate little and covered kilometres every day on Nicolò's bicycle.

At least a small tummy was easy to conceal. Nobody would ostracise her and point at her as an unmarried, pregnant girl like they did with Alba, a girl from Bastiani who'd had to flee in shame. With a small tummy she could still run in the darkness of night, hiding in the woods to help the *Banda*. There was so much to do in her mission as a *staffetta*. There was the bridge on the Biferno to bomb to stop the Germans and to aid the Allies in their advance.

Nina sighed. A swift caress of her tiny bump. She whispered, 'Thank you. Thanks to you, my baby, the Molise doctor saved me.' She blew a kiss. A lock of hair fell on her face. It reminded her of when Nicolò's fingers moved her hair away from her cheeks, before kissing her. The baby she was carrying was Nicolò's. Their child was there to help her continue to do what they had started together.

Chapter Thirty-Five

When the German officer with a long spindly neck ordered Don Simone to instruct the villagers of Bastiani to leave their homes, the priest at first refused. The officer's hair was clipped short, his face hollow, sunken. There was a shadowed sagging beneath her eyes, soft and bulbous.

Maybe this is not easy for him either, Ambra thought as she stood next to her father in the square, wrapped in her thick coat against the biting wind. She watched as Don Simone reached out, his fingers trembling. He clutched the officer's coat sleeve.

'Please sir, I beg you, spare Bastiani. Why destroy it? What is the point? We are a small village of poor *contadini*. We have not harmed you. Many here even support your cause.' He pointed to the villa standing solemnly in the grey light. 'The former superintendent of the surrounding camps lives there.'

The officer's pale eyes were empty. 'This is war.' His voice was emotionless, stony. Final.

'What must burn, will burn. What must be destroyed, will be destroyed. Otherwise, our enemies will have an advantage.'

'So, are we your enemy now?' Renzo's voice shook. 'We were home to your soldiers. They drank at my bar, listened to our Molise melodies, played football with our children. Why are you determined to destroy us?'

The officer stamped his foot against the frozen ground and stretched his arm in the Roman salute. 'Orders of the

Wehrmacht. We are to adopt a scorched-earth policy. We burn, destroy, scatter mines and booby traps. We must slow the Allied advance, ensuring the enemy finds only devastation. A wrecked landscape.' A silence followed. A muscle twitched in his jaw. 'Troops are authorised and obligated to use any means necessary in this war. That even includes against women and children. We are warning you now—you must leave. Stay, and you will be killed.'

'We are not your enemy,' Don Simone tried again, his mouth sunken, his face hollow. But his entreaty was pointless.

Bastiani was on the list.

A bolt of fear surged through Ambra and weighed like lead on her heart. She must document what was about to happen. But first, she needed her Leica.

A ripple of panic spread through the square, quiet at first then emboldened and wild like a winter's storm. Sentences uttered in terror hovered in the icy air around her, whispers, cries, pleas.

'What do we do? Where do we go?'

'We must save our crops and our homes.'

'No, we must leave. Listen to the words of the commander.'

'They are going to kill us.'

Ambra felt Ivo's hand on her shoulder. 'We must leave too,' he said gently. 'Come, Ambra. I need to go back to the Post Office, gather some food, sort things out in the storeroom.' He stopped and surveyed the square. Bringing his lips close to Ambra's ear, he whispered, 'I must ensure Esther is safe.'

Mariolina was waiting for them in the Post Office storeroom, hands twisting together, eyes narrowed. The muscles in her jaw tensed and tightened, her skin was a deathly white.

'I don't know where Nina is,' she said, voice raw with distress. 'I fear she's been arrested by the *Fascisti*. We were caught last night.' Her breath was slow and shallow. 'And now the Germans are here. They are chipping away at us. We think it is over and then it just gets worse. We were a village intact, whole, but now we are fractured.' She indicated to the space behind the safe, her voice soft. 'I'll hide here with Esther. I cannot leave my sister-in-law alone. If the Germans find her, she will be shot on the spot. I may have lost Nina, but I will do my best to save Esther. If she dies, I will die with her.'

There were dark, swollen shadows beneath her eyes. She looked exhausted beyond her years. How heroic Mariolina was, Ambra thought, torn between admiration and resentment. How easily she gave herself up for another! A true partisan, a *staffetta* through and through. Ambra had never been selfless like Mariolina or Nina. A shiver ran along her spine. Had Nina really been caught by the Italian Fascists?

'And Nina?' She turned towards her father.

Ivo placed two hands on her shoulders. 'We will find her, I promise, but now we have to leave our Post Office, our home. If we stay here we will be killed, do you understand?'

Ambra nodded and ran upstairs while Mariolina and Ivo gathered supplies from the kitchen. Time felt suspended, thick. She grabbed her Leica from its hiding place beneath the bed. She wrapped the camera in a blanket and placed it in a satchel, which she swung over her shoulder. Whatever was about to happen in Bastiani, she could not afford to lose such a precious possession. A generous gift from Werner. Her currency to show the world what was happening in Italy.

That night was a dreamlike fog—a twisted blend of the comforting past and the disquieting future. In the damp, freezing barns scattered around Bastiani, the villagers huddled like refugees from their own homes, shivering in the icy darkness, stomachs twisted with hunger. They heard the distant crack of gunfire, smelled the thick, acrid smoke curling through the valley. And they could do nothing. Nothing except clutch their rosaries, wring their gnarled hands, their faces etched with worry and grief, wondering what would remain of their village in the cold light of morning.

Ambra and Ivo found shelter with Renzo and Santino in a barn just beyond the fields. The olive trees stood heavy in the frosty air, their branches drooping as if in mourning for Bastiani. Clouds churned, swirling above the church spire like restless ghosts.

Then, the sound came.

A crackling, then a pop. Then more. Flames leapt into the sky, licking at rooftops, devouring timber, spitting embers into the night. Black smoke curled and thickened, spreading like a sickness.

A clatter, a clang, the thud of bricks collapsing—again and again and again.

Bastiani was burning.

Post Office

Cold, rain, mud, November's chilling breath is amongst us.

The sky is bruised with heavy clouds, yet they pale in comparison to the billows of smoke spiralling from the ruins of the square. The bridge over the River Fastino, blown to smithereens, is a mass of debris. The river's once clear waters are now a turbulent flow of twigs, mud, stones.

Bar Renzo is a pile of rubble. Our church, the heart of Bastiani, remains unscathed but the octagonal bell tower is in ruins. Don Simone sits crumpled, his head in his hands, weeping and praying. A gaping hole is now all that remains of the roof of the villa. The once noble branches of the old oak tree are now draped in a shroud of ash.

They came. Destroyed. Left.

Only I remain untouched; the village Post Office, walls intact but a wounded soul. Buildings can feel, you know. I'm not just a static presence. I suffer.

The German military left my Post Office standing, perhaps as a cruel jest or a tactical decision. Amidst the wreckage and destruction, I remain a fragile remnant of what once was. A glimmer of hope for what the future might hold.

The leaf of my paper calendar is veiled in dust.

It is the 2nd November, 1943, All Souls Day.

Today is the day of destruction.

Chapter Thirty-Six

Sunrise bled through the blackened clouds. The air was thick, acrid and curled into Ambra's lungs. Her heart felt heavy, like a stone on her chest. Smoke drifted in slow tendrils, black and murky as if the earth itself was mourning. A trickle of villagers emerged from the fields. Wails of despair rose into the air. Somewhere a child whimpered.

Ambra reached for her father's hand. It felt frail, small as if he had shrunk overnight. His face was smeared with dirt, his clothes soiled. Did she look the same? Did they all? Her fingers found the camera in her bag. She pulled it out, gripping it tightly.

'It's my third eye,' she murmured. 'I will record this.' Her heart hammered loudly in her chest; she was sure Ivo could hear the clamouring.

A procession formed, slow and deliberate, as if it were one of the saint's days, but this was no celebration. The women's black skirts billowed in the wind, their feet moving soundlessly over the cobblestones, eyes hollow with grief. They walked past cottages, where doors leaned against broken walls like drunks. Frightened hens darted between the wreckage, feathers like snowflakes swirling in the frosty November air. Ambra's eye was glued to the lens as her finger clicked the shutter. Image after image.

'They have gone,' Don Simone muttered. 'They came and destroyed us, just as the officer said they would.' His voice was raw, stripped of hope. He wiped his eyes with the back of his trembling hand, but the tears kept falling, tracing lines through the dust on his face before dripping onto his shoes.

The piazza was unrecognisable. Geraniums lay crushed in their broken pots. Bar Renzo had been reduced to shards of glass and broken chairs. The terrace was littered with the jagged remains of empty bottles.

Santa Croce still stood, but its octagonal bell tower had crumbled, its bricks and stones strewn in a chaotic heap at its feet. Pietruzzo and Celestina's bakery had been ransacked, the windows shattered, flour scattered across the floor. The till lay on its side, broken open, its contents stolen.

Ambra raised the camera to her eye and clicked. She had to capture it all. Every wound.

Only the Post Office stood untouched, defiant. A single reminder of what Bastiani had been. Even the basil and geranium pots remained intact on the windowsill.

Sitting by the oak tree in front of the Sansone villa was a hunched figure. Soft moans in the silence of the morning reached Ambra's ears. There was a strange depth to the rasping sobs, a nightmarish quality, in and out like a saw against wood.

'Nina,' Ivo screamed and rushed towards the huddled shape. 'You're safe. Thank God you're safe.'

Slowly, Nina turned towards them, shoulders heaving. But this was not the Nina Ambra knew. This face was swollen and bruised, stamped with yellow and purple contusions—cruel imprints of what she must have endured. The delicate features Ambra had once known were twisted in grief.

'What happened to you?' Ambra screamed.

But Nina only shook her head and pointed towards the wrought-iron gates of the villa.

'*Mamma*,' was the only word that escaped her lips. A solitary cry over and over. A prayer, a plea that brought tears to Ambra's eyes. Nina bent over and clutched her abdomen as she continued to call for her mother. Then another sound clawed its way out of Nina's throat, a guttural cry, raw and broken. It burrowed into Ambra's chest, wrapping tight around her ribs.

And then Ambra saw her. By the entrance of the villa, lying face upward, arms crossed over her chest as if in defiance, was Marta, apron still tied around her middle A pool of blood, thick and dark, carpeted her head. It seeped into the earth beside her.

They had shot her.

Ambra stepped forward and squeezed her camera through the iron bars of the gate. She had to capture it. But how could she ever truly capture grief? How could an image hold the weight of a village in pain?

She turned the lens on Nina, the shadow of her sorrow framing the photo. *Click*.

'We have to record this,' she whispered fiercely as Ivo and Celestina tried to stop her. 'We must show the world what they've done.'

There was a melting, a sense of sinking and swimming, like she was floating away.

But she had to be strong.

They stumbled through the Post Office door. A film of dust on the counter and coating the floor lent an ancient, abandoned look to the building. Letters were scattered throughout the room, like forlorn leaves, whispering forgotten tales of love and longing. Ambra and Ivo balanced Nina between them. She could barely stand.

'You will live with us,' Ivo insisted, his arm wrapped around her. 'You will be safe here. And I will send a message to Gino via Mariolina or one of the other couriers. He needs to know what has happened to his mother.'

Nina simply nodded, tears spilling silently onto her cheeks.

Again, Ambra lifted her camera. *Click*.

'We are alive,' Ivo's voice cracked. Tears carved paths through the grime on his cheeks. He stroked the till, patted the metal plate of the scales. 'And our Post Office is standing. We are lucky, Ambra. This will be Nina's home from now on.'

It was the first time Ambra had seen the secret hiding place behind the storeroom. She had often wondered where they were hiding Esther but never dared ask. When Ivo and Nina whispered the words '*oggi piove*' she felt a shimmer of something like jealousy, despite herself. Her father and Nina were so close, he trusted her to share this space, this secret code, but had never shared it with her. She had never even seen the secret passageway between the bakery and the Post Office. With a key hidden in his trouser pocket, Ivo opened the door. Inside the secret chamber, Esther and Mariolina were huddled together. They blinked in the semi-darkness, relief flooding their faces.

'We didn't know who it was. We were terrified we would be found,' Esther said in one tired breath.

'You're safe.' Ivo's voice was gentle. 'But they killed Marta. Shot her in the head.'

Esther covered her mouth; a muffled sob escaped her lips.

'And Nina?' Mariolina asked.

'She's here,' Ivo said. 'She's been beaten, but she's alive.' He pointed to the figure in the corner slumped to the floor. The women jumped up and wrapped their arms around

Nina, cradling her head, kissing her cheeks with loud, uncontrolled sobs.

Ambra was overcome with a hollow sense of detachment. A numbness that took over her entire being. She could not bear to see any more grief. Any more destruction. Any more pain. As soon as the Allies arrived to liberate Bastiani, she would leave. She would go to Campobasso and begin a new life.

She would finally find a way to leave the Post Office behind.

And she would never look back.

Chapter Thirty-Seven

Ambra woke up to the whirring of engines and deep voices in a language that sounded different from the German she had become accustomed to. She jumped out of bed and wearing her winter coat over her nightie, leant out of the window, the bracing cold hitting her face.

'They are here at last,' she screamed to her father. 'It's our turn now to be liberated, after Campobasso.'

She ran back to her bedside drawer and grasped hold of the Leica. Perching on the windowsill, Ambra scanned the piazza and beyond, camera poised ready to click at the scene below.

Don Simone, cassock flapping behind him, was running towards Piazza Garibaldi. Allied soldiers, rifles strung across their shoulders, helmets bobbing on their heads, marched into Bastiani, their heavy footsteps reverberating across the square.

Celestina's scream rose into the air, '*Benvenuti.*' She waved her hands with joy. 'Maybe my Giovannino will come home now.'

The soldiers offered chocolate, sweets and smiles with perfect white teeth.

Ambra clicked away.

The chiselled cheekbones and healthy skin of the Allied soldiers contrasted with the pale, yellow-tinged faces of the Bastiani folk with their sunken cheeks and bloodshot eyes. A blond-haired soldier lifted his helmet and raised his chin towards Ambra, his clear blue eyes twinkling in the morning light.

'Ciao, bella signorina.' He winked at her. She waved back, her body fizzing with the anticipation of a new conquest, even new romance.

But their intimacy lasted only a few seconds as the handsome soldier turned and handed a bar of chocolate to Nina standing in the crowd.

She clicked again as Nina reached out and snatched the shiny bar and tore open the packaging with her teeth devouring the sweet treat. Nina's gaze met Ambra's.

'The Royal Canadian regiment is here. We are free,' Nina shouted up to Ambra as Gino and the *ex-carabiniere* Russo along with other members of the Bastiani *Banda* arrived in the piazza, holding their rifles high above their heads and shouting, 'We did it! Bastiani is free!'

They must have descended from their hideout in the Matese mountains, Ambra thought. Their trousers were tied up with string, boots caked with earth, stubbled chins and hollowed cheeks.

She watched Gino's eyes scan the crowd, head moving left and right. When he saw Nina, he hugged her close, his hand wiping the tears streaking her cheeks. Nina's fingers stroked Gino's hair as she rested her head against his shoulder. Gino pulled her closer. Two heads entwined like the branches of the willow trees along the riverbank. The closeness of their bodies moved Ambra. She stopped clicking. She placed the camera on her bed and ran downstairs through the open Post Office door to join them.

Her father was standing next to Gino and Nina. '*Generalfeldmarschall* Albert Kesselring's troops have retreated north,' Ivo said to Ambra, one arm around Mariolina, the other draped on Esther's shoulder. 'No more danger, no more plots, no more whispering in the storeroom. Esther, you are free now.'

'Yes. No more hiding in the cubbyhole behind the storeroom, waiting for you to bring me food,' Esther whispered in relief. Her eyes were hollow, empty, like the eyes of a dead person, Ambra thought.

'But the struggle is far from over, Ivo! And I will not rest, not until the entire country is free of Fascists. I'm going up north to help the *partigiani* there.' Gino's words trickled amongst the cries of jubilation. 'I'm not fighting to be a hero,' he added. 'It is the only decent thing to do, to honour our country and those who have perished, like my mother.'

A warm, pink sun rose above the steeple of the church. The bells continued to peal loudly. A small crowd gathered on the terrace outside Bar Renzo. Below, the waters of the River Fastino sparkled red and gold. Renzo popped open a bottle of *spumantino* and offered it to the Canadian soldier.

'We are all friends now, sharing this liberation with countries that are now our friends, not our enemies.'

'*Italia, Italia*,' the soldiers cheered, clinking their glasses before gulping down the fizzy wine as if it were water.

A large, well-built Canadian soldier whistled and began to sing in English, words that had no meaning for them. Ambra watched as Nina approached him, tugging at his jacket sleeve.

'Nicolò Sansone?' she pleaded. 'Nicolò Sansone, *conosci*, you know him?'

He freed his arm, smiled and marched on.

Nina dashed after him. 'Nicolò Sansone?' she repeated with an urgency to her voice.

Ambra pulled her away. 'What are you doing? There are so many Allied soldiers all over Italy. It's highly unlikely they know Nicolò.'

'I ask everyone I can. I must find him,' Nina said and turned to face Ambra. A deep pool of sadness emanated from her eyes, a veil of darkness shrouded her frail body, despite her weak smile and words of celebration.

It was as if all the pain Nina held trapped inside her was now visible to be seen and acknowledged: the tragic death of her mother, the night spent in prison, the Caruso farm ransacked and still no news of Nicolò. Ambra felt a wave of regret, a punch of guilt.

'Ambra, are you sure there haven't been any letters for me, from the Winter Line?' Nina asked, her voice faint against the clamour of jubilation around them. Ambra jolted. It was as if Nina were listening to her thoughts.

It would be easy to say yes and hand the letters over now on this day of liberation. It wasn't as if Nicolò was still writing to Nina. The words he wrote were emblazoned on her heart.

My dearest love, do not despair if this is my last letter. I am going where the battles are raging.

But how could she explain the reason why she had kept the letters scribbled by Nicolò and now buried in her tin box and placed in the drawer of her chest of drawers. Was it jealousy and envy that had driven her? Jealousy and envy towards Nina, her friend; towards Nicolò, who chose Nina and not her. Yet how could she admit she had sold her friend for money, for a better life? To a Fascist, to a German, to Signora Sansone. It would be far easier to pretend she hadn't heard Nina's plea. Her game had gone too far, for too long. It was too hard to stop, now.

She shook her head slowly and deliberately, lips sealed, body rigid with yet another lie.

Truce

1944–1949

Post Office

The winter of 1944 settled over the village of Bastiani with a ferocity that turned the earth to frozen mud and cloaked the piazza in a heavy blanket of snow. The freezing wind cut through the remnants of a shattered village like pieces of shrapnel. Only the Bastiani spirit helped our villagers overcome the cold, brave the wind. By combining lime and sand from the nearby mountain with water, the villagers cooked freshly made bricks over open fires. The air smelled of dust and smoke but stone by stone, brick by brick they began to rebuild their homes, the roofs of their houses, the steeple of the Santa Croce church and the shattered windowpanes of Bar Renzo.

A combination of languages fills our piazza and cobbled alleyways whilst the storeroom lies silent. Mariolina and Esther no longer whisper and plot with Ivo; the need for action in Bastiani has faded with the melting of the snow.

Pale and drawn, yet more rounded than usual—is it the chestnut flour the villagers use to make bread, due to the paucity of grain?—Nina has taken over Ambra's duties in the Post Office.

Ambra is no longer in Bastiani. She is a Campobasso girl now.

Since its liberation from the German troops, Ambra could not resist the allure of the vibrant 'Canada Town', also known as Maple Leaf City, pulsating with the presence of Canadian soldiers. During her weekly visits home

Ivo would frown at her newfound sophistication, as she effortlessly rolled the new names of streets and squares off her tongue in English: Crown and Stripes Club; Piccadilly Circus; Trafalgar Square; Briscotti's Bakery; and the Royal York Hotel.

The changes were surreal, a blend of the familiar and the foreign much like our lives during that interminable winter. Yet the heart of Bastiani beats on, resilient against the encroaching cold, resilient against the announcement of bombs raining down on Montecassino, the battle of Monte Marrone, bridges and roads blown apart all over Molise. Partisans, Allies, Germans, all with their own agenda. A baffling, confusing time for our people. Still, each of us clings to fragments of hope and the promise of a spring yet to come.

December, January, February, March, April—months strung together in a cold, unyielding chain, each link forged in the deepest chill. Day by day, my calendar sheds its leaves, weeks and months filled with hardship and suffering.

The leaf of my paper calendar lies stiff with cold.

It is the 3rd April, 1944, Saint Sisto I Papa's feast day.

Today is the day of bafflement.

Chapter One

The calendar hung high on the wall. Nina reached up and tore the leaf off the previous day. It was Sunday, 9th April, Easter Sunday. A day of celebration. A day of rest. She opened the window and inhaled the fresh, clean air. The oak tree outside the abandoned Villa Sansone had begun to bud its first leaves. Nina lifted the geranium pots and placed them on the windowsill outside the Post Office. She arched her back and began to massage the muscles along her spine with a circular movement. A splash of sunlight warmed her cheeks.

Despite the arrival of spring, Nina had remained frozen inside as if it were still winter, her body stiff and cumbersome, numb to the soft breeze ruffling the water of the River Fastino and tickling the petals of the blossom trees. With the warm April days and the shedding of thick winter garments it was becoming increasingly challenging to hide the presence of the baby. Her mother's loose, black dresses, her knitted navy-blue cardigan offered Nina a solution. She tricked herself into believing her baby would disappear, by keeping her pregnancy a secret, concealing its existence within the folds of material.

Don Simone made the sign of the cross and recited a prayer for her mother's dead soul whenever he saw her kneeling at the wooden pew in the Santa Croce church. Celestina patted her hand, whispering, '*Carissima* Nina, you keep your mother close by wearing her clothes. You miss her. We all do in Bastiani.'

And she did miss her mother. And Gino too, hidden away with the partisans in Emilia-Romagna. She wished she could still use her body for battles and fighting like Gino, but her days as *staffetta* Luisa pedalling on Nicolò's old bike through fields of corn, along dusty lanes, had ended when the *Banda* had dissolved in January. She was no longer needed.

The war in Molise had come to an end with the arrival of the Allies and Malka was safe in the fishing town of Santa Maria al Bagno. The first letter Nina received from her was full of hope and gratitude. Nina smiled when she read the words Malka wrote in large, sprawling writing. She could picture Malka with her skin now bronzed from the winter southern sun, looking out of the window at a sparkling, turquoise sea and majestic palm trees. How different it was from the view of the cobbled alleyways and the shrivelled leaves of the oak tree opposite Palazzo Nonno in Vinchiaturo. At the bottom of the letter Malka had drawn a beautiful house where she was now living with other deported Jews. *Casa Rossa*, because of its red facade.

Nina was relieved Malka was safe and away from the crowded, stifling rooms in Vinchiaturo, where the stench had overwhelmed her. But a part of her wished Malka was not so far away. She felt Malka could be the one to confide in about the baby she was carrying. She wouldn't chastise her, judge her, call her undignified names. Malka would understand. And would Ambra? How many times had Nina rehearsed what she would say to her so-called friend? And how many times had her lips remained sealed?

Her musings were interrupted by the arrival of Ivo returning from Sunday mass. 'There is a letter for you on the table, in the storeroom. It arrived yesterday. I'll get it for you.'

Nina's heart jolted, her fingers tingled with anticipation. It might be from Nicolò, she sighed within. A feeling of lightness enveloped her, only to disappear when Ivo dropped a white, crumpled envelope into her hands bearing the black typed postmark of the detention camp number 34.

'It's from Malka, from the displaced persons' camp in Puglia.' As much as Nina was pleased to hear from Malka, her voice was tinged with sorrow. Had Nicolò forgotten her? Was he even alive? Anguish cloaked her belly; his child kicked as if it felt it too.

She slid her finger through the envelope. A leaf of paper floated to the floor. It was a drawing of a bay. In the background, four ancient stone towers were surrounded by palm trees. Strokes of light blue pencil formed the ripples of waves. In black were the words: the Ionian sea of Santa Maria al Bagno. Nina lifted the paper close to her face. She could almost smell the salty sea air. A feeling of nostalgia washed over her. Nicolò had promised to take her to Termoli and savour the freshness of the seaside. It had been their dream. Would it ever happen? Her eyes filled with tears. She lowered her chin to her chest and mumbled to Ivo, 'I'm going up to Ambra's room to read Malka's letter before Ambra arrives for her Sunday afternoon visit.'

'Let's see what Signorina Campobasso brings us today.'

'I hope it's chocolate.'

'I hope it's not chewing gum.'

'The tray of *fiadoni* I made for our meal is in the kitchen.'

'Let's hope Miss Ambra with her new-fangled ways still enjoys our Molise Easter dish made with chicory, anchovies and olives.'

They giggled.

Upstairs in Ambra's bedroom, Nina lowered herself onto the mattress, which for the last few months had become her new bed. Ivo and Ambra had both insisted Nina sleep in Ambra's old bed now that she had set up home in Campobasso. Yet Nina felt more comfortable on her own mattress from the Caruso farm. Santino the cobbler had helped her roll it up and fling it across his mule Spillo, flies buzzing around its sleepy eyes. Together with Nicolò's fountain pen in her pocket, the friendship handkerchief she had made with Ambra many years ago and a bundle of her mother's old clothes that had been strewn across the floor when the Germans ransacked the farm, they trundled through the cobbled alleyways to the Post Office.

She stretched out her legs, undid the buttons of her cardigan and began to read.

Cara *Nina,*

I think of you, your brother Gino and your friend Nicolò. I thank you and the Banda *every single morning when I wake up in my own bed, the sun rising over the shoreline of Santa Maria al Bagno. You all risked your life to help me escape, to free me from the horrors of what could have happened to me if I had been captured. I am ashamed to admit it feels like a holiday here.*

The population is kind to us and the food is good; we eat freshly baked bread we bake ourselves from supplies from the British soldiers. I gave a crusty loaf to a local man standing outside the gate. He came back the next day with fish he had caught for us detainees in Casa Rossa. I haven't eaten fish since the war broke out.

And to think Leanda could have enjoyed this too. If only she had not fled. Impatient, wild, she ran to find her own freedom. And I couldn't stop her. My heart sinks when I think of Leanda. Hopefully she is safe wherever she might be.

I have started to draw again. An American soldier lets me use his coloured crayons. He is an artist like me. His name is Samuel.

I hope the drawing I have included gives you a glimpse of the beauty of where I live. Stay safe, cara *Nina. I send you many kisses.*

Your friend Malka

Nina folded the letter, a soft smile creasing her cheeks. Malka's letter, sweet drawing and hint of freedom brought a ray of light amidst Nina's fears and grief.

A click-clack of heels on the stairs startled Nina. With haste, she buttoned up her cardigan and bunched it up to conceal her small, compact bump.

'What are you reading there?' Ambra's high-pitched voice made Nina turn her face towards the door. Ambra was wearing a tight-fitting dress with a white collar and shiny shoes. Her hair, swept up into a neat chignon, added depth to her face; her nose and cheekbones appeared more defined, regal even. She looked out of place in her own bedroom, above the Post Office.

'Malka, the Jewish refugee we helped, has written to me. Now I know where she is, I can write to her.'

Ambra's facial muscles relaxed. She flashed Nina a smile and lowered herself next to her on the mattress. Nina glanced down at her long bulky cardigan and black skirt, afraid Ambra might detect her swollen belly.

'That's nice,' Ambra replied with indifference. 'But look what I have brought you and *papà* from my new Canadian boyfriend. Powdered milk and two cans of pea soup.' She giggled as she dropped them onto the mattress with a thump, then her eyebrows arched into a worried point. 'You look tired, pale. Are you ill, Nina?'

Nina shook her head, the rope of her hair banging against her shoulder blade. Ambra wrapped an arm around Nina's shoulders. Nina sniffed the air.

'You smell of roses, Ambra.'

'Perfume from my Dick, the Canadian. It's the scent of independence, and freedom.' Ambra patted Nina's arm. 'Come on, Nina.' A pretence of cheer echoed through Ambra's words. 'It's Easter Sunday, a feast day at the Santissima Addolorata, Our Lady of Sorrows. Celebrations have already started.'

Ambra gathered herself up and opened the window. She tilted her head to one side.

'Can't you hear the singing, Nina?'

Muffled voices flew through the open window from beyond the wheat fields, the surrounding forested mountains. Ambra pointed to the procession of women from Bastiani and Castelnuovo snaking along the winding path, armed with rosary beads and tapered candles.

'You see, it has already started,' Ambra urged Nina with an inviting smile. 'Let's go. We must thank the Madonna for freeing Molise.' She offered Nina her arm.

'And pray for the safe return of Nicolò and all our men,' Nina added. 'There is still no news from Nicolò. I ask around all the time and I know your father is keeping an eye on the mail for me. I'm worried, Ambra. I'm thinking of writing to the Sansones in Salò.'

'You know you can't write to *La Repubblica Sociale Italiana*. Mussolini is still in power in the Republic of Salò; he's controlled by Hitler. Come on, let's go to the sanctuary now.'

Ambra linked her arm through Nina's and led her downstairs, through the Post Office and out into the square.

The late afternoon sun shimmered low in the sky donning the bricks of the recently rebuilt Santa Croce church with a pink hue. A promise of hope nestled in the mild April weather; a promise of renewed friendship despite the secrets locked away in their hearts.

Chapter Two

The air was fragrant, the fields verdant green, the river greeny-blue. A soft breeze caressed the new leaves on the trees. The cobblestones warm beneath their feet, Ambra and Nina sucked in the sweet heat of spring. It surprised Ambra to discover the bucolic atmosphere of Bastiani was what she missed most in Campobasso. But she would never give up the party life, the buzzing bars filled with soldiers from Canada and New Zealand, America and Britain, keen to receive her photographs and reward her with silk underwear, perfumes, novelty food, crisp dollar notes. Or her new boyfriend Dick, with his slicked-back hair, shiny teeth and modern ways, so different from Werner's obsequious method of courting.

As they turned the corner, Nina doubled over, clutching her lower abdomen.

'Nina what on earth's the matter?'

'It's nothing. Only a stitch.'

'I'll help you.' Ambra gathered Nina up and held her by the elbow. She looked pale and forlorn. Red filaments patterned the whites of her eyes. Nina's lustrous black hair was dull and hung down her back like coarse rope. Gaunt, dark circles shadowed her skin.

Remorse tightened around Ambra's heart, raw shame like sand and salt knotting her throat. She tried not to think of Nicolò's words in one of the letters he had written: *Your beautiful heart-shaped face is like the first morning star, bright and clear. You are my hope, my pool of courage.*

Was it her fault that Nina looked fragile, skin like paper, veins on her hands like tight coils? She instantly dismissed the thought. Why blame herself? There were countless reasons for Nina's decline. Nicolò was only one of them.

Ambra reached for Nina's hand. It felt strangely cold yet clammy at the same time.

'I feel better now.' Nina's lips stretched into a soft smile. She straightened up, placed a hand on her lower back. Colour returned to her cheeks. Ambra pulled Nina close; together they walked hand in hand. She wondered if from far away they still looked like close friends.

Trembling flames dotted the forested mountains with golden flecks. The procession of Bastiani women, heads covered with black lace veils, curled along the grassy lanes leading to the rounded dome of the Church of the Santissima Addolorata, Our Lady of Sorrows, erected in the exact spot where the Madonna, with Christ in her arms, had appeared to two young shepherdesses in 1888. Sweet voices chanted the Hail Mary, fingers deftly clicking along the beads of the rosary. The notes of the hymn and the fragrance of the blossoms thickened the air.

Ambra began to sing along, *'Oh bella vergine, oh cara signora.'*

'Do you remember the first time we joined the procession? We were young girls of twelve. We squeezed our eyes shut, scared the Madonna would appear,' Ambra whispered to Nina in between refrains. 'We held hands. Like now.'

She turned to face Nina. In the flickering light of the candles, Nina's face was pinched, eyes squeezed almost shut. Small white teeth bit her lower lip. Her breath was jagged.

'What's wrong, Nina?'

'It's the same stitch but stronger this time.' Nina groaned, her chest heaving.

'Shall we go back to the Post Office if you're unwell?'

'It's already passed.' Nina's features relaxed. She even smiled. 'I'm fine now. A little rest will help.'

'Let's pick some flowers to offer the Madonna,' Ambra suggested. 'Then we'll join the procession again.'

They stepped aside. Women passed them, waving. Chanting voices cradled Ambra and Nina as they bent down to gather small posies of dandelions and daisies, heads almost touching, fingers brushing the blades of grass, silvery grey in the twilight. A warm feeling swept through Ambra. For a moment it was as if they were still two young girls at the *lavatoio* tying their handkerchiefs together, screaming into the air. Friends forever, they had promised each other.

A strangled scream sliced through the night.

Ambra flinched.

Nina's bunch of daisies dropped between her folded knees as she rolled to the ground. Raucous gasps escaped from Nina's nostrils; her forehead and the furrow between her nose and mouth glistened with droplets of sweat. Ambra unclenched her hands, scattering her flowers amongst the blades of grass. She knelt next to Nina. Nina, face crumpled, the muscles of her neck swollen, was overpowered by yet another spasm. With both arms around Nina's shoulders, Ambra yelled as loudly as she could.

'Please, someone, help us. Nina's sick.'

The refrains of the Hail Mary filled the air: 'Now and in the hour of our death.'

Ambra leaned forward and fanned the air around Nina, in the hope of calming her. She whispered an urgent prayer to the Madonna, 'Please, help us. Help Nina.'

Could abandoned love really be so powerful to cause such grief? Fear turned to guilt, guilt turned to fear. *What have I done?*

Ambra took hold of Nina's hand. It was shaking and slick with sweat, just like hers. Shock buckled inside her, as if she was sharing Nina's pain.

'Quick, help us!' Ambra screamed.

Celestina ran towards them clutching her scarf, her black skirt trailing behind her. Grunting sounds escaped Nina's lips. The steady groans that escaped from Nina's chest pierced through Ambra. She placed her hands over her ears to stop the sounds, but they kept coming, louder and deeper.

'Help her, help Nina.'

Celestina silenced Ambra with a wave of her hand, her attention now focused on Nina. Ambra leaned forward and tugged at Celestina's sleeve.

'Is she dying?' she mouthed. The words stuck in her throat like slivers of ash. Nina groaned, her face creased with pain.

'No, she's not dying, my dear.' Celestina shook her head, tendrils of grey hair peeking from under her scarf. She plucked open Nina's cardigan, one button at a time, encouraging her to slow her breathing. The cardigan fell open to reveal a round, swollen stomach. 'Look at her tummy. She's having a baby.'

A baby? Ambra choked. The air weighed heavily around her. Far away the tall, stained-glass windows of the church flickered with the flames from the candles.

Mass had begun.

Chapter Three

Nina's baby boy was born in April under a waning gibbous moon. Following the birth Nina's legs were raised into a sling, better for the shock, the Canadian nurses had reassured her in basic Italian. The military hospital in Campobasso was set up in the Palazzo della Provincia in via Roma.

Drowned beneath the starched hospital sheets, eyes fixed on the stark whiteness of the ceiling, Nina tried to make sense of what was happening to her. She lowered her hand under the sheets and touched the nightdress covering her stomach. Through the thin cotton she felt her skin, soft and flabby. Could this really be her, Nina, *staffetta* Luisa, of the Bastiani *Banda* in this hospital room with the stone floor smelling of disinfectant, whispers of words she didn't understand floating around her, weaving together a web of fear and uncertainty?

Since the day the prison doctor had confirmed her pregnancy, she had lived with the delusion that the baby would never appear, and now here he was in the outside world for everyone to see, to share, to condemn.

But for her to love. And it was love that had exploded in her chest when the blonde curly-haired nurse with smiling eyes walked into her room, carrying a bleating bundle in her arms. A small tuft of golden-brown hair peeked out from the top of the blanket. Nina's arms stretched out, as if they had a life of their own. The nurse settled the baby close to her chest. She felt the warmth of his skin, inhaled the honey-sweet scent of him. His curled fingers caught Nina's.

It was their first encounter.

Nina drunk in his features, her thumb exploring the contour of his face, tracing the creases of his wrist. She tickled his foot, stroked his warm belly. She kissed the baby on the tip of his nose and held him tight to her breast. The warmth of that tiny body next to her own unfurled a mellow longing in her heart.

His eyes of azure stared at her.

'His eyes!' Nina gasped.

'They're all like that at the beginning,' the blonde nurse declared. 'A dazzling blue but they'll revert to their true colour in a few weeks.'

'These are his true colour. They are just like his father's.'

She was not alone anymore.

*

Nina lay in bed and stared out of the hospital window. The pink light of dusk settled on the nearby roofs of Campobasso, burnishing the tiles gold. The sound of footsteps clip-clopping on the tiles of the corridor outside her room reached Nina's ears. The door creaked open and Ambra's head popped around the slate-grey door frame. Nina beckoned to her to enter the room.

'How are you? I've been worried since the ambulance took you away.' A look of sorrow mixed with trepidation settled around her eyes.

Nina reached for Ambra's hand and squeezed it. 'I'm very drowsy. They're keeping me sedated; to help with the shock of the birth.'

'It was a shock for me too.' Ambra massaged the skin in between her eyes as if trying to rub away a frown etched on her forehead. 'I've seen the baby,' she added, lifting her gaze. 'It looks like him.' Ambra pressed her face close to Nina's ear. 'Why didn't you tell me you were having his baby?'

Nina slumped back onto the pillow and adjusted her legs in the sling. Ambra's sweet, powdery perfume mingled with the disinfectant of the ward. Nina's cheeks and throat prickled with red blotches. For a moment she turned her gaze away from Ambra, unable to cope with the mocking she was sure she would detect in Ambra's eyes. But they were soft and questioning.

'You never told me. Why not? Didn't you trust me?'

'I don't know.'

When did she stop trusting Ambra? Was it when she went to Isernia with Nicolò to bring food to Tonino? Nicolò had made her promise to keep it a secret, especially from Ambra. That's why she'd kept quiet. After all, Ambra had made her political leanings very clear. Even Ivo had been worried about her interest in the Germans, especially when Ambra started dating Werner.

And then Nicolò had kissed her and told her he loved her. The political became entangled with the sentimental. Not only did Nina want to protect her political leanings, but also her heart. The discovery she was carrying Nicolò's baby only made her more determined to keep it a secret. The pregnancy had saved her, this was true, but what would happen afterwards when the whole village found out? Gino wasn't there to protect her; her mother was dead. So why hadn't she confided in Ambra? Because Ambra may have convinced her to get rid of the one thing Nicolò had left her? That's why she'd kept the baby a secret, Nina suddenly understood, to keep him sheltered, protected and loved inside her. He was hers.

'What do you mean, you don't know? We had a friendship pact, have you forgotten?' Ambra's irises enlarged in amazement. She fidgeted with her fingers and kept her eyes fixed on the crumpled sheets on the bed. Strangely, she seemed ill at ease.

'I thought everyone would call me a sinner, my baby a bastard. I was afraid you'd make me get rid of it,' Nina whispered, her eyes shut tight.

'What nonsense!' Ambra poured Nina a glass of water. 'A baby is an innocent creature, and babies need their mothers like trees need water.'

'What will happen to me now? Can you imagine what the Sansones would say if they found out their son had fathered a child with me, a partisan, an anti-Fascist, a *contadino*'s daughter. And I haven't heard from Nicolò in months. He might be dead or he might have forgotten me.' Silent tears rolled down her cheeks.

'I'm sure Nicolò hasn't forgotten you,' Ambra said curtly as her fingers wiped away Nina's tears. She cleared her throat and continued in a business-like tone. 'But look. We are all behind you at the Post Office. We want to help you. Everything is arranged. I will ask my Canadian boyfriend to find a driver to take you and the baby to Monte Marrone in a military truck. You'll stay with Teresa, Don Simone's sister. She will help you with the baby. It's a liberated village and you'll both be safe there for a while.'

Nina reached for Ambra's hand and whispered the words, 'Thank you, Ambra.'

Ambra lowered her cheek close to Nina's and asked, 'Have you named the baby?'

Nina closed her eyes. A string of names circled around her brain—Diego, Angelo, Domenico, Gaetano after her father. Or perhaps she could name him Nicolò, after the baby's own father?

Nicolino Libero? The name had a pleasant ring; a reminder of his father and the freedom they both believed in.

But Nina shook her head. 'He has no name. Yet.'

Chapter Four

The sky was tinged with thin, vaporous clouds streaked with pink from the late afternoon sun when Ambra left the Campobasso hospital. She raised her eyes and sniffed the air, pregnant with the fragrance of almond blossom. Laughter from the surrounding bars filled the newly named Trafalgar Square. Lights from Castello Monforte perched high on the hill glimmered in the distance.

Ambra quickened her step and walked towards Piazza Gabriele Pepe and the Lupacchioli Café now known as the Crown and Stripes Club. Inside the bar Canadian and New Zealand soldiers mingled drinking together, laughing and smoking.

The light and effervescent mood made it hard to believe a war was still raging in Rome, Naples, the north. Only a few kilometres away, civilians were being killed, towns and villages destroyed, food a luxury. Ambra sometimes felt a hint of embarrassment when she tasted bread, so white and fresh under her teeth, or biscuits sweetened with real sugar. But the guilt lasted only a few moments. She couldn't resist the opulence offered by the Allied forces in Campobasso, newly christened Maple Leaf City. She knew it was her weakness, but she enjoyed the luxuries of the Campobasso lifestyle too much to give them up.

An image of Nina's baby lying crumpled in his hospital cot flickered across Ambra's mind. His wrinkled face, tiny fingers clenched into a fist as if he already knew life ahead would be tough. Wasn't it hard enough to be born in wartime amongst the destruction and bombs? And without a father?

The long mirror lining the wall behind the bar dappled with marks of condensation presented Ambra with her own fragmented reflection. It jolted her like the zapping of an electric current rippling through her chest. Was this a true reflection of her inner state of mind? For a moment she hated the confusion she felt.

A click inside her as if someone had switched on a light in the darkness. The shock of the birth had shifted her. The needle of the compass was changing direction. Hadn't she done enough damage? Should she now put things right between her and Nina, try to amend the wrongs she had done to her?

Dick waved at her from a corner of the bar. Two women clad in elegant dresses stood near him at the counter. They tossed their heads back with laughter, cigarettes in their mouths, lips pouted over thin yellow paper, leaving a mark of red lipstick on the rim. Ambra weaved her way through a group of soldiers and Campobasso women to reach him.

'You look pensive.' His voice rose above the rhythmic music played by impromptu jazz musicians, notes mellow and sweet lingering in the air. He offered Ambra a cigarette from a packet of Chesterfields and slid it between her lips. Ambra took a long drag and blew ringlets of smoke into the air above Dick's head. He laughed and pulled her close. 'What is bothering you, *mia cara*?'

Ambra blushed, 'I need an army truck.' The nerve on her eyelid fluttered like the beat of a drum.

Dick stepped back and stared at her, his hazel eyes, flecked with specks of bottle-green, blinked in surprise.

'An army truck? You can't even drive.' Dick guffawed in the loud manner that now filled the Campobasso streets and cobbled alleyways. Ambra had become accustomed to this booming laughter but now she felt he was mocking her. And she resented it.

'If you don't find me an army truck, I'll find someone else who will. I have other admirers, you know,' she huffed, pouting. 'And for the record, I know the area around here better than you despite all your maps. Will you give me the truck or not?'

'The trucks are the property of the regiment. You never stop intriguing me, *cara* Ambra.' He blew into her ear and wisps of her hair landed on his lips. 'Tell me what you need it for.'

'I need to drive a friend and her newborn baby to Castelnuovo al Volturno, a village in the mountains, where the fighting on the Winter Line took place.'

'I could arrange a private to drive her there, but I cannot allow you to drive one of our trucks. And I have to account for the fuel.'

'I will steal the fuel for you, don't worry. But I have one more request.'

'Steal the fuel?' Dick threw back his head and laughed. 'Your courage never ceases to amaze me.' The blue veins on his neck quivered as he stared at her. Nobody had ever looked at her in such a way, intense longing combined with curiosity. Not even Werner.

At every stage of the game, she had played her cards right, picking the right man at the right time: men who fell for her wiles, her prowess, her charm. She had a way of making men feel important, needed but with a daring and audaciousness that was unusual in women from rural Molise.

A waiter passed by. He was balancing a round tray with two tall glasses on it, both filled with amber-coloured liquid and a heap of ice cubes. Dick passed one to Ambra. 'What else do you have up your sleeve?'

Ambra downed the *poncio* liquor in one go. It burnt her throat. She slammed the glass down on the bar counter and sidled up to Dick. Placing her fingers around his neck she pulled him close. The stubble on his cheek brushed against her skin; she inhaled the soapy scent of his shaving foam and breathed her request into his ear: 'I need you to find an Italian man called Nicolò Sansone. He is a translator with the Allies.'

A slight nod of his head; he placed one arm around Ambra's waist and led her past the couples dancing the boogie-woogie.

She had won.

Now it was her turn to repay him.

Chapter Five

It was the beginning of May. Nina bumped along, next to the Canadian private Ambra's boyfriend had commanded to drive her from the Campobasso hospital to Castelnuovo al Volturno. He had oily skin and greasy black hair. The scent of petrol and sweat clung to his uniform. He barely spoke a word of Italian: a mere clumsy '*buongiorno, signorina*' when Nina climbed into the army truck, Nicolino nestled in her arms.

'Signora,' she corrected him in a brisk tone of voice, but she could tell by the smirk stretching from cheek to cheek that he didn't believe her. *Let him think what he likes.* She didn't care what anyone thought. But she had been grateful when Ivo had pressed Agostina's wedding ring into her palm, the last time he'd visited her at the hospital. 'I've kept it in a wooden box in the storeroom safe all these years,' he'd said. 'Wear it. It makes you presentable in the eyes of those who judge you.'

'*Bambino, bambina*?' the private asked pointing at Nicolino.

'*Bambino*,' she replied. 'Boy. Father, Nicolò Sansone. *Tu conosci?*' she continued in a mixture of basic English and Italian.

He shook his head, his eyes glued to the winding mountainous road. Another negative answer. Nobody seemed to know who he was, where he was. But she would never stop asking.

The truck snaked around the curves, whirring and groaning with the effort. Poppies dotted the roadside, and the sunflowers were vivid yellow, heavy with bright green seeds. Nina held Nicolino close to her chest and watched the countryside fly past. Wheat in the nearby fields had turned from sage to gold. The olive trees lining the road into Castelnuovo al Volturno merged with the grainy rock of the mountains stretching like swords into the sky above.

Wedged at the edge of Monte Marrone, this quiet mountain village had always infused Nina with a sense of calm. She had visited Castelnuovo a few times in the past. The villagers here were connected to the people of Bastiani by music, feast days and their *contadini* roots. Nina recalled a visit with her father Gaetano when he'd accompanied Aurelio the *zampognaro* to play music to the village folk, or when more recently she drove with Ivo and Don Simone in Ivo's van to visit Teresa, Don Simone's sister. She was a courageous woman who had worked tirelessly with the Bastiani *Banda* hiding internees from the surrounding camps.

Teresa Torti was standing at the entrance of the village when the truck ground to a halt in a cloud of dust. 'Welcome, Nina.' She embraced her with warmth. Her eyes were a soft tan like the leather of Nina's old school satchel and her skin was white and papery. 'Welcome to your new home. We are a modest bunch here, trying our best to survive.'

She took Nina's hand and led her towards the entrance of the village with its cobbled streets and dusty alleyways.

'This is our small school,' she explained as they crossed Piazza Roma and Teresa pointed out a stone building at the corner of the square. 'I have been teaching the younger children to read and count ever since our brave Esther was expelled. I am all they have,' she explained. 'We were lost without her but now that we are liberated and she is safe, I hope she will return here to teach.'

Nina nodded. She knew that Teresa had taught the children of Castelnuovo when Esther had lost her job as a result of the Racial Laws. But did Teresa know they had hidden Esther behind the storeroom for months until the liberation? Did she know Esther's hands shook constantly, that her skin was pale, her eyesight poor as a result of the incarceration? Nina kept quiet. There were things Teresa no doubt kept from Nina regarding her work with the *partigiani* and the internees. Missions, confidences. The war was over but as a *staffetta*, her loyalty to the secrets of the past remained buried tightly inside Nina's heart.

Nina followed Teresa past derelict, crumbling cottages clinging to the mountain slopes, past *contadini* with puckered faces who lifted their caps in silent greeting. With a stiff flick of their sticks, they urged their mules forward, the steady clip-clopping of hooves against the cobblestones the only sound.

Teresa lived in a humble two-room cottage beside the church. 'It is from the fourteenth century and filled with old frescoes,' she told Nina, a quiet pride in her voice. 'They're more beautiful than the frescoes in Bastiani. Our cottages are small and dim but our church makes us proud.'

Inside, Nina glanced around the sparsely furnished cottage. A thin straw mattress lay on the stone floor.

'That's where you will sleep,' Teresa said, then pointed to a helmet next to the makeshift bed. 'And this is for your baby. The women of Castelnuovo use the helmets of Allied soldiers as cribs for their newborns.'

Nina stared at the helmet, her pulse quickening. A soldier's helmet? A dead man's helmet!

A knock at the door interrupted her thoughts. It was Lidia, the wife of the *zampognaro* and Teresa's neighbour. 'I have knitted you a blanket.' Lidia stepped inside the tiny room, a woollen bundle in her hand. 'It will protect your baby's head.'

She bent down and placed the white woollen blanket inside the helmet patting it down with bony, arthritic fingers. 'It's what all the new mothers of Castelnuovo use.' A smile crossed her crinkled face. 'Aurelio found this one. It belonged to one of the British soldiers who died fighting during the battle of the Marrone.'

'Luckily Nicolino Libero is small; he will easily fit inside,' Teresa said.

Nina stared at the helmet. Could she really place little Nicolino inside a dead man's helmet? But there were no carpenters in Castelnuovo, no Antonio to build wooden cribs, no gently rocking cradles like the ones in Bastiani.

She crouched down and carefully laid Nicolino in the helmet, tucking the blanket around him. To her relief he curled effortlessly into his new cot, his tiny fingers coiling instinctively around the rough netting of the helmet. Then he whimpered. Nina rocked the helmet gently with her foot, astonished it was as successful at calming him as the wooden cribs for the Bastiani babies. Then she thought of Nicolò. Where was he? Was another woman in another village using Nicolò's helmet to rock her baby to sleep? But somehow, Nina knew that Nicolò was still alive. It was an intense sensation deep within her bones as if she could hear his voice whispering, 'I am here Nina, I haven't forgotten you.'

'And I haven't forgotten you either,' she whispered to the stark walls of the cottage. She requested a pen and some paper from Teresa. Even if Ambra had advised her not to, she decided to compose a letter to the Sansones in the Social Republic of Salò in the smallest chance they knew where he was. With no specific address she doubted they would ever receive it. But she had to try.

Post Office

Another summer, another June day. Beads of early morning rain cling to the geraniums and basil plants on the windowsill, shimmering like tiny diamonds against the green leaves. The storm has passed and now the blackened clouds disperse, revealing a sky, bright blue and clear stretching over the piazza.

Our village is still healing. A year pockmarked with ruin, loss and grief lingers in the cracks of the cobblestones and in the eyes of those who remain. But my villagers endure. I watch them toil tirelessly, kneeling in the streets, hammering doors back onto their frames, oil trickling through the metal to cushion the grating noise.

Ivo is standing by the door, his hand on the latch. His shirt is creased, a faint stain darkens the material near his shoulder and his hair, once neatly combed, is unruly. He does not smile these days. Though it is Sunday, piles of letters lie untouched on my counter, waiting for his hands to sort them. But he cannot. He suffers, just as I do.

No Ambra.

No Nina.

Gone are Ambra's hurried footsteps on my wooden stairs, the familiar clatter of pots in the kitchen. No soft hum of Nina sweeping my floor, dusting my counter. No warmth of broth and chicory in the early morning. The silence is heavy, thick with absence. I never realised how much Ivo needs them. How much I need them.

Shouts and cries, high-pitched and panting, cut through the stillness. Ivo startles as the voices float toward him. He opens the door, and they run to greet him. Mariolina—face flushed—Renzo, Santino, Celestina and Pietruzzo close behind them. Esther hobbles to keep up with them. Her bones are still weakened from months hidden away in the storeroom, where darkness was safer than daylight. But now, her eyes sparkle. They all have the same look I have not seen for some time.

Hope.

'*Roma è libera*,' Mariolina cries.

Ivo's breath catches. 'Rome?'

Renzo grasps Ivo by the arm and shakes him. 'After months of occupation, Rome is free, Ivo! Thanks to General Mark Clark, Rome is the first capital city to be liberated.'

'The people have crowded onto the streets to welcome the troops!' Mariolina exclaims. 'They are throwing flowers at the tanks that pass by. Renzo heard it on the wireless!'

Celestina presses a hand to her mouth; her voice breaks. 'Maybe now the Madonna will bring my Giovannino home.' How many times has she whispered that prayer, sending it into the wind like a plea?

Renzo pulls Ivo into an embrace. He lets himself be held, absorbing the weight of this moment. *Roma* is free. The world itself is taking a long, deep breath after so much darkness.

And yet, Ivo's heart is breaking.

And so is mine. We miss our girls.

The page on the calendar flutters free.

It is the June 4th, 1944, Saint Francis Caracciolo's feast day.

Today is a day of combined jubilation and melancholy.

Chapter Six

That first evening after rocking her baby to sleep in his helmet, Nina wrapped a shawl around her shoulders and stood by the small stone window. She gazed up at the dark, brooding shape of Monte Marrone with its deep canyons and thick forests stretching into the night.

Teresa joined Nina by the window and placed a comforting hand on her shoulder. 'This is our sacred mountain,' she murmured, her voice thick with emotion. In the dim light of the kitchen, Nina saw the shimmer of unshed tears in her eyes. 'The mountain is our saviour. And it can be yours too.'

A quiet knock at the door announced Lidia's arrival. She entered carrying a metal pot. 'Bean soup,' she said, handing it to Teresa, who placed it on the stove beside the stone sink in the corner of the tiny room.

A shadow fell across the open doorway. It was Aurelio, the *zampognaro* of Castelnuovo. He carried his bagpipes slung over one shoulder, a bundle of firewood in the other. 'In case Nina gets cold here in the mountains,' he said. 'Even in May the night air can freeze your bones.'

He stacked the firewood near the hearth. Soon the flames crackled, throwing flickering light across the room. Settling onto a stool beside his wife, he raised the *zampogna* to his lips, releasing a slow, mournful melody. The notes curled into the air like whispers from the past. Nina glanced at Nicolino, surprised that the baby did not stir at the lilting sounds of the music.

'I was telling Nina about our mountain,' Teresa said softly. 'How it saved us.'

'It was the holy week of Easter, only three months ago,' Lidia added, cheeks pink from the heat rising in the air.

The melancholic notes of Aurelio's *zampogna* filled the room as the voices of the two women transported Nina to the battle of Monte Marrone. It was one of the many conflicts fought on the various battlefields and defensive positions of the Winter Line. She had heard in Bastiani how the Allies had struggled to defend the Gustav Line against Kesselring's troops. So many had died. She glanced at the helmet where Nicolino slept—yes, that poor British soldier had perished trying to protect this very mountain and the villages it sheltered.

Teresa's voice became distant, reverent, as if reliving the memory. 'Just imagine, Nina. In under three hours, in the pitch-black of night, our Italian *Alpini* reached the peak of Monte Marrone.'

'They took Kesselring's troops by surprise.' Lidia clasped her hands tightly in her lap. 'The Germans never expected an attack.'

'Our brave *Alpini* forced them to surrender.' Teresa's voice trembled. 'If not for their courage, we would never have been freed.'

'They were accustomed to the mountainous terrain, from their native Piemonte, you see,' Lidia concurred. 'Unlike the Allies, they didn't understand the terrain, the pitfalls and crevasses of the mountain.'

'Our *Alpini* scaled the rocky face in the dark as if they were mountain goats.' Teresa paused, her voice breaking.

'Unlike the Allies, who lost so many men, our *Alpini* had the mountain on their side.'

Nina's gaze returned to Monte Marrone, imagining the scene—rough fingers gripping the jagged rock, torches flickering on helmeted heads, boots scrambling for a safe hold along the craggy ascent. She could almost hear the groaning of the men as they climbed, in the silence of night.

Aurelio lowered his bagpipes. 'The Allies tried to take the mountain last October,' he murmured. 'They were slaughtered. The Germans held their ground. But this time, with our *Alpini* leading the way, the impossible became possible. It was a great victory.'

The music ceased, and in the sudden hush, Nicolino began to cry. The sound pierced the air like the wails of wounded soldiers. Nina lifted him into her arms, swaying gently to calm him.

'Our mountain saved us,' Teresa repeated. 'Molise was liberated that night. And this victory opened the path to Monte Cassino, to Rome's liberation.' She made the sign of the cross, the furrow between her eyebrows deepening. 'And with the help of the Madonna, may the Allies soon liberate all the towns and villages in our beloved country.'

Nina stood by the window once more, Nicolino now fast asleep against her chest. Monte Marrone shimmered silver in the moonlight, its dark forests stretching like the shadows of disembodied spirits. A shudder ran through her. Was Nicolò fighting with the Allied forces somewhere along the Apennines? Was he even alive? She looked down at her son's peaceful face. His dark eyes flickered open, gazing up at her. She stroked the tufts of his hair, remembering how she once ruffled Nicolò's curls, streaked with copper.

The thought of her child growing into a man, resembling his father, filled her with unexpected warmth. She would do anything for her son. She would stay in Castelnuovo, hidden and unjudged, even if it meant pretending to be a war widow, like her mother before her. She had no choice but to embrace the roughness of this rural isolated hamlet.

In the days that followed, Nina began to adjust to her new life in Castelnuovo. The mountain towered over her, casting both shadow and protection. She did not know how long she would stay, and although part of her longed to be in Bastiani, the memories—the Post Office, Ivo, Ambra, working with the *Banda* and filling her days as a *staffetta*—began to feel more distant. Life in Castelnuovo al Volturno was different, and it wasn't merely the helmets used as cribs for newborn babies. From the stone cottages hugging the mountain slopes, their chimneys curling smoke into the cool mountain air, even in June, to the sleepy mules and furrowed faces of the *contadini*. In Bastiani the mountains framed the village like a gentle embrace, rising behind the cobbled streets and the turquoise waters of the Fastino. Here, the jagged rocky Monte Marrone loomed over Nina like a sleeping giant with its canyons and forests dense with oak and beech.

One morning, as light slanted through the cracks in the wooden shutters, Nina stirred, the scent of damp stone and hay filling her nostrils. She reached for Nicolino, still nestled in the helmet, his blanket snug around him. Outside, the village had already begun its day. Women scrubbed clothes at the communal fountain, chickens pecked at the dirt, a cart trundled past. A boy, no older than twelve, tipped his cap at Nina as he passed, his dark eyes bright with curiosity.

'Nina!' Lidia's voice called from across the piazza. 'Come, I need an extra pair of hands.' Lidia was kneeling beside a makeshift stall, arranging bundles of dried herbs. Nina adjusted her shawl and hurried over.

'You're settling in?' Lidia asked as she handed Nina a bundle of rosemary to tie with twine.

Nina hesitated, then nodded. 'I think so. It's different from Bastiani. Smaller. Quieter.'

Poorer, Nina thought, *more isolated.*

Lidia chuckled. 'Yes, we're small. Bastiani is like a city compared to Castelnuovo. We lie on the forgotten side of the mountain.'

Nina had noticed how the mountain often featured in the conversation of the villagers, how it dictated the village's rhythm—the men who trekked its slopes for firewood, the shepherds who guided their flocks to graze on its ridges, the women who gathered wild herbs from the foothills. It was neither welcoming nor cruel, but its vast, unyielding presence loomed like a sweeping giant. And as she sat beside Lidia, the soft, mournful notes of Aurelio's *zampogna* drifting in the air, Nina wondered which it would be for her.

Chapter Seven

The leaves on the trees surrounding the village had an exhausted summer air despite the breeze. Ambra hitched a ride from Campobasso, impatient to tell Nina the news she had received from Dick concerning Nicolò's whereabouts.

'All you do is click your fingers with requests,' he'd said, a half-serious expression crossing his angular face. 'But I have had notifications from the American forces in Lucca. Nicolò Sansone will soon be back in Campobasso.' She'd pulled him close, kissed him on the lips and promised to accompany him to the Theatre Savoy to see the Italian movie *Una Romantica Avventura.*

Ambra jumped out of the jeep and waved a thank you to the corporal from New Zealand for the lift. She waited until the truck had disappeared behind a cloud of dust, then pulled the Leica out of her bag. The last thing she wanted was to lose the trust of the New Zealanders and Canadians or, even worse, to have Werner's precious Leica seized. The photos provided her with her only source of income. If it weren't for the camera, how could she afford the rent for her room in Campobasso above Briscotti's Bakery? She was thankful for the added extras—stockings, perfumes, chocolate from Dick and the other soldiers she flirted with—yet she knew the only person she could truly rely on was herself. The photos she took gave her the *lire* she needed to live her new life away from Bastiani and for that she would always be grateful to Werner.

On the white chalky path leading up to the village Ambra snapped images of the mountain. She noticed a small procession of villagers, mattresses under their arms, their mules laden with copper pots glinting in the sunlight. Ambra, drawn to the play of light falling on their faces, placed the viewfinder close to her eye. Adjusting the lens, she could see their haggard faces and slumped shoulders.

'What's happening?' she asked a toothless man with a brooding mouth.

'We've been ordered to leave our homes.'

'I've come to see my friend Nina. She's staying with Teresa, the *maestra*. Have you seen her?'

He shrugged. 'She will be on her way to La Rocchetta, like all of us.'

Ambra dashed towards the entrance of the village. A bustling of activity—soldiers, noise, tanks, confusion surrounded her. She thrust the camera into her bag.

'What's going on?' she wondered aloud. Puzzled, she crouched behind the thick trunk of an ancient olive tree, the silvery leaves tickling her cheeks. Tightening her muscles, she kept as still as she could.

Were those tanks really German?

Were soldiers in American and German uniforms really laughing and chatting together? How could it be?

The Germans had retreated towards the north. She stifled a scream, rose and walked towards a soldier guarding the piazza.

'You can't enter here,' he said in broken Italian with a broad American slur. The man's lips smiled but his eyes were dark and fixed in a cold stare.

'Why not? Castelnuovo is a free village. I want to see my friend Nina Caruso and her baby.' A clammy sweat broke over her hands.

An arm holding a rifle reached out to stop her. 'We have evacuated the villagers, further down the valley, to La Rocchetta al Volturno. We have orders to carry out a disinfestation.'

Ambra's gaze moved from the soldier to the tanks and back to the soldier again. 'A disinfestation? Really?' She adopted a sweet, unsuspicious voice but inside her jumbled thoughts were curdling.

What is the disinfestation for? she wondered. And why are some soldiers wearing the uniform of the *nazifascisti?* She was mystified but she had learnt from experience, sometimes it was better to appear naive. The air was crisp with tension.

'You cannot stay here,' he repeated. 'Jump on the truck. It will take you to La Rocchetta.'

'But what is wrong with the village?' Ambra insisted and placed her hands on her hips. She stared with disbelief at the American.

The soldier raised his rifle to shoulder level and pointed it at Ambra's chest.

'Look here, *signorina*. Get on the truck. Now. Or I will send you to an internment camp in Calabria, do you understand?'

An internment camp in Calabria? Her, Ambra, an Italian in liberated Molise? These were the Allies, their friends. She bit the inside of her cheek in an attempt to control the rage jangling her bones. But she needed to remain calm if she were to find Nina and tell her where Nicolò was. So, she gave a slight nod of her head and climbed into the truck. The tart smell of freshly cut hay mingled with the pungent odour of gasoline.

*

At La Rocchetta Ambra jumped down from the truck. She felt the heat of the afternoon weigh heavily on her shoulders. Soldiers were guarding the crowd of villagers huddled together on the hillside overlooking Castelnuovo. Where was Nina? She searched for her heart-shaped face and head of hair like tar.

Boom. Boom. Boom.

The blast of artillery fire sliced the air in two. It shook the ground and Ambra's stomach churned with fear. A baby's wail shot through the air. Ambra turned. And there was Nina, cradling her baby close to her chest, Teresa standing behind her, an arm on Nina's shoulder.

Ambra ran towards them and reached for Nina's hand. She needed to feel the touch of someone familiar, real amidst the confusion around her. Nina turned to face Ambra, her deep brown eyes flecked with puzzled bewilderment.

'Ambra, you're here?'

'What on earth is happening to this village?'

'I don't know.' Nina's voice faded, swallowed by booming sounds echoing across the mountains to the crest of the hill. It was as if they were both suspended in the moment, waiting, wondering. The baby's cries became more intense. Ambra watched Nina rock him with care and love. Nicolino's blue-grey eyes stared at his mother. Nobody had looked at Ambra that way. Lust, yes. Desire too. But never pure love.

Aurelio, the *zampogna* tethered to his back, climbed a beech tree to survey the scene. His scraggly arms, burnt by the sun, clasped the branches as his legs nimbly scaled the trunk.

Rat-a-tat-tat. Rat-a-tat-tat. The sound of machine guns blasted across the landscape.

Dust. And more dust filled the cloudless sky.

'They are bombing our village,' Aurelio shrieked from the top of the tree.

'Are we dreaming?' A broken voice floated in the air behind Ambra. 'The war front of the Gothic Line is 700 kilometres away. Why is there a battle now? Here?' Ambra wondered whether this was Lidia, Aurelio's wife. She turned and saw her small scrawny body, her face wizened with alarm.

A soldier guarding the group shrugged his shoulders. 'Don't worry, we are disinfecting to make your village clean and safe.'

'This doesn't make any sense.' Ambra nudged Nina and whispered in her ear. 'Something is not right.'

Teresa screamed, her arms flailing in the air. 'Look, those armoured vehicles are charging through my potato fields. They are destroying my crop.'

Aurelio, balancing on a branch of the tree, shouted, 'They are destroying all the wheat fields around Castelnuovo. Our harvest is gone.' He scrambled down and jumped to the ground. 'I must stop them. This is our livelihood. How will any of us eat and feed our families without our crops?'

'*Calma. Calma*. You're not going anywhere.' A Canadian soldier with a long aquiline nose placed the rifle across Aurelio's chest and continued in perfect Italian. '*Paghiamo per danni*. You'll all be reimbursed for damages. Stay where you are.'

A sudden boom, stronger, louder, reverberated through the dust-filled air. A crashing jarring sound.

A shell, black and round, sped through the air.

Gasps lifted up to the lapis-blue sky. Breath held, eyes watched. The shell flew spinning towards the bell tower.

Crush, rumble, blast like the sound of a thunderstorm across the mountains. The bell tower crumbled to the ground as if made of flour not stone.

'They are dismembering our beautiful church. It's like a body with no head,' Teresa shouted.

A thick silence descended on the crowd as they watched their village reduced to rubble, stone by stone.

Nina screamed, her face grey-white with fear, 'Teresa, your house! Everything is gone.'

'The war has retraced its steps. They are ravaging our crops and our cottages. Will it be us next?' Teresa tilted her head towards the soldiers with rifles pointing towards them. 'We've seen this before with an army who pretended to be on our side.'

A breath caught in Ambra's throat as smoke choked the air. She blinked several times trying to make sense of what was unfolding in front of them. How could this be happening? This couldn't be a disinfestation. Her fingers itched with the desire to grasp the Leica and record what her eyes were witnessing.

She grabbed Nina's shoulder and whispered, 'You and Teresa, move over there and shield me from the view of the soldiers.' She pointed to a ridge surrounded by olive trees. 'I must take photos to record what's going on here.'

'I'll tell them I need to feed Nicolino,' Nina offered. 'The soldiers won't follow us if a woman is breastfeeding. It's an intimate moment. They'll leave us alone.'

'My baby needs feeding.' Nina pointed towards the clump of olive trees on the ridge. 'We're moving there.' A Canadian soldier with his helmet askew nodded and let them pass.

Teresa and Nina huddled around Ambra, guarding her. Protected by their presence Ambra knelt down in front of them. It was the perfect spot. She had a clear view of the battered village. She removed the camera from her bag. With trembling fingers, she pressed the shutter. *Click.*

Boom, boom, boom. Four houses destroyed by the artillery shots. *Click.*

Blast. Old oak trees mined with dynamite blown like planks of wood into the air. *Click.*

Soldiers sprinting, heads down firing machine guns. *Rat-a-tat-tat. Click.*

Smoke bombs exploding, dust, dirt, bricks flying through the air. Strident screams from gaping mouths. A soldier crumbled to the ground as stretcher-bearers arrived and carried the fallen man to a waiting ambulance, the cross on the green metal frame vibrant red in the sun's rays.

Resistance against her finger and a dull clicking sound. The film had reached the last frame. Ambra rewound and unloaded the used film and swiftly rummaged in her pocket for a new roll.

She jolted.

Two hands grabbed her shoulders and tugged her backwards. 'Photos are strictly forbidden.'

'What are you doing to me?' Ambra shrieked. She stamped her foot and elbowed her captor in the ribs. 'Leave me alone.'

'You are under arrest.'

'Robert, help me, this one is a traitor.' A soldier with floppy blond hair and a pinched face ran to the aid of the man holding Ambra. The butt of a gun pressed into Ambra's back.

For a moment she panicked. Her mind was fogged with fear then her brain clocked into clarity. A whoosh of adrenaline surged through her. Her words sounded calm and bold despite the blood rushing to her temples. 'I am

Italian; you liberated us. We are on the same side. You can't arrest me.'

'Oh yes we can. We don't like this camera of yours. You're coming with us.'

Ambra smoothed the hair from her forehead, cocked her head to one side and smiled sweetly at the soldiers. 'Of course I will come with you. But kindly remove the gun from my back and allow me to say goodbye to my friend. I am a free citizen.'

With her chin held high, Ambra took Nina by the shoulders and pulled her towards her. She held her tight.

'Not too close,' the soldier called Robert shouted.

A van was waiting by a clump of silver birch trees. The two soldiers pushed her onto the van, scraping her calves on the metal bumper. She slumped down onto the floor. Her bag now lay empty on her hips. Her Leica was in the hands of the Allies. They had no right to take it from her. It was her livelihood. She kicked the side of the van. How dare they! Only then, as the grey tips of the mountains whizzed past, did she remember the news she had wanted to tell Nina: Nicolò would soon be in Campobasso.

Chapter Eight

The roll of film Ambra had slipped into her hand felt like burning coal. It was all that was left of Ambra. Nina's eyes followed the military van rattling down the dusty trail past the houses of La Rocchetta. She wondered what was going to happen to her friend. A whizzing noise above her head made her look up. A small plane was spinning round and round in the blue afternoon sky smudged with smoke. A camera peeked out from the cockpit window. Nina frowned.

A voice boomed over the crowd, 'A roll of film is hidden somewhere amongst you. Line up. We will search you all.'

Fear knotted Nina's throat. She had to find a safer hiding place for Ambra's roll of film. She turned to Teresa and softly mumbled. 'I am going to make Nicolino cry again. Put your arms around me and pretend you are consoling him.'

Nina pinched Nicolino's wrist between her thumb and forefinger. She pressed hard. His blue eyes flickered open in surprise. He stared at her. She pressed the skin of his wrist again. Harder this time. The baby squeezed his face tight, the soft skin creased into tiny furrows. He let out a chilling wail.

Teresa, cheeks stained with tears, huddled over Nina and the baby, her soft, fleshy arms embracing them both. Hidden by Teresa's body, Nina slid the film from her clasped fist and tucked it into the triangular cloth swaddling the baby's bottom. Unlikely they will look here, she thought. A sliver of worry for Nicolino rushed through her. Was she putting her baby at risk? What choice did she have if she wanted to save Ambra and ensure the safety of the film? 'Keep this. Don't let anyone take it from you,' Ambra had whispered with urgency, her black eyes flecked with both courage and distress. 'I'm telling you, Nina. They are lying to us.'

Nina and Teresa lined up with Aurelio, Lidia and the other villagers of Castelnuovo. Soldiers walked up and down inspecting hands, peering underneath caps, inside trouser pockets, patting chests and tummies as if searching for gold nuggets. Nicolino was still screaming when Robert, the soldier with the floppy blond hair who had led Ambra to the military van, stood in front of them, his stubby fingers stretching towards Nicolino. Nina stopped breathing. She held her baby tighter, as if her arms were the only thing that could save him from the soldier's searching hands. Nicolino cries began to abate and a tiny smile appeared at the corner of his lips.

'He reminds me of my baby at home in Texas,' Robert said in broken Italian. With a sorrowful smile crossing his face, he stroked Nicolino's cheek. 'I miss him. Look after this young lad. Sorry for the disturbance, Signora.'

The soldier moved forward. Teresa squeezed Nina's hand. Whispers of the Ave Maria prayer reached Nina's ears. 'We are safe,' Nina whispered back and for the first time in many years, she made the sign of the cross, something her mother always did in times of peril or gratitude.

Nina turned her gaze towards the ruins of Castelnuovo al Volturno and with puzzled bewilderment watched the fallen soldier jump out of the ambulance. He pulled off his bloodied shirt and laughed together with men in the green-grey uniform of the German army, smoking cigarettes and gulping from tumblers. Baffled by this scene Nina swept the image from her mind. At least she, Teresa and her baby were safe. And so was the film Ambra had entrusted her with. 'Keep it safe. Please,' she'd breathed into Nina's ear. 'It mustn't get into the wrong hands.'

A sun of burning copper tickled the tiled roofs of the surviving houses of Castelnuovo. It threw hot, flickering rays onto the helmets of the soldiers. Nina glanced at Nicolino. The sunlight flooded his hair with streaks of gold. Kissing the tip of his nose she whispered, 'Nicolino, my love, we are moving again. La Rocchetta will be our home tonight.'

*

Bowls of bean soup provided by the villagers of La Rocchetta formed the evening meal for Nina and the other villagers banished from Castelnuovo. Beddings of hay were scattered over the floor of their new refuge in the Benedictine church of Santa Maria alle Grotte. Built within the silver-grey folds of the surrounding rock, Nina imagined what it must have been like to be one of the ancient pilgrims journeying to this isolated spot on their way to Monte Cassino.

'He will be our saviour and will protect us and your baby, Nina.' Teresa pointed to the effigy of Saint Christopher, protector of travellers, painted on the wall. Piled together in the dampened cave, the breath from many mouths warmed the air.

Nicolino began to cry. Nina picked him up and cradled him in her arms—a sweet tune of a lullaby escaped from her lips. Then a mellow sound rose into the air. Nina lifted her head. Aurelio picked up the *zampogna* that never left his side. During her brief stay in Castelnuovo, Nina noticed how Aurelio always carried the instrument under his arm as if it were a beloved child.

Aurelio's lips stretched over the mouthpiece as he blew into the hollow wooden pipe and squeezed the bag. The melancholic, sorrowful, yet vibrant melody enveloped the villagers.

A villager with a shock of white hair and a bristly grey beard began to sing, creating a symphony of sounds in harmony with the notes of the *zampogna*. Lidia joined in. Voices, like strands of thread, wove through the melody. Nicolino lowered his eyelids and drifted into sleep. Nina clasped him tightly. His tiny body infused her with an innocent warmth that moved her to tears. She scanned the room of villagers turned into a choir of singers and held together by the notes of the *zampogna*. They were one voice, one soul. An overwhelming void erupted in Nina. She missed her Bastiani people: Ambra, her friend; Nicolò, the father of her baby; Gino, her brother risking his life with the partisans in the north; Ivo, Esther, Mariolina; even the Post Office storeroom with its radio and black Olivetti typewriter.

A loneliness surged through her. A loneliness peppered with worry. The image of Ambra's alarmed yet resolute gaze when she slipped the film into Nina's hands and the image of her being led away in a military van, a rifle pressed against her back had stayed with her. Where had the soldiers taken her? She shuddered at the thought of Ambra imprisoned in a cell like she had been. She prayed the Allied soldiers would be kinder to Ambra. Nina raised her hand to her heart. There it was, near her breastbone, pressing against her skin. If only she could talk to Mariolina and Esther, they would tell her what to do with the roll of film.

The judgement and gossip of the Bastiani women, pointing at her, a fallen woman bringing shame not only on her family name but to the entire village, no longer seemed important. She was a *staffetta* and always had been. She would return to Bastiani: to her home, her people.

Nina's lids were heavy with sleep. She curled her limbs around the sleeping baby, inhaling the comforting smell of his milky breath. The music dwindled. The frescoes of saints decorating the walls glittered in the moonlight. She rubbed her nose against Nicolino's cheek and tenderly murmured to her son, 'You were born on the way to the Santissima Addolorata. My friend Ambra helped me and now it's our turn to help her. We will return to Bastiani where we came from.'

Chapter Nine

Nina bounced alongside Aurelio the *zampognaro* of Castelnuovo on his horse-drawn cart, Nicolino asleep in her arms despite the bumpy ride. A vast forest of green blanketed the Matese mountains, their peaks stretching toward a cloudless sapphire-blue sky. Heat pressed down on her skin as they trundled past fields, the colour of the chocolate the Allies had brought to Bastiani—rich and dark, a token of kindness shared with warm smiles and infectious laughter.

'Aurelio, drop me at the entrance of the village. I'll walk from there. I don't want to attract too much attention with the baby in my arms.' A flash of pink tinged Nina's cheeks. 'I don't know how everyone will react to my sudden return.'

'It's better to be back in Bastiani where you belong, Nina. There is little left in Castelnuovo now. We will rebuild our village, just like your Bastiani villagers did when it was scorched last year.' With gnarled fingers Aurelio pulled on the reins of his cart, urging the pony to a halt. 'Better to be here now,' he repeated and with a brisk movement, jumped out of the cart to help Nina down onto a path overgrown with red and yellow poppies, their heads nodding in the slight breeze.

'*Arrivederci,* Signor Aurelio. Thank you for everything. Keep playing your *zampogna* and bringing hope to Castelnuovo. One day, we will know the truth of what happened. One day it will all come to light.' She squeezed his hand.

Aurelio shrugged and with an unwavering voice of hope that made Nina feel both proud and sad, said, 'It's simply a disinfestation. We must trust what the Allies have to do and we must soldier on. We are *contadini*. We have strength.'

With her free hand, Nina lifted her bag from the cart and slung the straps over her shoulders. As the last wisps of dust vanished into the still summer air, she rummaged through the bag and extracted a small cylindrical object. She unbuttoned her shirt and tucked Ambra's film, a silent witness to the Castelnuovo disinfestation, inside her brassiere. She pressed the film close to her chest. A touching sense of nostalgia warmed her heart. It was as if the film had transformed itself into the knotted friendship pact of their youth. It wasn't only a silent witness to the events in Castelnuovo, but also proof that despite their differences, the bond between them was still vibrant.

Nina began to walk. It was early morning, and the sun had not yet reached its zenith. When she arrived at the River Fastino, she paused.

'This is where your father and I used to swim when we were young,' she whispered to the baby in her arms. Nicolino stared up at her, his milky blue eyes blinking against the sunlight. 'But the bridge is broken now. Look, Nicolino.' She pointed to the rocks placed in the swirling water as a means of passage for the villagers. She imagined them balancing sacks of newly harvested potatoes on their shoulders, hopping carefully from stone to stone, whilst their wilful mules waded through the water.

It had only been two months since Nicolino was born, since she had last seen Bastiani, but the village felt a different shape, a different outline from the one she remembered. The cottages had been rebuilt, their new doors hewn from the trees of the mountains, which had stood for centuries.

At the piazza, Nina sank onto a bench outside Bar Renzo, taking in her surroundings. The front window of the bar resembled a patchwork of square and triangular shards, salvaged from shattered windows and glass bottles. Hues of amber and forest green formed a dazzling mosaic.

Renzo stepped outside and wiped his hands on an apron tied around his waist. 'These are the colours of our new life.' He chuckled when he saw Nina staring at the bar. 'I'm hoping this design will attract more customers to our little Molise village at the foot of the mountains.' His eyes softened. 'It's good to see you back in Bastiani, Nina. And with your baby.'

A warm glow settled around Nina's heart. She waved, then crossed the square. The thick branches of the oak tree, heavy with lush, dark green leaves, loomed in front of the locked cast-iron gate of the deserted Villa Sansone.

'This was your father's home,' she bent forward, rubbing her cheek against Nicolino's head as she murmured. 'This is where we whispered secrets in the kitchen, where we planned how to help the internees. And this is where your *nonna* was killed.'

Tears streaked her cheeks as she gazed at the villa, its fractured roof, empty rooms and overgrown gardens. All that was left was a ghostly relic of life before war had darkened Molise, before her mother, loyal to the Sansones until the end, had perished alone. She walked with a determined stride across the piazza towards the Post Office. The door was open, allowing the morning breeze to stir the stuffy air inside. Pots of basil and geraniums on the windowsill basked in the sun. Ivo stood outside, plucking bright, green basil leaves, probably for his *minestra* or potato salad, Nina thought with a pang of wistfulness.

'Nina.' Ivo's voice, shrill with both bafflement and joy, flooded the quiet square. He stretched out his arms to embrace her, but she raised her hand, pressing a finger to her lips. He dropped his gaze to the bundle in Nina's arms.

'How did you get here?' Ivo squeezed her shoulder, his bushy eyebrows dancing with excitement, his lips stretched into a wide smile. 'We didn't expect you. Don Simone didn't mention it.'

'He doesn't know. Only Teresa knows I've come back to Bastiani. Aurelio dropped me at the entrance of the village. But please tell me, have you heard from Ambra? She was taken away by a soldier when she visited me in Castelnuovo, the day of the disinfestation. I haven't heard from her since. Is she safe?'

Ivo ushered her into the Post Office and placed the closed sign on the door. Nina lowered herself gingerly onto a chair so as not to disturb Nicolino.

'Ambra! That daughter of mine.' Ivo wiped his forehead with the back of his hands, his eyes glinting with flickers of concern. 'She is a constant worry.'

'What happened to her? Where is she now?'

'I received a call from her. Her voice was shaky. All she would tell me is that she was taken to a military prison in Campobasso.'

A military prison! Fear gripped Nina's throat. What if Ambra was tortured and forced to reveal that it was she, Nina, who had the film? Maybe the soldiers would come to Bastiani to find her. Would they take Nicolino away? She hugged her baby close to her chest. Nicolino let out a whining sound. Could he feel the film digging into his flesh? She released her hold on Nicolino and relaxed her shoulders. No, Ambra would never betray her. She was sure.

'It's because of the disinfestation in Castelnuovo by the Allies. There was something strange about it. And Ambra asked too many questions.' Nina chewed the inside of her mouth, her fingers tightening around the fabric of her shirt. Should she reveal to Ivo the eeriness of the scene—Allied soldiers, German uniforms, a battle on the ground, filming from the air. She clenched the muscles of her neck. She would keep quiet.

'But you know your daughter, she always manages to get herself out of trouble,' she said, trying to reassure him and herself at the same time.

'I hope you're right.' He squeezed her arm. 'It's good to have you back in Bastiani, Nina.'

'I want to be here in my piazza, to sit under the hazelnut bush by the River Fastino, to rock my baby to sleep beneath the shade of the olive groves.' *And if Nicolò ever comes back, he will know where to find me*, she thought, a sigh pressing on her chest. 'But I can't go home to the farm, with my mother dead and Gino still fighting in the north.'

Ivo nodded. 'You will always have a home here in my Post Office, Nina. And with your baby of course. I need help; it's hard managing on my own.'

Nina glanced at the counter, furred with dust, the stacks of unopened letters, the cobwebs swaying from the ceiling like lace curtains. Ivo's rugged face was wrinkled with lines; his leaden eyes no longer fizzed with excitement like they used to when they all worked together, helping the internees and working for the *Banda*. She sighed and patted Ivo's arm.

'Go upstairs and lay your baby safely on your mattress on Ambra's floor.' He smiled and clicked his tongue. 'It's still there and I'll make a nice cold *poncio* for us to drink.'

Nina climbed the staircase, her soft tread padding the wooden boards. She pushed open the door of Ambra's bedroom and lay Nicolino on the mattress, under the bedcover Agostina had embroidered for Ambra as a child. Nicolino gurgled, sucking his wrist.

'This will be much more comfortable for you than a soldier's helmet,' Nina hummed. She placed a hand on Nicolino's chest and rocked him until he fell into a deep sleep.

Slowly, she unbuttoned her shirt and extracted the film from the inside of her brassiere. She rolled it between her fingers for several moments, pondering what to do with it. Then she sprang up and opened the top drawer, where Ambra had hidden her friendship pact all those years ago. She rummaged amongst Ambra's underwear. The handkerchief was not there but Nina's fingers touched a metal box lying under a moth-eaten cardigan. She pulled out the box and lifted the lid. The film would be safe there, until she could speak to Ambra and see what she wanted to do with it.

Nina's fingertips brushed against shreds of cotton. She lifted them out. Strips were all that remained of the handkerchief with green and white flowers. A cry escaped from her lips. Why? When?

She was about to close the lid when she noticed notes of paper at the bottom of the box. Her eyes widened. She slipped her hand inside and with two fingers extracted a thin sheet of paper folded in two. A rustling sound filled the room, mingling with Nicolino's soft breathing.

Nina unfolded the square of yellow paper. As if in slow motion, she sunk to her knees, forehead furrowed into a map of lines. Her heart quickened.

Three words: '*My dear Nina*.'

She bit her lip and shut her eyes. She counted to ten before opening them. There it was again, '*Mia amata* Nina.' A melody in three words. She scanned the text that followed until she reached the signature. She didn't want to be mistaken. '*Tuo* Nicolò.' An ache and a longing for him surged through her body as the letter quivered between her fingers.

His words, a string of beads. *I miss you and I long to hold you in my arms once more*. Words threaded together, one after the other, recounting his days: *joined the Allies . . . translating and interpreting . . . I will keep you posted.*

It was too absurd, too unbelievable to cry. Here was his voice reaching her as if he were standing beside her. She continued to read, *and as soon as this war is over, we will be together, no matter what my family thinks.*

'Together,' she murmured as her heart skipped a beat. She clasped the letter close to her chest, its weight both comforting and unsettling. Slowly, she raised her hand and brought the letter to her nose, longing to inhale his scent—his sweet, intoxicating scent of coffee beans and ripe hazelnuts. All that lingered was the sterile dryness of the ink and a fleeting hint of glue. His essence was gone, vanished just like he had.

Nina folded the letter. She turned to look at Nicolino still fast asleep, tiny fist clinging to the scarf she had placed over him. His deep forehead, his nose, his clear sky-blue eyes were just like his father's.

As she reached into the box once more, her heart jolted with a blend of anticipation and dread. There were more envelopes, four of them, each bearing the handwritten scrawl '*A MANO*'. She pulled them out, sifting through them with a desperate frenzy. Nicolò had been right—there was a delicate web of couriers spanning partisan and Allied lines. They had somehow managed to transport the letters to the Bastiani Post Office. He had never abandoned her. He had risked everything for her. For a moment an overwhelming elation filled her heart, only to swiftly transform into searing rage towards Ambra.

How could Ambra have betrayed her? Hadn't Nina asked her countless times if any letters from Nicolò had arrived? 'Any letter from the Winter Line?' had been her constant refrain in those months of loneliness, always met with disappointment. And here they were hidden in Ambra's tin box covered by the shreds of the friendship pact; and now in Nina's hands at last.

She settled herself on the floor and started to read the letters in the order she had found them. Devouring one after the next, her eyes raced across the page. When she reached the last letter, an icy dread shook her to the core.

> *My dearest love, do not despair if this is my last letter. I am going where the battles are raging. My fate is unknown. Your beautiful heart-shaped face is like the first morning star, bright and clear. You are my hope, my pool of courage.*

Mind shaded by ghosts, limbs stiffened by the shock of her discovery, Nina unravelled herself from the hard floor. She sifted through the letters, their rustling carrying the echo of his presence. She pressed Nicolò's letters close to her chest. They were hers to keep now. From the bedroom window she enjoyed a clear view of the flowing waters of the River Fastino, dappled by sunlight. That river had always been her favourite spot in Bastiani. It had the power to calm her, as if by letting her gaze wander over its unclouded waters she could see more lucidly within herself. The fog in her mind cleared. She knew what to do next. She would find out where Ambra was staying in Campobasso and fearless, she would confront her, as if she were an enemy not a friend. Hadn't Ambra already torn friendship to shreds?

'Then you'll have to give me a straight answer, my dear Ambra,' Nina mouthed silently into the sweltering air of the piazza.

Chapter Ten

The clamour of the city seeped through the shuttered window of the *Liceo.*

Ambra glanced around the classroom of the Campobasso High School now transformed into a prison by the Allies. She had never liked school and here she was locked up in an empty classroom, a blackboard and torn posters of Mussolini lining the wooden floorboards her only companions.

From the other side of the door, she heard raucous voices yelling, heavy footsteps pounding on tiled floors. Amidst the uproar, the soft refrain of a Bing Crosby song she recognised from her evenings at the Caffè Lupacchioli, reached her ears.

Then a strident voice shouted, 'You have a visitor.'

The door swung open, and a head of slick black hair appeared.

I knew he would come to rescue me. Ambra exhaled with relief. She uncrossed her legs and jumped up. She smoothed her skirt and ran her fingers through her hair hoping to look more presentable. Dick had never seen her dishevelled. She was always beautifully coiffured and made-up whenever they were together. Now her pleated skirt was stained with grease from the army vehicle that had bought her here. Her skin felt grainy and grimy to her touch and her hair hung down her back in unkempt coils.

An irate voice jolted her from her thoughts. 'What the hell were you thinking, Ambra? You better have a good explanation.' His hazelnut eyes shot with specks of red, widened with fury. A film of white saliva formed at the edge of his mouth. Something inside Ambra hardened. She swallowed then flared back at Dick, 'What was I thinking? How dare you! It was your men who arrested me and confiscated my camera. It's you who owes me an explanation.'

Dick opened his mouth wide, flashing his white teeth. 'I owe you an explanation! Ambra, you put me at risk by taking photographs of a military operation. I've done everything to help you . . .' He stopped and stared at the ground, shaking his head as if he could not believe all that he had done to help her.

'I got a jeep to take your friend to the mountains, remember? I even paid for the gas. I helped you find a beautiful apartment above Briscotti's Bakery. I even searched for your friend Nicolò Sansone. And this . . .' He gestured wildly. 'This is how you repay me?'

Ambra's lips trembled. 'Look what I have done for you and your Allies. I've risked everything to give you my photographs. They are proof of the atrocities the Fascists inflicted on our villages, our people.' She could no longer contain the feelings spiralling through her. 'Without me, you'd have no record of the murders in Fornelli. No images of poor Tommaso and Rita hanging outside their *baita,* or Bastiani in ruins. None of it!'

How could Dick—her Dick—be shouting at her like this? And to think that Werner had never once raised his voice at her. Not even when the photos she showed him of Nina and Nicolò were worthless to the Germans. Not even when she'd failed him.

'We paid you well, so you could afford to leave your hole of a village, as you yourself call it.' Dick's voice was heightened with exasperation, loud and jarring like the hee-hawing of a donkey. Ambra covered her ears with the palms of her hands. Hot tears of anger pricked her eyelids.

'And this is how you repay me? By imprisoning me in this classroom and stealing my Leica?'

Despite herself Ambra began to weep. She was shaking now; her knees buckled. She slid down to the wooden floor. Loud, strangling sobs reverberated across the room.

Then Dick's thick, muscly arms encircled her and held her close. Kneeling on the floor beside her, he kissed her hair and stroked her neck. The familiar scent of his shaving foam softened the edges of her rage. The intimate sensation of his chin brushing her cheek gave her a flicker of hope. It will be all right, she repeated silently to herself.

Dick kissed the tip of her nose. 'We can sort this out, baby. I'll get you out of here, I promise.' His tone had softened to the one she recognised, a rasping tenderness mingled with desire. 'But I'm afraid you'll have to tell me where the film is.'

Ambra's sobs settled in her chest. With the back of her hand, she wiped her salty tears mixed with streaks of sweat. She lifted her head, gazed at Dick with misty eyes and whimpered, 'I threw it away.'

'You did what?'

'I threw it,' she repeated, firmer this time. 'Across the Mainarde mountains.'

Dick pulled away from her, his face shot with a mixture of disbelief and exasperation.

'Why the hell would you do that?'

Ambra shrugged. The silence between them spread and diffused into the walls of the classroom, thick like stagnant water.

He lifted her chin with his forefinger. 'Tell me the truth. You owe me the truth, Ambra.'

His eyes, greeny-brown irises flecked with copper and green flecks, bored into her. She felt a shiver in the air.

'I panicked. That's all. I was scared so I . . . I threw the film. Across the mountains.'

It wasn't the truth, not entirely. But lying had always come naturally to Ambra. Lies trickled from her tongue like water from a tap. Now she was lying to Dick, her boyfriend who had been kind to her. Hadn't he helped her to settle into life in Maple Leaf City, accepted her as if she were one of the Allied women? Wasn't she treated better than the Campobasso *signorine* who had to make do with war rations and unstylish clothes? Dick had introduced her to American films and food and fashion. He'd even taught her a smattering of English. If it wasn't for Dick she would still be the Bastiani Post Office girl. Yet, it was Werner and his Leica that had given her the opportunity to record wartime horrors, be rewarded in lire and dollars and finally better herself. Without him, without the camera, she would have been forever hidden away in the depths of rural Molise.

Dick scratched his head. 'We need to find the film, Ambra. If photos of this operation end up in the wrong hands . . .'

'They won't,' she interrupted him. 'The film is there somewhere scattered across Monte Marrone, amidst the bullets and helmets from the battle. Maybe a goat is nibbling on it right now. I was angry they confiscated my camera, so I threw the film where they'd never find it. There's nothing to worry about. I only took photos of the trees, the sky, my friend Nina and her new baby.'

Dick pulled away and held Ambra at arm's length, his fingers digging into her shoulders, pinching her skin. A sliver of moonlight stole through the shutters of the window, enhancing the taut lines of his face, the pallor of his skin. Beads of sweat gleamed on his temples.

'We'll tell them you panicked,' he said slowly. 'We'll say you threw the film in a moment of fear but there's nothing compromising to worry about. But we're going to find it. Together. We'll search for as long as it takes. Understood?'

Ambra nodded, acquiescent and dutiful. 'As long as it takes,' she echoed. 'But they have to return my camera to me.'

'Forget the damn camera, Ambra. There's only so much I can do. Now let's get you out of here.' He stood up, placed his arm under Ambra's elbow and hoisted her to her feet. He wiped the streaks of tears from her skin and kissed her lips.

She opened her mouth, sensing his tongue against her teeth. Ambra, flooded with a glow akin to pride and satisfaction, kissed Dick back. She may have lost her Leica, but she had protected Nina and little Nicolino.

Chapter Eleven

It was late afternoon when Ambra made her way to Piazza Savoia to meet Dick. He had chosen the wrought-iron gate at the entrance to Villa De Capoa as their meeting place. Ambra had visited the gardens once before with Werner. He had loved wandering along the labyrinthine paths lined with towering sequoias, cedars of Lebanon and cypress trees. Dick usually preferred the polished ambiance of the newly named Savoy Hotel or the lively bustle of Piccadilly Circus. This choice felt different.

When she saw Dick, pacing in front of the gate, dressed in civilian clothes, loose slacks and a chequered shirt, the muscles of her chest stiffened with worry.

He ran a hand through his hair and beckoned her towards him. He was shifting his weight from one foot to the other and looking around in a restless, agitated manner. When she approached, he didn't embrace her or utter a greeting. Instead, he swept his hand under her elbow and steered her swiftly through the gate and down one of the tree-lined paths. As they passed stone statues and ornate fountains, Dick glanced around them, behind them, as though convinced they were being followed. His face appeared longer, hollowed out. Shadows bruised the skin beneath his eyes.

'What is it, Dick? Is something wrong?' Ambra asked, attempting to break free from his grasp.

'I'll tell you when it's safe.'

'Safe?'

He didn't reply, just tightened his hold and led her to a grotto, hidden beneath the vast canopy of a sequoia tree. Only then did he turn her to face him, his hands settling gently on her shoulders.

'Ambra.' His voice dropped. 'You are in danger.'

'Me. Why? Is it because of my Leica?'

Her heart rate quickened. Had the Allies uncovered her relationship with Werner? That an enemy soldier had bribed her with a camera? Did the Allies believe she had been spying for the Germans? Would they arrest her for treason?

Dick scanned the area, again checking they were alone. He pulled Ambra towards him and brought his lips close to her ear.

'That disinfestation you witnessed: well, it wasn't what it seemed.'

'I thought so. I had a feeling there was something suspicious about it.'

'The Allies were making a film.'

'A film?'

'Yes, a propaganda film.'

Ambra's brow creased into a deep furrow. His words didn't make sense.

'They are making it for the folks back home,' Dick explained. 'To show how well the war effort is going, the battles we are winning, the victories, our successes. They want people to believe it's all worth it, that we're beating the Germans at every turn.'

'But why would the Allies destroy an innocent village in liberated Molise? Why would they make a film that was a lie?'

'It was staged because they can't show the truth of men blown to smithereens. Or how treacherous it is to cross the Apennines and free villages and towns surrounded by mines, bullets, grenades.'

Dick, with his skin bronzed from the Molise sun and hearty laugh, had never spoken to Ambra of the horrors he had witnessed during his time in Italy. These were clearly truths not meant for the ears of the civilian population. Yet sometimes words had floated in the air, hissed between gritted teeth in English and Italian: waste of young life, fighting for what, torn flesh, shattered skulls. Dick carried himself as though the anguish he witnessed was a burden he could bear, as though it were merely part of his duty. But perhaps his courage was a mask, and beneath the warm smile and jocular demeanour, he bore silent wounds.

'If they ever find that film, you'll be in danger,' he continued. 'Tell me the truth, did you take photographs of the mission?'

Despite herself, she could sense her cheeks flood with heat.

'No, I've told you. I simply panicked. I was worried about the Leica, so I threw the film across the mountain.'

But she could tell he didn't believe her. She could see it in the flashing of his eyes, the creases around his chin. Without thinking, Ambra reached up and smoothed a wisp of hair that fell across his forehead. He caught her hand and pressed his lips to her palm.

'And there is more.'

'What, Dick? What?' Ambra sensed a flurry of fear travel along her spine and wrap itself around her heart.

'They know your secret, Ambra. You've never shared it with me.'

Like a burning flame, shame engulfed her.

'So you know.' Unshed tears misted her eyes. 'That was then. I have changed like so many others in our country. We were enemies back then; now we are friends. And I've proved it with everything I have done to help you. You've benefited from the images I took with that German Leica. Without them you would not know what they did to our villages, our people.'

'But you could be arrested, branded a traitor.'

'For what?' she hissed the words through closed lips. 'For having a relationship with a German? Or for seeing the truth?'

'For hindering the Allied war effort.'

Hindering the war effort? Is that what she had done when she passed the film over to Nina? And where had Nina hidden the film?

'I have protected you up to now but . . .' He hesitated. 'How long before they come to find you and me?'

'Are you in trouble, Dick?'

'Not yet, but we haven't found the film. We searched the mountain yesterday and it's not there.'

'I told you I don't have the film.'

'Listen, I am leaving the country. Come with me. You don't have a choice. I can't protect you if you stay here.'

'What do you mean you are leaving?'

'My father has had a serious heart attack. He's dying.' He stroked Ambra's cheek and stared straight ahead. 'I'm now excused from active service. I'm an only child, you see. I'm leaving Campobasso tomorrow night. I have a passage from Bari to Southampton and then across the Atlantic to Canada.' He hesitated then continued. 'Come with me, Ambra. Come with me to Montreal. I don't care about your past. Marry me, and we'll start a new life far away from war-torn Europe.'

Canada. Freedom. Skies without war planes whizzing above. Another country, far away, where the war in Europe was a hazy speck on a distant landscape.

The temptation was there. Was she ready to leave her country?

'Why are you helping me, Dick?'

'Because I love you. Come with me, Ambra,' he repeated, almost pleading. 'Meet me tomorrow at the station.'

'I can't,' she whispered. 'It's too quick and I don't have any documents.'

'I have arranged everything for you.'

Something exploded within her. What appeared as freedom suddenly felt like a trap. And Ambra didn't like it. She wanted to be the one to choose when and how.

She turned and walked away leaving him standing there alone, her heels clacking against the cobblestones. She could feel his gaze boring into her back, following her as she passed the stone fountains and elaborate statues under the deep crimson sky.

By the time she returned to her apartment, dusk had settled over Campobasso. The shutters over Briscotti's Bakery were closed for the night, but the air still carried the faintest trace of baked bread. Ambra climbed upstairs and stopped in front of her apartment. The door was wide open. Her heart clanged in her chest. She knew she had locked the door. She stepped inside and looked around—clothes scattered on the floor, earth from the overturned pots of geraniums soiling the balcony floor, her bedside drawers half-opened.

Her hand flew to her throat. What had they done? She began to shake and couldn't stop. They were looking for the film. They had come to her apartment.

She could be next.

Chapter Twelve

The narrow, steep alleyways of Campobasso, eroded by centuries of town folk marching up and down, reminded Nina of a spider's web. And here she was trapped inside. The paving stones gleamed white under the bright midday sun. They hurt her eyes, forcing her to squint. The oppressive heat of the day weighed heavily on her chest, much like her thoughts.

In the piazza, Allied soldiers were lounging at oblong tables along the bustling main street, drinking and smoking, laughing loudly. Nina stopped in front of the bakery, glanced at the note in her hand, scribbled with Ambra's address in Ivo's handwriting. She climbed the staircase and with a shaky hand knocked on the door of Ambra's apartment.

'Nina? Has something happened.' The delicate skin under Ambra's eyes, thin as eggshells and tinged with faint purple veins, bore traces of sleepless nights. 'Is *papà* unwell? Tell me, is he ill?'

'Your father is fine. But something has happened, you're right about that.'

'Is it about the film?'

Ambra reached out to take Nina's arm and steer her down the corridor to the tiny bedroom, but Nina jerked her arm away.

'I was trying to find a place to hide it in your bedroom and . . .' Tears pearled on Nina's lashes and for a long moment, she stood motionless. 'How could you, Ambra, how could you betray me?'

There was a curling of her lips, a defiance in her posture.

'What are you talking about?' A white ring framed the curves of Ambra's lips; her chest rose and fell with deep, uneven breaths.

Nina rummaged inside her bag and pulled out a brown envelope, the kind Ivo sold at the Post Office. She tore it open with her teeth and with trembling fingers withdrew four pieces of paper, slightly yellow at the edges. She began to shake them in front of Ambra's eyes. The papers fluttered like flags in the wind.

'What are these letters, addressed to me, doing in your tin box hidden underneath your torn friendship handkerchief?' Nina's voice rose louder and shriller. 'What have I ever done to you, Ambra? I thought you were my friend. But you're not, you're my enemy. You stole letters from me, letters that would have meant so much during those long months when I kept my pregnancy hidden from the world. They were mine to read. Not yours. I should have known not to trust you.'

'I meant to tell you. I swear I did.' Ambra drew a deep sigh. 'After you gave birth to little Nicolino, I felt so ashamed. The easiest thing was to dismiss everything I had done wrong to you from my mind. Instead I did whatever I could to help you keep little Nicolino.'

'But why?' Nina's voice cracked with raw pain. 'Why would you hide those letters from me and tear our pact to pieces?'

'You pushed me away. You made me feel like I didn't matter to you. And when the first letter arrived, I was so angry I showed it to the Sansones.'

'You did what?' Nina's face flushed crimson with fury. 'You gave Nicolò's letter to his parents?' She stabbed her finger at Ambra's chest. 'So it was you, who told them about us? We wondered how they knew we were delivering food to the internees.'

'I was angry with you. And hurt. Nicolò was everything to you and I, your friend, was nothing. So when they asked me to keep all future letters safe until they returned from Salò, I agreed. The Sansones didn't want Nicolò's letters falling into the wrong hands. He would be arrested for being an anti-Fascist. They said it was to protect him and they promised to pay me.'

'Pay you?' Nina's rasping voice crackled with rage. 'Pay you for spying on me, for stealing their son's letters?' The words writhed on her tongue like droplets of poison.

'Think! In a way I protected you both by hiding them. Think what would have happened if they had fallen into the wrong hands.'

'Yet you were happy to betray us both.' Nina's head was spinning. 'And now I'm going to betray you.' Nina pressed her teeth into her lower lip. She pulled the roll of film from her pocket and shook it in front of Ambra's eyes. 'I'll hand the Castelnuovo roll of film to the Allies.' Eyes tight, mouth puckered, Nina fired the words between clenched teeth.

'Don't.' Ambra stepped forward and tried to reach for the film. 'You mustn't.'

Nina grasped the film tightly in her fist and hid it behind her back. 'I won't give it to you.'

'There is more to it than you think. Much more.'

Ambra began to reveal what Dick had told her about the false disinfestation in Castelnuovo, about her being branded a traitor. She waved her arm around the room. 'You can see it was ransacked last night. The Allied military government was searching for proof against me.'

When she finished she sank onto a chair, fingers pressing her temples. 'You see now why it's important we keep the film safely hidden.' Ambra kept her gaze directly on Nina. 'Dick is going back to Canada. His father is dying. He asked me to marry him and go with him.'

'You're leaving Italy?'

'I think it's for the best.' She hesitated. 'If they discover I have information about the disinfestation that the Americans want to hide, I could be in grave danger. You are safe, don't worry. Nobody knows I passed the film to you.' Ambra puffed the air out of her lungs. 'You must keep it hidden somewhere safe. It's the only proof we have of what they did.'

Ridges creased Nina's forehead into a deep scowl. 'The Allies have abandoned Castelnuovo. The village is still in ruins. Teresa hasn't returned to her home. Aurelio and Lidia wander around Molise with their *zampogna*, trying to raise money to rebuild the church, the homes.'

'Do they really believe the village was ruined for a disinfestation?'

'They do.'

Nina's shoulders relaxed, the skin of her face softened. Ambra was right. That film had to be kept hidden, no matter what Ambra had done to her. And she, Nina, would be its keeper until the right moment came.

'They won't find the film, Ambra. But I'm not doing it for you. I'm doing it for Castelnuovo, Teresa and Aurelio and for everyone in Bastiani. For our country still shaken by war.'

Incandescent slivers of sunlight filtered through the gaps in the shutters. Particles of white dust floated around the room. Silence dropped between them. Ambra coughed. 'Nina, I have something else to confess. I know where Nicolò is.'

Nina's heart galloped, pressing against her ribs. 'And you're telling me now?' It was as if a grenade had exploded at her feet. The muscles of her tummy clenched.

Nicolò. Nicolò. Nicolò. A tear squeezed out of the corner of her eye.

'Is he alive?'

'He's wounded. He's in a military hospital, not far from here.'

'Why didn't you tell me the moment you found out?'

'I tried. I came to Castelnuovo to tell you. But I was bundled away in an army vehicle and so much has happened since. It's this war that has taken the best and the worst out of me. I'm so sorry.'

Promises made and later broken. Lies, deceit, betrayal. Nina felt the weight of their friendship pact heavy on her heart but there was joy. Nicolò was alive and in Campobasso, almost within her reach.

Nina held the roll of film in the palm of her hand.

'Put your hand on it,' she ordered Ambra in a sharp tone. 'I will never forgive you for what you have done to me, but this is our new pact now. Not between us, but a promise for our people of Molise.'

Ambra stepped forward and carefully paced her hand on top of Nina's.

'This film is yours now. One day, we will need the photographs and we will tell the story of Castelnuovo.'

When the war and its shadows are far behind them, together they will decide when to reveal what happened that day at Castelnuovo al Volturno. One day the truth will come to light.

Chapter Thirteen

Outside Ambra's apartment swallows jostled and swooped in the midday air. A rhythmic clip-clopping of hooves made Nina raise her head. A local *contadino* trotted past her on his mule, his cart brimming with potatoes and tomatoes. He tipped his cap to Nina and smiled a broad, toothless grin. Streaks of soft sunlight painted angular shadows across his weathered face, catching the stubble of his chin.

Thunderclaps rumbled in the distance. Nina climbed the steep alleyways towards Castello Monforte. A cluster of leaden clouds loomed above its four thick towers. The wind was picking up, fast, warm against her cheeks. The air felt clammy against her skin. Her breath stung under her ribs as she breathed in the moist July air.

Nina felt dizzy from nerves. Pleasure, anxiety: a tumult of feelings she couldn't name. She increased her pace and arrived just as hot drops of rain soaked the cobblestoned street.

Inside the hospital walls, she was assailed by the constant passing by of frenzied doctors in white coats, nurses in blue uniforms and white veils, the cacophony of clattering, shrieks and odours. She flattened herself against a wall in the corridor, feeling like an intruder in such a hive of activity. A sense of nausea overwhelmed her. It was the overpowering stench of wounds, perspiration, blood. She shivered. This was the outcome of war. Men and women, casualties of the madness of other people's power, of the conflicting forces of politics.

What did it matter if Molise was liberated? Conflict and battles still raged in other regions of her country. Gino was fighting somewhere in the Apennines of Emilia-Romagna. There was hope Tuscany would be the next region to gain freedom. And maybe soon Gino could come home. At least Nicolò was back. Nina's gaze wandered along rows of camp beds occupied by men in bandages, plaster casts and slings. She searched for him amongst their shattered, forlorn faces.

A thunderclap resonated through the sky with a sudden, deafening roar. A blast of cold air blanketed Nina then a window in the corridor slammed shut.

She jolted and turned her head.

Was that him, lying on the bed?

'Nicolò?' His name felt unfamiliar on her lips. It had been a long while since she had allowed it to venture from her thoughts to a sound.

His mouth broke into a weak smile and Nina noticed the gaps where his teeth were missing. A thick dressing covered one ear, held on by a narrow bandage wrapped around his head. A plaster cast encased his foot. He raised his head and peered at her. His blue eyes had lost their former brightness and had borrowed instead the hardness of stone. She shuddered at the thought of the pain and fear he must have endured.

'Nina?' His mouth silently formed her name. His eyes seemed to soften. She gave him a sad smile, mouth dry, throat parched.

'Nina,' he pronounced her name again, softly this time. 'How . . . did you . . .' His brown coppery hair hung around his face, gaunt, emaciated but still handsome.

To her ears, his voice sounded like waves washing against rocks, stirring vivid memories of their time together when he whispered tender words of affection. Memories of those summer weeks when the sun and the stars witnessed their love. That was only months ago. It felt like an eternity.

Their eyes reached out towards each other, but their bodies remained still. The desire to run her fingers across his lips, trace the line of his jaw and feel his breath against hers overwhelmed her. Her throat ached with tears. She longed to stroke his cheek, his wounded ear, to whisper: 'nothing has changed, my love.'

But then everything had changed.

Bastiani was not the same village, the villa lay empty, the gardens in ruins. And his son . . . How would he cope with knowing he was a father?

She leant over him. His skin was ashen, as grey as a winter sky; his sunken cheeks made his nose seem more prominent than Nina remembered. New fine strands of silver streaked his hair. It was as if these changes were a testimony to the horrors he had witnessed. He looked so frail.

Nicolò stretched out his arm, cupping her tiny hand in his large one. She noticed it trembled, like his lips. He guided it towards his mouth. She swallowed, a sensation of sweet warmth stirring in her belly. With a gentle pressure of his half-opened lips on her fingers, he blew a soft kiss into the middle of her palm. She caught a glimpse of his blue eyes brimming with tears and saw in him both the child he had been and the child she'd given birth to. Their faces merged in her mind. She had to tell him she'd given birth to his child. She twitched when he held her right hand and stroked her finger, Ivo's metal ring shining against her sunburnt skin.

'You're married? That's why you never wrote back. I understand now, Nina.' His gaze pierced through her.

She lowered her eyes. 'It's not what you think, my love.' Her voice was steady despite tangles of unease pulling at her heart. She removed the ring from her finger and let it drop into one of the large pockets of her dress.

Words rippled through the air as she related her story. The letters Ambra had concealed in the tin box, the discovery she was pregnant whilst locked up in the cells of the Italian Fascist police, her work as a *staffetta* under the name Luisa, the sudden birth, the days in Castelnuovo. The baby boy, who reminded her of him every moment of the day. She told him all this slowly, watching his reaction, not wanting to say too much and at the same time not being able to stop. Words slipped from her lips like water gushing from a rock. But she kept the details of the film to herself. For now, that would be her one remaining secret with Ambra, the last shred of the friendship they'd once had.

Nicolò listened, the nerve on his eyelid fluttering like the beat of a drum.

'Our baby was born on 9th April, 1944, on the way to the Santissima Addolorata. I named him Nicolino Libero, to remind him and myself of you, his father and the freedom we fought for.'

Tears welled in his eyes; a dreamlike look appeared on his face. 'A son. My son?'

'He has your blue eyes, your wide forehead. When I first saw him, my heart melted. It was as if it were you in my arms.'

He pulled her closer. Nina inhaled the whiff of medicaments, a blend of disinfectant and herbal ointments. It was Nicolò's smell now, she told herself, with a pinch of her heart. She placed a hand on his wounded ear and kissed it.

Careful not to hurt him she pressed her forehead against his cheek, the soft stubble of his beard a comforting sensation against her skin.

He pulled himself up on the bed, creases at the side of his eyes. 'Am I still important to you?'

'I love you, Nicolò. I have never stopped loving you. I couldn't imagine loving anyone other than you, and our little Nicolino.'

'Nina, I dreamt of you every single night. I've seen so many terrible things and it was your heart-shaped face and raven hair that kept me going.'

The storm had ceased. The clouds had dissolved to reveal the expanse of a peach-coloured sky. Speckles of sunlight filtered through the window, tinting the bed sheets the colour of ripened wheat. She wished she still knew the small things that mattered to him: the cigarettes he smoked, the wine he drank, the books he read.

'What happened to you, my love? Tell me what you've been through, all the things you had to witness.'

A brief glimmer of fear shot across his eyes. 'We were caught somewhere on the Winter Line, trying to reach Forlì.' His chin quivered. 'We were crossing a river in the dark. There was a landmine. Then shelling. Metal fragments from a hand grenade tore through my ear. A bullet shattered my foot.' He pointed to the plaster cast. 'And I was just the translator, helping the Allied forces navigate the language. I didn't have to fight, I had no weapons and yet . . .' His voice trailed off, heavy with memories. 'I got away lightly. Some of the others didn't make it; they didn't stand a chance.' He took several breaths, holding back tears. 'They were flung into the air, pieces of limbs scattered around me like crumbs of bread.' He took a deep inhale. The depth of weariness and pain in Nicolò's blank eyes touched Nina's core.

'How did you get back to Campobasso?'

'They carried me for miles, then took me by mule until I could get some form of medical aid. Finally, I was transferred to a vehicle and brought to this hospital.'

'You're safe now. You can recuperate, mend your wounds.'

He blinked and uttered softly, his voice stirring the air with a deep sadness, 'Some wounds can never heal.' A dense sorrow settled over Nina. She stroked a lock of hair from his forehead.

Would he ever be able to return to the life he had known before? She hoped her love for him would heal the wounds of his soul.

He faced the window then returned his gaze to Nina. A shard of light warmed the greenish tint in his deep blue eyes. She gathered his frail frame towards her.

'We've found each other now. Don't speak. Just rest.'

Nina pulled up a chair next to Nicolò's bed and laid her head on his chest. He caressed her hair. He ran his long fingers through the thick flowing curls cascading onto her shoulders. He ruffled it, then stroked her cheek.

'It's the three of us now,' he whispered through the locks of her hair.

Nina nodded. A silence pregnant with expectation filled the air like a lover's breath.

Their past, present and future were merging into one.

A sensation of fragile peace sifted through Nina. It settled around her heart.

Post Office

The sun dips low over the purple-glazed mountains of Molise, casting an amber glow across the piazza. The afternoon light is hazy with apricot-orange clouds. The scent of freshly turned earth lingers in the air, blending with the faint aroma of roses and lavender.

The Post Office, a symbol of connection, bears the weight of new beginnings. It seals the memory of what has been and the hope of what could be. Bastiani has changed but its heart, like my humble stone building, has endured.

I stand as a silent witness to the passing of time and the upheaval of battles. The last vestiges of German occupation have disappeared from our shores. 8th May, 1945, Germany unconditionally surrendered its military forces in Europe. Italy is free, liberated. A truce finally brokered. Millions rejoiced. For how long will the traces of war stain our fields, our hearts, our bodies? Fascists slink back to their postwar lives; some now imprisoned, others pardoned as if nothing has happened. Like a slate wiped clean, we continue with the day-to-day effort of harvesting our fields, picking olives from the silver branches, sowing seeds, baking bread, teaching our children and sending letters to loved ones. But the loss of human life is far from over. Unexploded shells and bombs lie hidden in our fields, sown by two opposing armies, harbingers of more deaths yet to come.

It took Gino several weeks to return to Bastiani, his cheekbones sharp and pointed. He is back home, living on the Caruso farm with Nina, Nicolò and his nephew Nicolino. It was a relief to his worn-out body, after surviving for months amongst the partisans in the mountains outside Forlì, washing in streams, fighting for his beliefs, fed by some civilians, betrayed by others. The storeroom is vibrant once again. This time guarded whispers are replaced with loud voices determined to make the world a better place. Indignant and passionate, Gino talks to Esther and Mariolina about starting a new socialist party in Bastiani. Ideas flow, voices rise and there is fire in their eyes.

Now Gino has a new mission: he is to battle for the rights of the *contadini* and demand compensation from the new Italian government for the partial destruction of Bastiani and the villages nearby. There is always a wrong to put right, he shouts. Anger flares in the storeroom as they discussed the disinfestation of Castelnuovo, the brutal murders of Fornelli, the many Italian men still missing in action in Greece, Albania or in the mountains of our own land, the hundreds and thousands of Allied soldiers, Italian and German men killed in battle.

When the Sansones are mentioned, the storeroom settles into a hushed silence. Nicolò has helped to arrange a pardon for his parents together with a promise to raise funds to rebuild the village and their villa and purchase a new bell for the Santa Croce tower. Not everyone is happy. Gino, Esther and Mariolina say nothing, but their contempt is palpable. It is another wound to bear. But Ivo and Don Simone believe in the redemptive power of justice.

We are a family again, but a different one. Ambra, my Post Office girl, is far away across the ocean in her new home in Montreal. Nina comes most days to help Ivo sort the mail, organise letters into piles, invoices into folders. She checks the ink has not dried out in the rubber stamps. She seems at peace here among my walls. Nina and Nicolò, married by Don Simone the day Nicolò returned in a military van from the hospital in Campobasso, have settled into the farmhouse with their child and Gino. They are slowly rebuilding their lives. Most days, Nicolò accompanies Nina up the path through the arch to the Post Office with a walking stick in his hand. The rusty metal nails in Nicolò's leg cause him pain and a limp that he will carry for the rest of his days. His back is bent, his jaw clenched with exertion. In his free hand, he guides little Nicolino who toddles next to his father. Nicolò's wounded ear has healed but he remains partially deaf. Yet, the dentists in the military hospital fitted him with brand-new teeth before his release. He is almost whole.

Stone by stone we rebuild our village; we mend our souls and we spare a thought for Celestina's son Giovannino, still missing somewhere on the battlefields of Albania.

The end of war has brought peace but below the surface other battles rage. Italy is free, we are all free, but the political and the personal are bound together. Sometimes the shackles of the past take time to heal. And the scars remain embedded, deep and unyielding, in the soil of our earth.

Fleeting moments, fleeting lives, we are all almost whole.

The radio crackles. An announcement. *It is finally the end of the Second World War, not just for Europe but for the entire world.*

The page of the calendar rustles.

It is the 2nd September, 1945, Saint Zenone martyr's day.

Today is the start of a new chapter.

Chapter Fourteen

The apartment on the corner of Henri-Julien and Jean-Talon was modest by Canadian standards but larger than the cramped lodgings in Campobasso and more airy than the rooms she'd shared with her father in the Post Office, with its small kitchen nestled at the back.

Everything was different about life in Montreal. The vast skies, the red-bricked buildings and tram-lined streets were a world away from the cobbled piazza and mule-drawn carts of Bastiani, from the pomp and elegance she had observed in Villa Sansone. In Montreal, life was buzzing and vibrant with jazz clubs and movie theatres, many more than the ones she had visited with Dick in Campobasso. A new one seemed to pop up each week, Ambra noticed with excitement. Yet there were threads of familiarity in the sounds and smells around her. Dialects from every corner of Italy mingled in the air, their lilts and rhythms tugging at her heart. The tavernas and shops that sold specialities from different Italian regions gave Ambra a sense of belonging.

Shortly after they arrived in the apartment, Dick asked Ambra to close her eyes and open her hands, palms up towards the ceiling. She obediently did what she was asked, and when she felt the weight of the heavy box in her hands, she immediately knew what it was. Her eyes snapped open. She focused on the box in her palms.

'It's a camera!'

'A Kodak Vigilant with an optical viewfinder and an adjustable lens,' Dick said, a note of smugness and pride filtering through his words. 'I promised you I'd buy you another camera.' Ambra placed the box containing the Kodak on the coffee table next to the tall glass door leading onto the balcony and flung her arms around Dick's neck.

'*Grazie*, Dick,' she sobbed in Italian and then switched to English. 'Thank you. Thank you. Now I can record all the sights of my new city. There's so much to capture, so much to remember.'

They laughed. Dick placed his hands on her waist just under her ribs. He lifted her off the floor and swung her around the small living room, her feet almost knocking a lamp off the table.

Dick was a good man, kind and attentive. He treated her well. He was aware of how much Ambra loved going to movie theatres, something Bastiani with its cobbled street, old *lavatoio* and stubborn mules could never have offered her. He took her regularly, buying her popcorn and holding her hand as they watched film after film. And for a while, Ambra was happy.

That night, she accompanied Dick to the Loew Vaudeville theatre in Little Italy to watch a screening of *Gone with the Wind*. She was excited to see the elaborate dresses Vivienne Leigh would be wearing. She dug her hand into a carton of popcorn Dick was holding. She licked her fingers and settled into her seat to watch a short documentary film before the main feature. The background music filled the theatre with a booming sound. The screen flickered in black and white to a mountainous scene.

'That looks like my Molise,' she whispered to Dick.

The camera zoomed in over a rocky landscape to a tiny village of stone dwellings perched on the slopes of a mountain.

'Wait a minute. This is Castelnuovo.' Ambra turned to Dick, a feeling of dread gnawing at the mouth of her stomach.

A frenzy of action filled the screen. Mesmerised Ambra witnessed the stones of the bell tower collapse to the ground. Then there were hand grenades, artillery. Amongst a cloud of dust German and Allied soldiers clashed in the piazza, engaged in hand-to-hand combat. A wounded soldier was lifted on a stretcher to an ambulance.

Fury bubbled within Ambra. Her eyes popped with rage and injustice as she relived the scenes she had witnessed with Nina three years ago.

'This is not possible. It's a lie. These scenes are fabricated. Say something, Dick,' she whispered and squeezed Dick's fingers.

He whispered back, 'Shh, my darling. I can't do anything now.'

'This was staged,' she shouted aloud. 'I know because I was there. And it was our *Alpini* forces together with Moroccan soldiers who conquered Monte Marrone. The English and Americans couldn't conquer that impregnable mountain.'

'You need to keep your voice down, Ambra. Just watch the film and we'll discuss it later.'

'I can't keep quiet, Dick. They've taken a peaceful, impoverished village and turned it into a battleground to prove how successful the war effort in Italy has been. It's a disgrace.' The words hissed from Ambra's tight lips.

As other viewers in the rows close to Ambra began to twitch and mutter at her disturbance, she picked herself up and marched outside. She pulled a cigarette from her handbag, lit it and puffed angry wisps of smoke into the crisp night air. The sky above was littered with stars. Ambra raised her eyes and thought of the night skies in Bastiani where the mountains loomed above the village and the moon hung low. For the first time since her arrival in Canada she missed her home, her father. She wished she could be there to tell them what she had just witnessed. Two hot, angry tears slid down her cheeks.

Dick sidled up next to her, Ambra's coat draped over his arm. 'Are you okay, my love?'

'I can't bear to stay and watch the movie,' she spat out the words, indignation clogging her throat. 'Not now. Not after what I've just seen. There was no battle, Dick. No disinfestation. The villagers were conned. We were all conned. You told me yourself.'

Dick sighed, his breath clouding in the night air. 'Ambra, we've all suffered. All of us. Don't think just because I say nothing to you, that I don't dream night after night of air raids, combat, hunger, my men dying in a foreign land so far away from their own homes, their own families. This is war. Let it go.'

'Let it go!' she cried. 'But this battle wasn't a war. How many times do I have to repeat it. It's a lie. Castelnuovo was a liberated village. We were getting on with our lives trying to recover after the German invasion of Molise. We were trying to live again.' She began to sob, her whole body shaking uncontrollably. 'The truth must come out. We owe it, Dick. I owe it to my people, to my country.'

He placed his hands on Ambra's shoulder. 'Ambra. Don't rock the boat. You are here now. You've married a Canadian.' He shook her, as if trying to make her see sense. '*You're* a

Canadian. This is your new home. What good will it do to dredge this up?'

Ambra shook herself free from Dick's hold. 'What good will it do?' She was screaming now, her words a torrent of fury. 'When we arrived here in Quebec, you proudly told me the motto of Montreal, is *Concordia Salus*, "well-being through harmony". The city is open to the world, you told me. Everyone lives in harmony in Montreal. But in order to have harmony, we must have truth. Dick, we have a duty to reveal what really happened that day in Castelnuovo.'

Ambra stopped shouting and took a deep inhale. Tears pooled in her eyes. She collapsed against the wall of the movie theatre, deflated. A couple with their arms entwined passed them on the pavement, staring, tutting, wondering what the row between two lovers could possibly be about.

Dick's stare bored into Ambra. There was something she had never seen before in his hazel irises, in the compact and stubborn setting of his jaw. His breath came thick and wild through his nostrils.

'You do nothing, you hear me? Nothing. You mention it to no one. Now you can see why you needed to leave Italy. Forget what you have seen. This is the country you have a duty towards now.'

With that, he turned and marched away, his long strides disappearing into the shadows of Henri-Julien Street.

It was their first row.

Something clicked inside her, like a light switched on in a darkened cellar. The day she had been waiting for had finally come.

That night Ambra slept alone in the apartment. She didn't know where Dick had gone or whether he would return the following day. She pulled out a pen and a sheet of crisp white paper from the top drawer of the counter in the kitchen and began to write.

The next day she posted the letter to Nina and walked with her Kodak camera all the way to the St Lawrence River. The sun was high in the sky, dazzling, glittering. She focused the lens. The reflection of sunlight on the river, like patches of shimmering gold, reminded Ambra of the River Fastino stained with red and orange smudges from the Molise sunshine. She pressed the shutter, again and again. Images of her new life merged into memories of her old one. She lowered the camera and gazed at the swirling waters of the St Lawrence River.

'What should I do?' she muttered into the still morning air as if willing the river to whisper back.

'Do I stay? Or do I go?'

She stood there for a moment, watching, waiting. Then she placed the Kodak back in its case, turned and began to walk slowly towards the streetcar that would take her back to her apartment on Henri-Julien Street.

Chapter Fifteen

The silver-leafed olive trees shimmered in the oblique sunlight. The orchard trees bowed under the weight of small golden plums, and the hazelnut bushes were heavy with leather-coloured nuts. Outside the farmyard, the path to the village arch was dappled with light. The trees overhead swayed gently in the September breeze. Several leaves were russet brown from the heat and lack of summer rain. In the morning light the mountain tops were grainy white and the air smelled faintly of autumn—earthy, crisp and bittersweet.

Wherever Nina walked, the ghosts walked with her: her parents, the shadow of the village Bastiani once was and Nicolò and Gino, both shadows of the men they had been before the war. At night, Nina felt those scars most acutely. Curled up with Nicolò in the bed they shared, she listened to his breathing, uneven and shallow. She would awaken to his strangled cries, knowing he was trapped once more in the horrors of memory. In those moments, she would press her body against his, whispering soothing words, her voice steady even as her heart ached.

In the next room, Gino also slept fitfully, his rest punctuated by shouts and screams. Nina often thought of the two men and how the war had shaped them into fractured mirrors of each other; Nicolò quiet and burdened, Gino brimming with a restless energy that seemed almost reckless. The weight of the past lingered over them, a presence that neither could escape.

That morning the piazza was quiet. Soft splashes of water interrupted the stillness. Ivo was watering the basil and geranium pots adorning the outside walls of the Post Office. Nina watched him for a moment, before crossing the piazza to join him.

'This is my job,' she said with a chuckle and took the watering can from his hands. Her voice carried an edge of familiarity that spoke of three years of shared routine. Ivo grinned and kissed her on both cheeks.

'How would I ever manage without you?' His weathered face creased with warmth. Then, as if only just remembering, he added. 'Oh, Nina. There are two letters waiting for you on the counter.'

He scratched his head. 'One is from Ambra, from Montreal, another from the south.'

'Another letter from Ambra? But we only just received news from her yesterday.'

'It's marked "PRIVATE AND CONFIDENTIAL" on the envelope.'

The vein on the back of his hand pulsed visibly, as though he could already sense the weight of the letter's contents.

Nina finished tending to the plants then placed the watering can on the ground next to a pot of basil. She walked inside and sidled up to the counter. There they were, waiting for her to bring to life the words written on the pages. The postmark of *Campo Accoglienza, Santa Maria del Bagno* on one envelope and the writing 'PRIVATE AND CONFIDENTIAL' on the other.

She held the envelopes in her hands, wondering which one to open first. Ambra's letters came as regularly as the passing of weeks and were usually addressed to Ivo. They were a lifeline for the village. Ivo would beckon everyone into the Post Office, packed with villagers huddled around him, eager to hear the latest news of Ambra's life in Montreal, a fantasy to those who remained in Bastiani.

Ambra wrote about the different foods she ate, the orange juleps and daiquiris she drank, ice-cold bottles of Coca-Cola, the movies she saw with Dick at the Leuwe Vaudeville cinema, the large cars and wide sidewalks. As an Italian war bride, she felt at home in Little Italy, with the Jean-Talon market and ample movie theatres nearby.

But that day the words 'PRIVATE AND CONFIDENTIAL' on the envelope addressed only to Nina alerted her. Yet she decided to take some time to compose herself. She would read Malka's letter first.

Dear Nina,

A new life is ahead of me. The Red Cross has found me passage to America. In a week I will leave Santa Maria del Bagno with new documents and regular visas. Anna Rossi will once again become Malka Schwartz, the real me.

As she read, Nina heard Malka's soft voice, her Italian accented with the melodious tones of her native Polish. Nina could picture Malka's fleshy lips, her greeny-blue eyes shining.

I will never forget what you all did for me. You had the courage to go against the rules of the camp in order to alleviate our confinement. As a sign of gratitude, I have drawn a small picture that I slipped inside this envelope. Think of me.

Con tutto l'affetto,
tua *Malka*

The drawing was the size of a child's hand. Nina held it with two fingers, a smile of surprise sketched across her face. It was Palazzo Nonno in via della Libertà. She even included the oak tree with its sprawling branches where Nina and Nicolò would wait to deliver baskets of food.

Nina placed the drawing on the counter and sat down on a stool. Emotion and memories of that time washed over her. Only last week when visiting *Maestra* Anna, she'd noticed the door of the palazzo was half-open. The windows were shut. She'd decided to step inside. To her surprise, the air was still thick with the smell of cooked cabbage and sickness, remnants of a time when the house had been full of struggles and pain. The small stifling rooms with their cracked walls seemed to close in around her, sucking out her breath. Memories of faces pressed down on her. Those stark white walls were alive with the presences of the women who had been interned here, urging her to listen, urging her to remember.

She folded the drawing and placed it on top of Malka's letter on the counter.

Beside it was the shiny white envelope with Ambra's familiar, sprawling handwriting on it. It seemed as if it was pulsating, beckoning her to read what was written inside. What was Ambra about to reveal to her? Nina ripped open the envelope and read with caution.

Dear Nina,

This is for you alone.

Dick and I were at the movie theatre tonight. A documentary was shown on the screen. Nina, you won't believe it. It was the battle of Castelnuovo. It was exactly what we witnessed that day. They're using it to glorify the war effort, pretending Castelnuovo was still occupied, and pretending the Allies had won the battle against the Germans.

I could hardly breathe. I squeezed Dick's hand so hard I'm surprised I didn't break a bone.

Nina stopped reading. Ambra had always known a day would come when they would finally get to talk about what really happened at Castelnuovo al Volturno. But to hear that footage was being shown in Canada, perhaps all over the world, as a triumph of the Allied campaign felt like a cruel joke.

Her eyes drifted back to the letter.

I know and trust you have kept the film safe for me. But now is the time. You must print those photos and send them to a national newspaper. The world has to know what really happened in Castelnuovo that day in June three years ago—not the victory paraded across the screen that I witnessed this evening, but the chaos, the loss and the unspeakable cost.

Nina lowered the letter. Her thoughts turned to poor Teresa, still unable to live in the derelict cottage she had willingly shared, opening up her warm heart to Nina and Nicolino. Then she thought of Lidia and Aurelio dressed in their traditional cloaks and hats, trailing their *zampogna* all over the region in an attempt to earn a crumb.

Nina held the letter against her chest, her breath shallow.

Do whatever you can to get the images developed. Together, we will prove what really happened.

Tua affezionata *Ambra*

Her mind was spinning. Nina had kept the film, hidden in that battered tin box where she had found Nicolò's letters and the torn friendship handkerchief, knowing its power, its truth.

It was now time.

The weight of Ambra's words pressed down on her. It was Ambra's film, but it wasn't just Ambra's story. It was hers, too. That was the pact they'd made.

*

The roll of film fitted perfectly into the palm of her hand. Nina closed her fist around it, until she felt the hard metal piercing her skin. Shots of adrenaline sizzled through Nina's bones. She opened her fist. The black case gleamed under the pearly morning light. She felt as if Ambra were here, next to her. Holding the roll of film in her hand was like clasping the *fazzoletto*, the friendship pact they had bound together all those years ago. Their friendship, with its highs and lows, had brought them to this point. They were in this together, just like when they sat in the Post Office, their fingers poised over the keyboard of the Olivetti. But this time there would be no betrayal.

Nina descended the stairs from Ambra's bedroom and settled herself at the portable Olivetti typewriter in the storeroom. She slid the sheets of white paper through the rollers, interweaving them with mauve carbon paper to obtain more copies. Thoughts and sentences tumbled from her mind. She wished she could type faster. Her fingers trembled over the keys, her knuckles creaked, her palms were coated with sweat from concentration rather than from the heat of the day. She cursed when she typed an extra 'c' before the 'k', for the name of the American General Mark Clark who was in charge at the time. She wrote about Teresa, who had welcomed her and Nicolino into her humble home; about the searching hands of the soldiers as they inspected all the villagers for the hidden roll of film, their bodies shaking with fear, their minds quivering with uncertainty. Nina's heart swelled with affection, her fingers flew over the keys as she typed the lines praising the courage of the photographer, Ambra Tizzani.

Nina stretched her arms upwards to release the tension that had gripped her body. A sense of satisfaction and accomplishment filled her, knowing she had made progress in revealing what really happened that summer's day in June 1944. With a swift movement, she slid the papers out of the typewriter, the ink still fresh on the crisp sheets.

Epilogue

Bastiani 1949

Post Office

I have stood here for decades, nestled in the heart of this village, my walls kissed by frost in winter and warmed by heat in summer. I have seen the comings and goings of every letter, every parcel, every whisper of resistance, hope and tears that have passed through my doors. And today, I feel it—a hum, a pulse of something extraordinary in the air. I see a village standing tall, unbroken, its voice carried beyond these hills for the world to hear.

The cold January air settles over the piazza, but no one seems to mind. They come slowly at first—Santino, Don Simone, Pietruzzo, Celestina and Renzo, Gino, Mariolina and Esther, amidst the other villagers, all bundled against the chill. And then come Teresa, Lidia and Aurelio from Castelnuovo and *Maestra* Anna from Vinchiaturo. They trickle into the piazza, wrapped in shawls and coats, their boots crunching on the frosted ground. The women's traditional Bastiani costumes are proudly on display: thick black woollen skirts sway as they walk, their lace-edged blouses bright and crisp, like wedding linens brought out of trunks. The men's knee breeches and white shirts mirror the stark contrast of snow and soil, while the women's shawls—scarlet, emerald, cobalt—add streaks of colour to the piazza. Celebratory music fills the square. Tambourines jingle, accordions breathe and the mournful notes of Pietruzzo's and Aurelio's *zampogne* swell and fade. The villagers' breath rises like steam, curling into the pale afternoon sky. Children dart through the crowd, cheeks flushed, scarves flapping as they race through the snow to the Post Office.

I have seen gatherings before, but none quite like this. Today, we celebrate not a feast day, nor a marriage, nor a harvest. Today, we celebrate words written by one of our own, images taken by another. Both hold our stories and our struggles.

It is Ivo who stands here now, hammer in hand, pinning the last sheet of newspaper to the wooden board outside my walls.

Bang. Bang.

Each blow of the hammer echoes through me like a heartbeat. Ivo steps back and smooths the edges of the newspaper with mittened hands. Powdery flecks of plaster fall to the ground like flour from Celestina's fingers.

'There!' he says, stepping back to admire his work. Nicolino clutches Ivo's hand and cranes his neck to see. His small finger shoots up, pointing at the bold capital letters printed across the page. 'Mother's name! Look, it says Caruso, Nina!' the boy exclaims. Ivo chuckles and ruffles Nicolino's curls.

'That's right, Nicolino, your mother, the new *maestra* of Bastiani, wrote those words. And see the photographs? They were taken by my daughter, your *Zia* Ambra. If only she were here with us today. How proud she would be to see her work displayed in the pages of *Il Paese*.'

My Ambra, I would shed a tear if I could. She is so far away in the city she has called her own, with oceans and land separating us. Ambra Tizzani, now a photographer for the *Standard Magazine* of Quebec. Even here, her name carries a quiet pride. I admire how she has forged a life for herself, a career and a new love after divorcing Dick.

The villagers gather around the noticeboard, their breath clouding the air as they press close together to read the article. Some squint, their fingers tracing the printed words as if to feel the weight of their meaning, when the words themselves make no sense to their illiterate eyes. Others murmur the words aloud, stringing together the sentences in bursts of understanding.

'Nina!' someone calls. And there she is, hurrying through the wrought-iron gates of Villa Sansone where she now lives with Nicolò and her son. Nicolò follows close behind, his limp barely noticeable now, though his gait is measured and careful. When Nina reaches the noticeboard, she pauses, her eyes scanning the page. 'It's here,' she whispers, almost to herself.

'It's here,' Nicolò repeats, his hand resting lightly on her arm. He leans in, his voice low. 'For everyone to see, for everyone to know.'

Our Nina, our Luisa, the brave *staffetta*. How many letters have I sent on her behalf? How many envelopes and scraps of paper have passed through my hands, carrying her name but intended for some poor internee? Today, she stands before me, cheeks flushed from the cold, hair pinned back. Loose strands escape and brush her collar.

'Read it to us,' Santino shouts. Nina turns to the crowd, her voice steady. 'All right,' she says. 'I'll read it. The words are mine, the photographs are Ambra's.'

Ambra, Nina, joined together on these pages, just as they were when they were young girls, scribbling, typing, giggling. Then war came and they took different paths, made different choices. Ambra left. Nina stayed. But their bond survived despite the cracks.

The villagers fall quiet. They cluster closer together, their faces upturned like sunflowers in summer. Nina begins to read, her words slow and deliberate.

'Molise resists. In this small, rugged region of Italy, where mountains rise steep and rivers carve their way through ancient stone, the scars of war remain vivid. Villages like Bastiani, Castelnuovo and Fornelli have borne the weight of destruction and yet continue to stand, their people bound by resilience and hope.'

A murmur runs through the crowd. Heads nod, shoulders straighten and eyes glisten. Nina continues, her voice growing stronger as she reads: 'Though homes have been reduced to rubble and barns shelter families still, the spirit of the people remains unbroken. Castelnuovo al Volturno, the site of a staged battle by the Allies weeks after Molise was liberated, paid a very heavy price. And yet, as the new Republic of Italy emerges from the ashes, this village stands as a testament to how we must fight for compensation, for all our villages.'

They murmur in agreement, their voices low but strong. Mariolina and Esther dab their eyes with handkerchiefs, while Gino stands beside Nina, arms crossed over his muscled chest, his face a blend of pride and resolve.

'We ask not for pity,' Nina reads, 'but for justice. For the bridges and houses to be rebuilt, for the aqueducts to flow again. For the children of Castelnuovo, Bastiani and Fornelli to inherit more than scars. We cannot fail to remember those unfortunate internees incarcerated in internment camps nearby, by a ruthless regime. Agnone, Vinchiaturo, Boiano Isernia and Casacalenda, we will not forget you. We demand recognition, restitution and the chance to begin anew.'

The crowd erupts in cheers; their voices ring out against my walls. I feel their joy, their defiance, their hope. From the edge of the piazza, Leanda stands alone, her presence quiet but steady. She has found work with Santino at his cobbler's shop and Celestina in the bakery. She watches as the crowd surges toward Nina, their voices raised in celebration. Her life is entwined with ours now. She has found her place here, as much as a Sinti can ever settle down, a woman whose journey took her from Palazzo Nonno in Vinchiaturo to the caves and forests of the Molise mountains and finally to Bastiani. Her life has folded into the villagers' lives like a page into a book. She steps forward, her hand brushing the edge of the noticeboard as if to thank it for bearing this story.

The new bell of the Santa Croce church, donated by the Sansones on their return from the north, rings loud and clear. The bell's peal carries over the snow-clad mountains. Determined to settle back into normal life, the Sansones returned to their home in Campobasso promising to pay towards rebuilding the church.

Nina and Nicolò watch the celebration unfold, fingers entwined. The noticeboard, now adorned with Nina's words and Ambra's photographs, bears witness to the pride and resilience of our Molise.

For every loss, there is survival. For every ending, a beginning. And as the bells ring once more and the laughter fills the air, I know this: Bastiani remembers. Bastiani resists. Bastiani endures. And I, the old Post Office at the heart of this village, will hold Ambra and Nina's story for as long as my walls stand.

The page of the calendar shines like snow.

It is the 21st January, 1949, Saint Agnese's feast day, virgin and martyr.

Today is the day of rejoicing.

Afterword

Until today no compensation has been received by the community of Castelnuovo al Volturno either from the Italian Republic or the countries involved in the Allied invasion of Italy. Even though Castelnuovo has not yet received compensation, eighty years later, some of the relatives of the men put to death in Fornelli finally received a share of twelve million euros awarded by an Italian court as compensation for their families' trauma.

A Note from the Authors

This novel is a work of fiction inspired by the events we unearthed in Molise, a small, relatively undiscovered region in south-east Italy.Writing a story about our two main characters Ambra and Nina living in a fictionalised town, Bastiani, in Molise, we discovered compelling facts about the area during the Second World War. We incorporated our discoveries of the internment camps of Vinchiaturo, Isernia, Boiano, Casacalenda and Agnone into our novel, as well as the fake battle of Castelnuovo al Volturno. Nina's work as a *staffetta* was inspired by research into the women couriers at the time who risked their lives to help the Allies and the various groups of Partisans, the Bande, stationed around the area.

We pay tribute to the Trivento Banda in particular, and to Mary Neiman who inspired the character of Esther. Together with her husband Giovanni and her sister-in-law Domenichina (the inspiration for Mariolina) this group of partisans helped to defend the area of Trivento and are inspirational in their bravery and courage in fighting fascism.

We must also remember the internees of the Vinchiaturo female internment camp and the children of the Scuola Primaria in Vinchiaturo whose pupils under their teachers, Maria Pistilli, Luisa Infante, Orsola Perrino and Maria Lucia Caruso crafted a beautiful book recreating the lives of the internees with powerful drawings and texts. Our characters Malka and Leanda were based on two internees at this camp.

A tribute is to be made to Giuseppe Laurelli of Fornelli who lived for justice and freedom and fought against the Fascist ideals of the era.

We would like to thank all those who helped us with the research for this novel. In particular Christian Rossi who highlighted the story of Castelnuovo al Volturno in his book *La Guerra nel mio Paese*, as a history project whilst still at school. Thank you for the time you devoted to us in explaining these extraordinary events.

Of all the many resources we used during the research for this book, we are deeply grateful to:

Christian Rossi, *La Guerra nel mio Paese, Ricordi e testimonianze della Seconda Guerra mondiale a Castelnuovo al Volturno*, Edizione Cisav, Marzo 2024;

Giovanni Cerchia, *Il Molise e La Guerra Totale,* Collana Storia e Documenti, Cosmo Iannone Editore, Isernia, 2011;

Fabrizio Nocera, *Le Bande Partigiane Lungo la Linea Gustav. Abruzzo e Molise nelle Carte del Ricompart*, Studi, Convegni, Ricerche della Fondazione Giorgio Amendola e dell'Associazione Lucana Carlo Levi, Edizioni il Rinnovamento, Torino;

Giovanni Artese, *La Guerra in Abruzzo e Molise 1943–1944*, Vol.I, 2022;

Carlo Spartaco Capogreco, *Mussolini's Camps: Civilian Internment in Fascist Italy (1940–1943)*,Taylor & Francis (2019);

Ilaria Renzi, *Le dinamiche di gruppo nei campi di concentramento nazisti: il Molise*, from the web, Fondation Auschwitz;

Il Quaderno della Memoria, Istituto Omnicomprensivo "Matese", Scuola Primaria G.G.Iacobucci, Classi IV e V, 2011–2012;

Atlante Stragi Nazifasciste, compiled by Giuseppe Angelone;

Winter Line Museum, Venafro;

Museo dell'Eccidio di Fornelli, Fornelli. Especially for the information referring to the German division responsible for the act.

Let's not forget all those who fought and risked their lives against the evils of Fascism.

Per non dimenticare mai

Lest we never forget

Stone placard outside Palazzo Nonno in Vinchiaturo in memory of the women internees. Translation: Between 1940 and 1943, this building housed a women only internment camp where Russian, Polish, Hungarian, Yugoslavian and foreign Jews were interned by the Fascist regime. Lest we never forget!

About the Authors

Amanda and Silvia first met at a creative writing course in London. Bonded by their love of writing, literature, Italy and Italian food and culture, they wrote stories as a means of improving their own craft and deepening their friend-ship. They became 'sisters in writing'. Over many years one of their stories evolved into *The Lost Secrets of the Italian Post Office*. The research for this novel brought them to Molise and the discovery of its strategic importance during the war as well as the beauty, history and generosity of its people.

Amanda studied Modern Languages at the University of East Anglia, followed by a PGCE at King's College London. She worked as a French teacher and then for many years she ran a company in International Advertising Sales. She currently works as a copywriter for a care home in London for older people. She is the author of *The Italian Bookshop Amongst the Vines* published by Embla, 2023. This is her second novel.

Silvia Mazzola, Milanese by birth, London resident for many years, art historian and passionate about art, literature, theatre and food (even British food) is the author of *La Miniaturista* (Fazi in 2011), a novel which has eighteenth-century Venice and a woman artist as protagonists. She has also published in *Italy La lingua nel piatto* (Mursia, April 2006), *Londra e contorni* (Mursia,

April 2009), *Mangiamore* (Ugo Mursia Editore, 2007) on British culture, its cuisine and language. She is co-author of the comedy script *The Wily Widow* (2017). She guides tours at the Victoria and Albert Museum, London.

About Embla Books

Embla Books is a digital-first publisher of standout commercial adult fiction. Passionate about storytelling, the team at Embla believe our lives are built on stories – and publish books that will make you 'laugh, love, look over your shoulder and lose sleep'. Launched by Bonnier Books UK in 2021, the imprint is named after the first woman from the creation myth in Norse mythology. Embla was carved by the gods from a tree trunk found on the seashore; an image of the kind of creative work and crafting that writers do, and a symbol of how stories shape our lives.

Find out about some of our other books and stay in touch:

X, Facebook, Instagram: @emblabooks
Newsletter: https://bit.ly/emblanewsletter